'Terri Thal, who was at the center of the Greenwich Village folk music bohemia, has some great stories to tell about the people she knew and loved and didn't love so much. But like the best memoirs, hers mainly tells her own story, as an experimenter and expeditionary, a doer as well as a seeker, part of some amazing crowds but always her candid self.'
Sean Wilentz, Professor of American History and author of *Bob Dylan in America*

'I was fascinated, amused, and very pleased by Terri's memoir. Fascinated by a unique view of a scene we usually only see from the perspective of performers, and too often from male performers—I was sometimes reminded of Diane DiPrima's memoir of the beats in an overlapping period. Amused because of the lightness, humour, and quirky individuality of Terri's writing. And pleased because it gave me a better understanding of Dave Van Ronk, one of my dearest friends and deepest influences, as well as new insights into other friends and influences, from Roy Berkeley to Bob Dylan. It is an important addition to the growing body of work on the Greenwich Village scene of that time, putting the folk scene in a broader perspective, and a tale well told.'
Elijah Wald, Musician and author of *Dylan Goes Electric*, and co-author with Dave Van Ronk of *The Mayor of MacDougal Street*

'No one was closer to all of it in Greenwich Village than Terri Thal.'
Tom Paxton, folk singer-songwriter

'Terri Thal's candid and deeply personal memoir of the mythological Village of the Sixties answers questions so many of us have had--and adds to our knowledge of the iconic musicians she befriended and worked with.'
David Browne, author of *Fire and Rain: The Beatles, Simon and Garfunkel, James Taylor, CSNY, and the Lost Story of 1970*

'Here's a new book that features Bob Dylan that Bob Dylan will actually read.'
Eric Andersen, folk music singer-songwriter

'A fabulous glimpse into an era of music and politics that changed everything. Just as fascinating as Terri Thal's remarkable role as manager, muse, and confidante to legendary musicians who spoke to a generation, is how she got there, and what happened next. With her compelling self-confidence and sexy nonchalance, it is *she* who should be seen in the cover photo leading the men, instead of the other way around.'
Richard Barone, musician and author of *Music + Revolution: Greenwich Village in the 1960s*

'Terri Thal changed the course of my life when I was 16 years old, and she managed my sister Maggie and me. She took us under her wing, introducing us into the now legendary world of Greenwich Village musicians in the 1960's. More than any one person I can think of Terri is responsible for setting me on a life path of Music. I will forever be grateful to her. I'm thrilled she is finally telling her story in this book!'
Terre Roche, singer, songwriter and founding member of The Roches

'The burgeoning folk music revival from the late Fifties through the Sixties in New York's Greenwich Village was a halcyon time, and Terri Thal was an "insider" for all of it. Her insights about her life and the talented, colorful, somewhat eccentric characters that she knew make for a fascinating trip through that historic era.'
Happy Traum, folk musician

'Terri Thal's memoir is told from the privileged position of not only having been there for the crowning, but as a woman on the cultural front lines. Her detailed recall brings a fresh perspective on the Greenwich Village folk scene of the '60s.'
Marc Eliot, best-selling author of *Phil Ochs: Death of a Rebel*

'A fascinating book by a fascinating woman who has led a fascinating life, and along the way married Dave Van Ronk and was Bob Dylan's first manager. And would Bob Dylan be where he is now if not for her early guidance? She obviously isn't done, and I, for one, want more, more, *more*.'
Christine Lavin, singer-songwriter, transcriptionist for Dave Van Ronk, author of *Cold Pizza for Breakfast: A Mem-wha??*

'When I began writing *Bob Dylan In The Big Apple*, there were a small number of key people that I was keen to interview. People who were integral not only to the Bob Dylan story but also to Greenwich Village and even New York itself. The most important of them all, Terri Thal, remained elusive. She was Dylan's first manager, the spark at the heart of 60's Greenwich Village, and was eventually persuaded to contribute to my book. The most vibrant and informative of chapters. Of course. I whooped with delight at the news that Terri would give a rare interview to me... and finally with this book, the world at long last gets the whole story.'
K G Miles, author of *Bob Dylan in London, Bob Dylan in the Big Apple* and *Bob Dylan in Minnesota*

'Love the book. So easy to read and very interesting. Such a remarkable woman. I will definitely recommend it to friends.'
Dr Michelle Selinger, principal consultant and advisor

'I opened this book expecting to revive the memories of a magical decade and I was not disappointed. Along the way, I was reminded of much that we found remiss and our struggles to make things better. Terri's journey, so eloquently narrated here, weaves the music, news events, and culture of the last half century into a story we might all recognize, leaving me envious of her honesty, compassion and achievement.'
David Wilson, Former Editor, *Broadside of Boston*

'Terri Thal, with her razor sharp wit, takes you right back to the late 50's and early 60's Greenwich Village folk scene along with behind the scenes on being Bob Dylan's first manager. She was a huge link in Bob's chain of success. This is a must read book!'
Marc Percansky, co-author of *Bob Dylan in Minnesota, Troubadour Tales from Duluth, Hibbing and Dinkytown*

'Some years ago I urged Terri Thal to write a memoir—and I couldn't have been the only one. From her central position in the Venn diagram of folk music and radical politics, she knew everybody and was present for everything. And, mirabile dictu, she remembers it all clearly—even that oversexed Capuchin monkey at 190 Spring Street—and shares her recollections vividly. She's always been a remarkable woman, and this is a brilliant book.'
Lawrence Block, author

'She was there and survived to tell a marvelous story.'
Richard Kostelanetz, author of *Soho: The Rise and Fall of an Artists' Colony*

MY GREENWICH VILLAGE
Dave, Bob and Me

Terri Thal

Published by McNidder & Grace
21 Bridge Street
Carmarthen SA31 3JS
Wales, United Kingdom

www.mcnidderandgrace.com

Editor: Caroline Peden Smith
Publisher: Andy Smith

1st edition hardback first published 2023
© Terri Thal

All rights reserved. No part of this work may be reproduced or transmitted in any form or by any means, electronic or mechanical, including photocopy, recording, or any information storage and retrieval system, without permission in writing from the publisher.

Terri Thal has asserted her right to be identified as the author of this work in accordance with the Copyright, Designs and Patents Act 1988.

Every effort has been made to obtain necessary permission with reference to copyright material. The publisher apologises if, inadvertently, any sources remain unacknowledged and will be glad to make the necessary arrangements at the earliest opportunity.

Image credits: cover photo, Jim Marshall Photography LLC.

A catalogue record for this work is available from the British Library.

ISBN 9780857162489 hardback
ISBN 9780857162496 ebook

Cover design: Tabitha Palmer
Designer: JS Typesetting Ltd
Printed and bound in the Czech Republic by Finidr

Dedicated to
Jacob L. (Jack) Beller, who told his 11-year-old niece that she should grow up to be an authoress.
Paul Solomon Orentlich and Dave Van Ronk, who told me I could succeed at anything I chose.

FOREWORD

It's a little over a half-century since I first came upon the name Dave Van Ronk. It was 1972 and I was reading Anthony Scaduto's biography of Bob Dylan. I was scarcely into my teens and the journey that would take me deep into what I came to understand as "the New York folk revival" had begun some three years earlier when, fumbling with my first guitar chords I encountered an album called simply *Joan Baez Vol 2* in my sister's modest record collection. Its sole recommendation was the cover photograph – a young woman playing a Spanish guitar. In a rudimentary way, I quickly mastered most of the songs and hastened to the library to seek out other Baez records, whose songs and detailed sleeve notes provided a sort of Venn Diagram through which to explore 20th-century American culture and politics. Many of the names and songs were buried deep in my subconscious, for in those days Britain had very few radio stations and even fewer TV channels; families listened and watched together. And "folk music," in mostly polite, middle-class arrangements, had made it on to BBC Radio, including a schools' broadcast called *Singing Together*.

Scaduto provided many new signposts to follow and the radio serialisation of his book, *Bob Dylan: An Intimate Biography*, put voices to many of the names, in speech and in song. Among them was Van Ronk. He sounded a jolly fellow, laughing asthmatically as he told the now-famous story of how Bob Dylan had "stolen" his arrangement of "House of the Rising Sun" for his debut album.

My interest in this music and a place called Greenwich Village quickly deepened into an obsession, one that led over the years to all sorts of encounters, including Robert Shelton, the now-late *New York Times* critic who wrote the first reviews of Baez and Dylan. He was living in London by then, but he'd been a neighbour of Van Ronk and his wife Terri Thal and had been both an observer of, and participant in, the 1960s Village folk scene. It was my restoration of *No Direction Home* – "the author's cut" in 2011 – that led me to found a festival celebrating Greenwich Village.

What always fascinated me, long before I could articulate it, was a sense that everything somehow came together in the Village. The music and the politics, and much besides. Washington Square Park was where everything intersected on its way out into the world – and did so long before Terri and Dave came to the Village, and long before Dave and Bob and the many other folksingers and songwriters about whom Terri writes clambered on to the rickety, makeshift stages in the clubs that studded the crooked streets around the Park.

Terri's memoir brings it all to life. But *My Greenwich Village: Dave, Bob and Me* is about much more than folk music. It's an account of what it was like growing up in the dull-grey Eisenhower years, the weight of nice Jewish middle-class family expectations on your shoulders, when all you wanted to do was cut the ties that bind and escape suburban Brooklyn for bohemia and a bunch of left-wing folkies. It was the time of "the great folk scare," a phrase credited to Van Ronk, whose FBI files would turn out to be voluminous.

Terri more than held her own amid a scene that was overwhelmingly male and macho, and her account is a fascinating companion to Suze Rotolo's *A Freewheelin' Time*. A rare eyewitness account from a funny, feisty, independent-minded woman who was Dylan's first manager and lived to tell the tale.

Wasn't that a time!

Elizabeth Thomson
Greenwich Village, July 2023

CONTENTS

Foreword	By Elizabeth Thomson	vii
Chapter 1	Where I Came From	1
Chapter 2	My Introduction to Folk Music	19
Chapter 3	Young Sex … and a Word About Elderly Sex	27
Chapter 4	It's a Small World	33
Chapter 5	Jesus Christ, the FBI	35
Chapter 6	Eleven Years and One Month	43
Chapter 7	Greenwich Village Folk Music in the '60s	85
Chapter 8	The Business of Folk Music	111
Chapter 9	Dylan, Friend and Client	133
Chapter 10	Socialism, Here I Come	151
Chapter 11	There's Life After Folk Music	163
Chapter 12	The Revival of the Folk Revival	175
Afterword	My Other Passion	183
Folk Singers and Related People in New York City, Mid-Late 50s Through Mid-Late 60s		189
Acknowledgments		195
Bibliography		197
Index		199

Chapter 1
WHERE I CAME FROM

"You were the first woman we knew who had balls," folk singer John Winn wrote to me a while ago.

I was flattered. That's partly how I want to be remembered.

John was writing about the folk music world of the 1950s and '60s, when most women were regarded as objects. I wasn't an object. I was a participant in a world of music, excitement, political passion, and fun. I managed folk singers; I was married to one. I was involved in non-Communist left-wing politics. I worked for civil rights and civil liberties and against the war in Vietnam. It was a passionate time, and I made my mark on it.

At age 18, halfway through Brooklyn College, I met Dave Van Ronk, a folk singer who was also committed to social change. We were together for eleven years. It was a fun, politically exciting time, although I struggled with my wish to be independent and my realization that I had tied my personal self into Dave's career. When we found ourselves turning each other into nervous wrecks, we separated, but remained friends until he died.

A year after we separated, I lived with a man twenty years older than me for twenty-seven years, until he died. He didn't share my politics but was incredibly supportive of my career, and I immersed myself in the work I did for not-for-profit organizations. Four years after he died, I wound up living with a land conservationist, and my involvement with environmental health issues and his protection of the land and water in our community meshed. When he died, I was 78, and I've lived alone since then, immersed in environmental and social justice issues.

My commitment was: every man, woman, and child on this planet should have enough food, water, shelter, healthcare, and basic amenities to live comfortably. This is what socialists believed in the 1950s and '60s; and I still do. It's why I wandered into the world of folk music. At that time, there was a relationship between folk music and left-wing politics, although I was more entranced by the stories the music told than the rabble-rousing songs so many of my peers liked.

My parents were immigrants, Jews from Russia and Austria-Hungary who had moved up from cold-water apartments with toilets in the outside halls to a house in Brooklyn, where they had three children. I'm the middle child; my sister Joyce is three years older; my brother Leon was five years younger. He died in an airplane accident in 2007.

Both of my parents came to the United States in 1921. My mother's father was a tailor; he made, remade, and repaired clothing. My father's father was a barber who also sold birds in his shop in Brooklyn. Each of my parents was one of six living children; each family had lost three others—one of my father's siblings was killed in his mother's arms by Russian soldiers in their home back in Stanislav.

My father had gone to work when he was young. I've been told that when he started to work for a dental mechanic in Harlem, he walked to work from Manhattan's Lower East Side to Harlem every day—fifty blocks, which is about 2½ miles (4 km)— to save the nickel trolley fare so he could telephone my mother.

He apprenticed with someone, learning to make teeth and restorative devices such as bridges or dentures, until he was able to open his own laboratory in Bedford-Stuyvesant in Brooklyn, where we lived. My father worked long hours—and inhaled so many chemicals that he developed lifelong emphysema. He had a heart attack when I was 10, and his doctors insisted that he find a profession less strenuous than making teeth. Their advice may have saved his life; continuing to breathe the chemicals could have killed him. He then went to work for his oldest brother, who had started a textile manufacturing company in Massachusetts with offices in the Empire State Building, where my father handled yarn purchasing and fabric pricing until he retired.

My father's original surname was *Lichtenthal*. He changed it to *Thal* when he went to work for his brother, who had changed his last name when he started his textile business. I was 11, and resented the name change, which may have been partly why I've always kept my own last name rather than adopt one that belonged to a husband or lover. When I was about 8, I read a biography of Franz Peter Shubert, who was born in the town of Lichtenthal in Austria. I was excited that a town had been named after us—only years later did I learn that Jews in Eastern Europe generally took or were given the name of the town where they lived.

My parents encouraged us to read. They wanted us to be smart, and they wanted us to continue their Jewish heritage. They didn't want me to screw around, to live with and marry a non-Jewish folksinger or, subsequently, to live with a man who was twenty years older than me, or to dedicate my life to human rights—all activities that were unusual, but becoming less so on the part of young people who were struggling with the culture of America after the Second World War.

To my parents, who always lived in a two-family house with some members of my mother's family, the people who counted the most were my mother's sisters and brothers and their children. We were part of one of those wonderfully close families in which everyone is safe and, if not always adored, is included and forgiven.

My mother was the oldest of six children, and came to the U.S. from Russia with her family. She became responsible for shopping, cooking and generally caring for her siblings when my grandmother found it hard to cope. She was intelligent and a fast learner, and wanted desperately to go to an academic high school, but my grandfather insisted that she get a business diploma and go to work. Her teacher visited her parents to support her request, but my grandfather was adamant.

"I never wanted to have girls," my mother often told my sister Joyce and me. "Being a woman stinks." Not because she didn't like girls, but because "women get screwed." She never became a feminist, which I think was unfortunate; she might have felt better about herself if she had found a social cause to join. I'm sure consistently and frequently hearing that being a woman is lousy was one of the reasons why I was determined to be an independent person, and why I wanted to be treated like a man. It also may have been why I have been drawn to working on women's issues professionally and as a volunteer.

When I was an adult and my mother was ill with Parkinson's disease, I found her high school diploma from Seward Park High School. She was then in her last years of illness, and her memory had diminished. Still, she looked at the diploma, shook her head, and said, "That's not a real diploma." She meant it wasn't an academic diploma. My god ... what a damned tragedy.

When I was growing up, I absorbed only my mother's disapproval and criticism. Maybe she had lost any ability she once had to show affection, but whatever the reason, I don't remember her ever hugging me, saying "I love you," or congratulating me on an accomplishment, except when I was skipped from one grade to another in school. My father did offer me that, but he worked long hours in his dental laboratory, wasn't home weekdays, and I suspect he didn't hear about the positive things I might have done. Years late, after my mother died, my father told me she had loved me. By then, I was 50, and had recognized it through her actions, such as leaving her seat in her Orthodox synagogue to stand next to me when I foolishly walked in wearing a pants suit and carrying my handbag—Orthodox Jewish women don't wear pants and don't carry things, especially money, on holy days—or by suggesting to my father

My wonderful maternal grandmother, Jenny Beller

that they give me their summer house when Paul and I were thinking about whether and how we could move out of Greenwich Village. But growing up, I wasn't aware of it. I craved affection and approval.

I got those things from my maternal grandmother Jenny Beller, and from aunts and uncles. *Bubbe* (Yiddish for 'grandmother') hadn't been able to cope with bringing up six kids in America, but she adored her grandchildren, especially Joyce and me, who were the first and second. She listened to us and didn't criticize.

Once, when I was living with Dave and he had started to earn money as a musician, and I visited my family in Brooklyn, my grandmother asked me why we didn't get married. "We're not ready to," I said. "Maybe we will be, but I don't feel grown up enough to get married. He doesn't either." *Bubbe* thought about it for a moment. Then she asked me, "When he comes home at the end of the week, does he give you his pay?" Dave hated banks and wouldn't to go to them. I had to coerce him into having a joint checking account; he had told me to set one up without him. So I honestly said, "Yes, he does." My wonderful grandmother shrugged and said, "Nu, not so bad."

Years later, I learned that long ago, back in a Russian shtetl, my grandmother had run away from home at a young age to marry my grandfather, and her family disowned her. My father told me that sometimes she would stand outside her family's candlelit home and just look at it, but her parents wouldn't let her in. I don't know why they disapproved of my grandfather. But it explains her attitude toward me.

My aunt Sandy was my mother's youngest sister. She worshiped my mother, and wanted to emulate her. It was odd, because Sandy was not like my mother. She didn't keep a perfectly clean house; my mother's was spotless. She had friends; my mother had no friends other than her relatives. And, like my grandmother, Sandy never criticized me. So I thought she approved of everything I did. I was grown up before I realized that she simply was kind and discreet.

Sandy's oldest son, my cousin Mark, has told me that when he was young, his parents criticized him so severely that he used to talk about himself to my mother. He got a feeling of approval from her that he didn't get at home. It's interesting that both women, I'm sure without talking to one another about it, were able to separate their expectations of their own children from the needs of their nieces and nephews. Sandy and her family, and my grandmother (until she remarried—my grandfather died when I was 8), lived in the other apartment in our two-family house. The back doors to the two apartments were never locked—except once, when I was 16 and my parents went away for a week, I gave my family heartburn by bringing home a man in his twenties and locking the back door. We didn't have sex, but only because he probably had drunk a lot of beer. Now, I'm glad that I didn't have my first sexual encounter at age 16 to someone I had just met on the bus.

The open-door policy meant that anyone from our apartment could go down to my aunt and uncle's at any time, and vice versa. I wonder whether there were times when my aunt and uncle simply wanted to be alone—especially after my grandmother remarried and moved away—but were too polite to lock the back door.

Every Friday evening, most of my mother's brothers and sisters would gather around the dining table, either in our apartment or my aunt and uncle's. We'd eat dinner and afterward, drink glasses of tea—no glass holders or teabags—accompanied by my grandmother's or my aunt Sandy's *pletzl* (poppyseed cookies), *kechel* (yeast dough cookies filled with jam), apple pie, or just Nabisco unsalted saltines and jam.

When I was in college and went to political meetings or to meet my boyfriend in Greenwich Village on Friday and Saturday evenings, sometimes I would have preferred to stay home with my family around the dining room table, talking about national politics or their known or unknown relatives. My mother's brother Irving often talked about how he won at the racetrack or about the gangsters he admired and hung out with. Irving sometimes brought home items that had "fallen off the truck." My mother wouldn't allow those things in her house, but I remember one cotton rain jacket that came from Irving's stash.

They never talked about coming to the U.S. in steerage in 1921, or about life in Russia. My aunts and uncles were too young to remember it, and my mother wouldn't speak of it. When my sister or I pressed her, she just said, "It was dirty," and clammed up.

My Heroes

Bette, my mother's other sister, occasionally swept me up and took me home to stay with her family during school vacations. Once, when I was about 10 and spending a week with them, Bette served dinner and then said to her husband—the writer Harvey Swados—"Esther [my mother] would shit if she knew what we were feeding Terri."

I was alarmed and curious. "What are you feeding me?"

"Spare ribs."

"What's wrong with them?" I wanted to know.

"They're pork," Bette told me.

I don't think I threw up, but I don't think I was able to eat them. I lived in a kosher home; you don't mix milk and meat, and you don't eat pork or shellfish.

Years later, when I was 15, Bette asked me whether I'd had sex yet. I was shocked. "Of course not," I said. "Don't you think I'm too young?"

Bette thought about it, and told me sooner was better than later.

"When Felice (my cousin, who is ten years younger than me) is my age, will you tell her to have sex?"

My aunt thought about it. "I hope I have the courage to," she said.

Sorry, Bette ... years later, I asked Felice whether you had recommended sex to her at age 15. You chickened out.

But when I was 17, I turned to Bette and said, "A friend of mine thinks she's pregnant. What should she do?"

Keeping a straight face, Bette said, "If you find that you're pregnant, you come to me."

I got my period a week later and forgot the conversation. Many years later, my aunt reminded me of it, remonstrating that "I sweated over you for months." I adored that woman.

My mother's middle brother, Jack, who lived out of New York most of those years, was always present in spirit. Jack was my hero. A pacifist, he was a chemist who helped design the fuse for the A-bomb. Later, he had a nervous breakdown. When he retired, Jack took consulting jobs, often for the government. In May 2007, eight months before his 90th birthday, he performed the calculations and projections used to create the infrared components of the James Webb Space Telescope, launched in December 2021, to view objects too old and distant for the older Hubble Space Telescope.

When Joyce and I were kids, Jack gave us wonderful books with holes punched in them. My sister and I loved them. We thought the holes meant that the books were special; years later, we learned that they meant that the books had been remaindered, and the holes were punched by the publisher so bookstores couldn't sell them as new.

As we grew up, I kept one of Joyce's books, *Book of Marvels*, written by an English adventurer, Richard Halliburton. It remains my favorite book ever, and for her 75th birthday, I returned it.

When I was 6 and Jack worked in Rhode Island, he sent me about a dozen postcards, like this one:

> If you get tired of staying home
> And want to take a trip,
> Just take a trip to Fairyland
> With your soft bed for a ship.
> There you'll see all the fairy folk;
> The Teeny Weenies, too, you'll find,
> And when you're safely home again
> They'll all be left behind.
>
> All except one little imp,
> And if you ask me who
> I'll tell you, little one,
> The little imp was you.

He sent similar postcards to Joyce and to our younger brother Leon. Of course we thought he was perfect. When Jack married, Joyce was 12 and I was 9. I remember a long discussion between us about what this meant. *Would Jack love us less? Would we lose him to this woman? Would they have kids?* That would be more than we could bear. He married a wonderful woman named Florence who adored him and cared about us, but no, he didn't spend as much time with us as before. No, they didn't have children; Florence had a physical condition that precluded childbirth.

Jack told me I should grow up to be an "authoress." When I was 18 and needed a diaphragm, he and Florence allowed me to use their address so my mother wouldn't see any mail I might receive from the Margaret Sanger Clinic (the first legal birth control clinic in the U.S. and forerunner of Planned Parenthood).

Before I started school, Joyce taught me to read. Weekend mornings, to keep me entertained so I didn't bother our parents, she told me stories. I didn't know then that she was telling me the American history stories she learned in school. I learned about George Washington and the cherry tree; the Revolutionary War; Patrick Henry. When I started elementary school, I was years ahead of my classmates. I was skipped from second to third grade, and by fourth grade, my teachers didn't know what to do with me and had me teaching Puerto Rican immigrant kids to read English. In retrospect, I feel sorry for all of us. I may have been intrinsically smart, but I lost a year of education during which I should have learned how to study and learn, and the Puerto Rican children certainly didn't learn very much from an 8-year-old.

In fifth grade, I was taken for a test at the headquarters of the NYC Board of Education. Before I took it, someone talked with me. "Do you know why you're here?" they asked. "Yes," I said. "You want to decide whether to put me in a special class for blind children." My vision had been deteriorating, I wore bright red glasses with thick lenses, I was supposed to use two lines to write capital letters and one for lower case letters, and no one had told me why I was going to the Board of Education building. No one ever told kids anything about what was going on back then.

It actually was an IQ test that resulted in my being approved by the New York City Board of Education for a special school for smart kids. I didn't go to the school; it was far enough away that my parents felt I had to be driven there, and my father had a major heart attack and wouldn't have been able to drive. I was broken-hearted.

Ethnicity and Religion

Until I was 11, we lived in Bedford-Stuyvesant in Brooklyn, a neighborhood that had housed Jews, Italians, and Irish-Catholics. By the time I entered elementary school in PS 57 on Lafayette Avenue, five blocks west of my home, a long stretch of streets running further west from Lafayette had become populated by Black people. Our block and the immediate surrounding ones were mixed—a few Blacks, mostly Italians and Irish-Catholics, a diminishing number of Jews, a small and growing group of Puerto Ricans, and a handful of Romani, who tended to live in small stores on a commercial street.

In that area, kids from various backgrounds got along but didn't socialize after school. I remember only a few of my schoolmates. Charlie, an Italian youngster, lived across the street and came to my backyard to dig in the dirt when we were about 4. Helen, a Black girl, used to re-tie the tie-belt in the back of my dresses when they became unknotted in school. Beverly, a Jewish girl, was my best friend for many years until she married a nice Jewish guy and I became involved with a non-Jewish folk singer. Janet taught me that young girls could enjoy fondling each other's

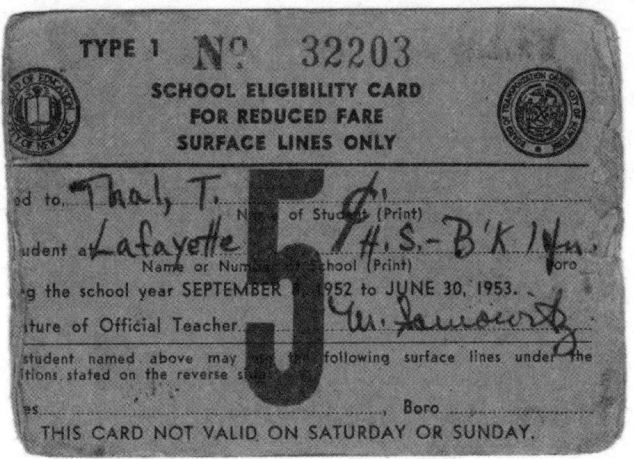

It cost 5 cents to take a bus to my high school

breasts, although I didn't have any yet. Philip was my Italian 'boyfriend' in fourth grade—I would stop at his house on my way to school and he would carry my books the rest of the way.

There was a considerable amount of Jew-bashing. Many of the Irish-Catholic kids went to a parochial school a few blocks from our house. Apparently, they were taught that the Jews killed Christ, and on their way home from school, when Joyce and I played outside our house, we were sometimes barraged with snowballs in winter and occasional stones in fall and spring, and cries of "The Jews killed Christ" or "Christ killers."

My friend Beverly's family moved to another section of Brooklyn, and when I walked from the bus to her building, boys standing on street corners often yelled "Dirty Jew" or "Christ killer" as I walked by. I was equal parts angry and scared, not knowing whether this would be followed by physical attacks.

Years later, when I told Dave about that, he said that when he had gone to Catholic elementary school in Bushwick, Brooklyn, only a few miles from where I had lived in Bedford-Stuyvesant, the nuns in his school told the students that the Jews had killed Christ and would be punished for it. Apparently, that was a common lesson in Catholic parochial schools in the 1940s.

How did those kids know I was Jewish? The youngsters who walked past our house daily on their way to school simply knew. The others? Maybe because I was chubby. In Brooklyn, you could tell someone's ethnic background from their looks: hair, facial structure, bone structure, clothes, their way of walking. By the early 1950s, white bucks (oxfords) and socks said *Jewish girl*. Black shells (flat shoes that looked like dance shoes but with no ribbons) and bare feet or stockings said *Italian girl*. A certain shade of off-blonde hair and freckles generally said *Irish girl*. Very slim with dark brown hair said *Puerto Rican*.

The ethnic and religious identifications were: Italian, Jewish, Irish-Catholic, Puerto Rican, Black. By and large, we didn't identify people by religion but sort of by ethnicity. The Italian kids were Catholic, but nobody thought of them that way; they were thought of as Italian. They were not anti-Semitic; Italian boys and Jewish girls dated. Some Jewish girls considered Italian guys bold heroes who smoked and looked sexy. Many of the Irish young people who had gone to Catholic elementary schools were anti-Semitic. The Puerto Ricans didn't think about it. The Blacks were Protestant, although no one I knew then considered their religion, just their race. There were Romanis, but not enough to have any identifying factor.

I'm sure all of this contributed to my later politics.

Feeling Jewish

I was 12 when I opened a desk in my parents' living room and found photographs that my father's youngest brother had taken when the Allies entered Buchenwald. It was one of the few times in my life when I was so upset I couldn't eat.

You may have seen similar photos. Mounds of bodies, mostly skeletal. Bodies stacked into wooden carrels on the side of the building and on the ground. Piles of dental fixtures. Piles of shoes. Those photographs are common now, shown in movies, magazines and books.

Like many Jews at that time, my mother had a *pushka* (Yiddish for 'little box') that she put money in for Jewish causes in a kitchen cabinet. The cans were picked up by elderly men with long beards. I understood that the money was earmarked to help Jews leave Eastern Europe, mostly to go to Israel. But other men came sometimes, and my mother sent us out of the kitchen when she met with them. I never asked who they were, but many years later, Martus, with whom I lived in the 2000s until his death, told me that when he was young, they had come to his house, too, and that he understood they were involved with the underground trying to smuggle Jews out of Russia.

In the early 1950s, a large part of my mother's family—Jews in Russia—disappeared. My parents and they had corresponded, and once, my parents sent them money and never heard from them again. I don't know how my mother learned that they had all been killed, but I remember her saying that perhaps they were killed because of the gift of cash. Did they die because they received U.S. $100?

No one ever really knew what happened. My mother felt guilty until she died. "What if our money killed them?" she occasionally asked, and she sometimes cried—the only times I ever saw her cry. Mostly, she was bitter and enraged about what happened to the Jews in Germany and in Russia. Initially, I was too young to distinguish between the Nazis and the Communists, but I knew that my relatives were killed because they were Jewish. I knew what was happening internationally but didn't yet understand the nuances.

As a teenager, I had fantasies about being part of a group of prisoners the Nazis were dividing. They put the Jews on one side of a courtyard and the non-Jews on another, and sent the two groups to different places. Clearly, the Jews were being sent to concentration camps to be killed. In that fantasy, I could have faked being a non-Jew. But I never did; I always proudly admitted that I was Jewish. I suppose I was making believe or hoping that I would be a hero. I don't know whether I thought I really would have made that decision. Eventually, I accepted the fantasy as part of my life. That kind of specter affected my sister Joyce, too.

Joyce later told me that she and a friend whose parents had escaped from Holland before the Nazi invasion used to fantasize about who in their families, if taken to a concentration camp, would have survived. Joyce says they thought our mother would have, because she seemed to be incredibly strong and independent. As Joyce got older, she realized that we all would have been killed.

The New Neighborhood

We moved from Bedford-Stuyvesant to Flatbush, a different section of Brooklyn, when I was 11. Flatbush was largely Jewish, but I was in the adjoining school district, which mostly comprised Italians. The block we moved onto, East 9th Street between Avenues L and M, was ethnically mixed. Young people of different ethnicities and races mingled—not a lot, but in some after-school activities. For a few years, until we went to high school, we played softball or stoopball in the street after school. I don't remember any racial, ethnic, or religious strife among either the kids or the adults. People seemed to get along. We may have gone our own ways socially, but the community was solid.

Carol, a Jewish girl who lived across the street, and I became friends, although we were very different. She was determined to socialize with the Italian guys who hung out in a candy store five long blocks away. Sometimes I went there with her. But, in my first two years in high school, I had reached my full height of 5'11" (1.8 m), and was still chubby. I didn't understand flirtation. I couldn't kid around with boys whose activities and attitudes both intrigued and scared me. What nefarious activities did they undertake? I didn't and still don't know. I doubt that they were much worse than riding loud motorcycles.

Carol later married a 'nice' Jewish guy who lived on our block. By then I was 17, and no longer a virgin. Carol once told me that she had 'gone down on' Lewis, which apparently was OK because it didn't affect her virginity. But she considered my sexual behavior shameful —I had 'gone all the way.' I found the distinction confusing. Sex was fun and I did it voluntarily with my then-boyfriend. I thought that what I was doing was honest, and that she was hypocritical. I wasn't invited to their wedding, but by then both of our lives had changed and our friendship had ended.

Stuart Ritterman was my closest friend during my last years in high school and my first years in college. Stu was fairly short, and I was tall for a woman. We were both a bit odd; Stu had painted his bedroom black and listened to Stravinsky; I would have liked to be liked by some of my classmates, but I was tall, chubby, awkward, and two years younger than any of them. Stu spent a lot of time at my house.

We spent one summer happily riding the rides in Steeplechase, a large amusement park in Coney Island, because he got passes from a relative. The following summer, I went to Cambridge, Massachusetts, to stay in my sister's room when she went to Mexico with some friends. After a few weeks of enjoying living away from my parents, I had sex with a married psychology professor who taught at one of the nearby colleges. A few days later, I called Stu and wailed, "I want to go home. Come get me." He did. He flew up the next day, spent an unsexual night in my bed because there was no place else for him to sleep except the floor, and took me home to Brooklyn.

More than 60 years later, although he lived in Canada, had politics I couldn't share, and was on a dialysis machine until he died in 2022, a part of me still believed—or wanted to believe—that if I were in desperate need of help, I could call Stu.

My 16th birthday and high school graduation both took place in June 1955. I didn't know whether or not I wanted to go to college or where I would like to go or what I wanted to study if I did. I thought it might be good to go to work, but, of course, I had no idea what work to do. New York City colleges were free; you just needed a high school average of at least 85% to attend. Brooklyn College was a bus ride away, so I went there. My parents were pleased; my sister was at Brandeis University in Massachusetts, and they wanted to have some of their children around.

Fitting In

During those years, I was developing a persona that, in retrospect, I realize I had adopted but which also fitted me.

I never felt that I fit in with any group. I know that's not unusual, but, of course, I didn't know it when I was a child or teenager. I just knew that I wasn't part of any coterie. When a bunch of people gathered, I wasn't one of them. Why not? I didn't know.

I'm not sure when that started.

Even at age 6 or 7, I knew I was chubby and clutzy. Then, I grew very quickly, so now I knew I was tall and chubby and clutzy. When I was 12 or 13, I told my mother that I wanted to study ballet. "Ballet dancers are graceful," she told me. "Not clutzy." So much for ballet.

By my 13th or 14th birthday, I was in high school and 5'11". I towered over almost all of the boys at school.

Several years ago, it occurred to me that while I liked being the youngest in most social groups, being two years younger than everyone else when I was in school probably wasn't a positive. I'd never before considered the possible social differences a two-year divergence in age made among kids.

The Campus Bohemians

In my sophomore year at Brooklyn College, I became, for the first time, part of a group of people I admired, who welcomed me and who accepted me. It was a small group known as the "campus bohemians," although I didn't know that until later. On my first day of classes, a student named Michael Eisenstadt was standing at the main gate to the campus handing out copies of W.H. Auden's poem 'The Unknown Citizen.' I've never been able to absorb much from poetry, but that one struck me—although I probably was more intrigued by the idea of someone distributing the poem at the campus gate than by the poem itself.

A year later, I became friendly with Michael and others in his small group of people who had graduated and returned to do graduate work, or who had been in the U.S. armed services and had returned to complete college. The eight people in the group, which included two married couples, were all majoring in mathematics or ancient Greek, and all planned to teach in colleges.

They adopted me. We hung out in the Brooklyn College cafeteria or in the nearby apartment of Sam and his wife. For a while, I dated Arthur, a mathematician who wanted me to be more attracted to him than I found possible. And somehow, several of them developed a rapport with my parents. I was surprised. My parents would have liked me to have 'normal' Jewish friends who were my own age. These people were unusual, nonreligious, and older than me. But three of them often came to the house for lunch on Sundays, and my father and Marty, another mathematician, chatted like friends. I'd never seen my father get along with anyone that well.

Even my mother, a very restrained person, was more than cordial to them. One very rainy weekday afternoon, Nagy was visiting, and had to go to a medical office in another section of Brooklyn. Getting there from my house would have involved taking two buses. To my surprise, my mother, who didn't like to drive, offered to take him there. Later, I asked her why she had done it. "He would have been late and wet if he took the bus," she said.

At the end of that year, most members of the group graduated, got teaching jobs in colleges, or went to other schools for more advanced degrees. Luckily, I met Dave the following fall, and found a new social life.

Needing to Control My Own Life

I wrote earlier that when our mother said being a woman was lousy and she wished that my sister and I were boys, Joyce and I understood that she meant that she would have preferred that we were of the sex that had power rather than the one that didn't. I think I absorbed a good deal of her assessment—but that I also took some of her dislike of being a woman personally. I'm sure that's partly why, for many years, I thought she didn't like me or love me. I'm sure it's partly why, while growing up and into my thirties, I wanted to be treated like a man, not a woman; it was why I tried to act like a man, selecting very visible, specific traits to adopt. I cursed like a man; I drank like a man. I had sex with men I barely knew, and sometimes with men I didn't know—just the way, I thought, men did with women. I scorned as boring any interest in marriage, and the appurtenances of marriage associated with women, such as dishes and tableware. Those traits lasted a long time, although I had to rein in the cursing and drinking when I left the music world; and when I lived with men I was monogamous, except toward the end of my marriage to Dave.

I've learned to soften those traits—and simply stopped drinking several years ago—but they haven't completely disappeared. Although I still have male friends, I now also have female ones and I find women as smart as and, often, smarter than many men. But I still say *fuck* much too often; I still tend to interrupt people in meetings, though I insist that's a Brooklyn-based trait; and I'm embarrassed to realize that I took care of the men I lived with more than they took care of me.

Money

This is where I admit I don't understand my own insistence on controlling finances. No one ever tried to restrict my earning money or handling it. Even before I became his manager, Dave said he didn't want to be involved with money. I had to insist that he co-sign a bank account; he didn't want to have anything to do with banks. I had to insist that we make sure that our apartment leases were in both of our names; he didn't want to sign legal documents. When a substantial amount of royalties came in from his co-authorship of a song that was recorded on Peter, Paul and Mary's first album, I deposited the payments in the bank and decreed that they didn't exist. Later, that money funded his rock group, Dave Van Ronk and the Hudson Dusters.

When we separated, we agreed on what to do with the money we had then, which was only a few thousand dollars; we had invested everything we had in the Hudson Dusters. I didn't ask for any of his future earnings. Later, I neglected to try to collect royalties for his recordings of the songs for which my publishing company, Obscure Music, held a copyright. I

DAVE VAN RONK AND THE HUDSON DUSTERS
TERRI THAL MANAGEMENT
190 WAVERLY PLACE NEW YORK, N.Y. 10014
(212) 255-2856

The Hudson Dusters, Pot (Phil Namanworth), Ed Gregory, Rick Henderson, Dave, Dave Woods

never would have been that careless with another client's funds, but I think not claiming those royalties was related to my need to be financially independent. I also think it was stupid—but it's much too late to be concerned about that.

For the rest of my life, I insisted on being able to take care of myself financially. I didn't ask Paul, my second husband, to contribute toward our household expenses—although he did so until he had to stop working when he hit his seventies. I did ask Martus, my third husband to contribute toward them, but didn't insist when I realized that his income as a land-saving lawyer was barely enough to cover his own financial outlays.

This wasn't a negative trait, but I think it's an odd one, and I don't know why I've always insisted on having financial control. I guess I realized it gave me a certain amount of power.

Chapter 2
MY INTRODUCTION TO FOLK MUSIC

My sister Joyce first introduced me to folk music in 1955, before I met Dave. Joyce went to Brandeis University, then a fairly new, sophisticated college with an extraordinarily liberal faculty. Socialists, ethnographers, cultural anthropologists, and a student body that was involved with what I thought then were major issues, such as whether *The Birth of a Nation*, a racist film directed by the famed D.W. Griffith, should be shown on campus.

Joyce had Pete Seeger's Folkways Records album of labor songs. I bought other albums—mostly ten-inch LPs of Lead Belly, Woody Guthrie, and Cisco Houston which featured music from what I thought was the world of American country people and of the working class.

I was impressed and delighted by the music. "This land is your land, this land is our land," Woody Guthrie sang. I was thrilled, as were thousands of others. There also were stories of seafarers, of the West, of miners, of tragedies that happened in Appalachia and on picket lines, and, of course, there were lovely traditional English songs about murderers and fair maidens, many of whom either killed themselves or were killed.

When I started to go to socialist meetings in 1956, I found that folk music was an intrinsic part of the culture of the Left. During the 1930s, the Great Depression had led many artists to join the Communist Party (CP), which talked about a world of economic equality. Some of the artists were folk singers or people who collected folk songs from the South.

By 1941, a group known as the Almanac Singers started to perform protest songs, often for radical causes, and tried to introduce the working class to folk music. By and large, the working class wasn't interested—but left-wing political organizations and artists were.

In 1946, a group of left-wing folk singers created an organization called People's Songs, which found work for radical performers. People's Songs musicians, some of whom never officially joined the CP, had a mission. Pete Seeger, Woody Guthrie, the Weavers, and many others carried messages about poverty, despair, and the need for industrial unions and for workers to organize.

A Socialist Boyfriend

My first experience with folk singers was at meetings of the Young Socialist League (YSL) in 1956. Roy Berkeley, a tall, slim folk singer wearing a snug black turtlenecked sweater was playing union songs. These were an outgrowth of the labor movement, including songs like 'Solidarity Forever'—which, from my perspective, still talks about a need in America; the writing is florid, but the message is clear:

> When the union's inspiration through the workers' blood shall run,
> There can be no power greater anywhere beneath the sun;
> Yet what force on earth is weaker than the feeble strength of one,
> But the union makes us strong.
>
> *Solidarity forever,*
> *Solidarity forever,*
> *Solidarity forever,*
> *For the union makes us strong.*
>
> Is there aught we hold in common with the greedy parasite?
> Who would lash us into serfdom and would crush us with his might?
> Is there anything left to us but to organize and fight?
> For the union makes us strong.
>
> *Chorus*
>
> It is we who plowed the prairies; built the cities where they trade;
> Dug the mines and built the workshops, endless miles of railroad laid;
> Now we stand outcast and starving midst the wonders we have made;
> But the union makes us strong.

Chorus

All the world that's owned by idle drones is ours and ours alone.
We have laid the wide foundations; built it skyward stone by stone.
It is ours, not to slave in, but to master and to own.
While the union makes us strong.

Chorus

They have taken untold millions that they never toiled to earn,
But without our brain and muscle not a single wheel can turn.
We can break their haughty power, gain our freedom when we learn
That the union makes us strong.

Chorus

In our hands is placed a power greater than their hoarded gold,
Greater than the might of armies, magnified a thousand-fold.
We can bring to birth a new world from the ashes of the old
For the union makes us strong.

Roy was a little taller than me, slim, with a slightly swarthy complexion, a gaunt face, and striking cheekbones. He sang union songs and English and American ballads. He was a socialist but refused to join any socialist organization. He was a journalism student at Columbia University, lived in a cold-water flat with the toilet in a cubbyhole in the hall outside the apartment, and had a slightly sour smell. Not unpleasant, not unclean … just slightly sour. I've never been able to identify it more clearly than that.

The music appealed to the *becoming a socialist* persona of my 17-year-old self. Going out with the socialist folk singer who had at least twenty fans fed my ego, and Roy was smart and funny. We dated for about six months, then drifted apart. During those months, my admiration for the music that told stories about America was strengthened.

It helped that a lot of the music Roy played fed into my own political predilections. In high school, I had devoured books such as Upton Sinclair's *The Jungle* and John Dos Passos' *U.S.A.* trilogy. Now I was reading *On the Line* by my uncle Harvey Swados, a well-known social-democratic writer, C. Wright Mills' *The Power Elite*, and struggling with Karl Marx's *Das Kapital*, and Friedrich Engels' *The Origin of the*

Family, Private Property and the State. I was becoming a committed socialist, although I found the theories promulgated by the various socialist organizations confusing.

Folk music, though, was clear. There were heroes and villains. Stories and action. Poetry and open space. Children's songs. The songs of people who suffered; the songs of working people who won power over their own lives. I wasn't interested in singalongs and 'togetherness.' I wasn't interested in hootenannies, just in how the songs showed cultural and political aspects of people's lives, and how America should react to the messages.

My interest in folk music was augmented two years later in an honors American Studies seminar I took in college. John Hope Franklin, then chair of the Brooklyn College History Department, showed us how historic events, music, literature, food, and other aspects of culture, meshed and were related. It was the most interesting, exciting class I had in college or later in graduate school—and it reinforced my interest in the narratives of English and American folk songs.

Dave, Me, and More Folk Music

When Dave Van Ronk and I started to go out in September 1957, he introduced me to a broader, even more fascinating world of folk music.

In 1957, a few older musicians such as Cynthia Gooding and Theo Bikel were still performing. But by then, People's Songs had dissolved and the very slight folk music boom of the 1940s and '50s had disintegrated—especially as HUAC (House Un-American Committee) investigated communists and purported communists.

Dave had left the merchant marine about six months earlier, had played in a traditional jazz band, and was determined to make a living through music. Politically, when I met him he considered himself an anarchist and was a member of the Libertarian League, an anarcho-syndicalist organization. Several of its members had fought in the Spanish Civil War, and while they were militant about their politics, they were among the personally warmest people I've ever met.

Dave's perspective on folk music was different from Roy's, although occasionally they appeared in small concerts together. (This hadn't happened during the months when Roy and I went out, so I hadn't met Dave then or known that he and Roy were friends). One of his aunts had loved jazz, and as a kid he had heard it on radio broadcasts; he was forced to take piano lessons; and when he was 12 he took up the ukulele. A few years later, he took guitar lessons from a jazz musician, then played tenor banjo in jazz bands.

When we met, he no longer was playing in jazz bands. He'd learned a style of playing guitar called 'fingerpicking' that was used by blues musicians, and spent a lot of time bopping between Washington Square, where the folk singers played on Sundays from spring through fall, and an apartment on Spring Street that hosted folk singers after 5 p.m. on Sundays. He went to 'picking sessions' in peoples' living rooms and gathered with friends in the Caricature, a small upstairs coffee house on MacDougal Street, whose owner allowed the folk singers to hang out and play in her small back room. He spent many weekday afternoons in the Figaro.

The Figaro was a coffee house on the corner of MacDougal and Bleecker Streets. It was a fairly large, white-tiled, bright room and served as a hangout for many of the Village folk singers; for my bohemian college friends and me; and for hundreds of other Village denizens. You could sit and drink a mug of coffee for 25 cents. There were no free refills, but you didn't have to buy more than one mug to spend several hours there.

Because of his jazz background, Dave was as interested in the music he played as he was in the lyrics. He couldn't read music, but he carefully worked out arrangements of songs he'd played with a jazz band, such as 'Cake Walking Babies From Home,' or 'Tell Old Bill,' which he learned from Bob Gibson, who probably learned it from Carl Sandburg's *The American Songbag*. His personal passion was for blues, the music of the south that had been recorded by people such as Lead Belly, Sleepy John Estes, Lightnin' Hopkins and other Black musicians.

There weren't a lot of recordings of those songs around. There were some old race records—recordings of Black musicians produced by record companies to sell to Black listeners—and jazz recordings of blues, but few of acoustic guitarists. The major source of folk and blues was *Anthology of American Folk Music*, a six-record set released by Folkways Records, comprising songs recorded in the 1920s and '30s by traditional musicians. It included blues, ballads, fiddle tunes, country music, and other genres, and was the basis for the repertoire of most American folk singers during the 1950s.

Where did I fit into this? In the beginning, I didn't. I was a fan and Dave's girlfriend. I didn't play an instrument, couldn't carry a tune, lived with my family in Brooklyn, went to Brooklyn College, and could only be around any folk music activities weekends.

As the girlfriend of a folk singer, I had little status in that world. Girlfriends were relegated to the background—some even carried their boyfriend's instrument as they schlepped along behind the guy. I didn't schlep and I didn't carry Dave's guitar. We were proud of each other, and I was very clear about wanting not to be seen only as his girlfriend but as someone who controlled her own life. Dave supported that, and I'm delighted to remember that his actions never undermined his words.

The Folksingers Guild

There were few ways for me to function in the folk music scene. My realm was Brooklyn College and, more importantly then, socialist activities. Until Dave and I started to live together in July 1959, I participated in only one folk music effort: the Folksingers Guild. In 1957, a group of folk singers—or would-be professional folk singers—organized themselves to protect folk singers from being asked to play without pay. Since there wasn't anyone around, except for one coffee house, who wanted them to perform, with or without pay, there wasn't anyone to protect themselves against. So, to generate an audience, they produced their own small concerts.

Membership Card for the Folksingers guild, 1959

The best-known performers featured in Folksingers Guild concerts were Paul Clayton, whose clear voice produced ballads and sea shanties, and Logan English. Both men were in their mid-twenties, making them distinctively older than Dave, Roy, Luke Faust, Ellen Adler, Gina Glaser, Phil Pearlman, Ben Rifkin, and the other young would-be musicians. Paul Clayton had also recorded albums of ballads and sea shanties, and drew a larger audience than anyone else.

Folksingers Guild concerts were presented in small auditoriums, sometimes in schools. They gave members a chance to appear on stage, to get some experience, to be heard by their friends and a few other supporters. We charged very little—perhaps 50 cents or a dollar, and proceeds after expenses were divided among the performers. The only expenses were renting the auditorium and postage for press releases. The smallest amount performers earned in the least-attended concert was $1 each. At least they didn't get nothing.

I didn't play a role in organizing the Folksingers Guild. But I wound up handling its press. Someone else made flyers and pasted them up throughout the Village. I wrote press notices and sent them to newspapers and the two radio stations I thought might be interested. It was my first taste of public relations, and years later I realized that I had been good at it—even though doing it for the Folksingers Guild had been a baby effort. I didn't even always send full press releases, just hand-written postcards ... but I wrote each one that I sent to a print outlet in the style that the publication used for its listings.

The *Village Voice* and the *Villager*, both weekly newspapers, ran listings of events (although no one we knew read the *Villager*), so I sent them notices. Also the *NY Post*, an NYU student newspaper, and the *Columbia University Spectator*. Oscar Brand had a show on WNYC; George Lorrie had one on WNCN-FM; and WBAI, a small, non-commercial station, had returned to the air in 1955 after a two-year hiatus. They all received notices. There may have been some other media outlets; I don't remember which ones.

The Music I Love

When Dave and I moved in together in July 1959, I was heavily influenced by his taste in music. I'm glad that I was. I reacted viscerally to the blues.

What are the blues? Technical definitions and interpretations describe an 8-, 12-, or 16-bar form that uses 'blue notes'—that is, the flatted third and seventh notes of the major scale. None of that means anything to me. To this day, I simply recognize the sound and feel of a blues song when I hear it.

I was entranced by the driving, minor tones of the music, and by the lyrical, often joking notes of the blues singers. This book is retrospective—I'm writing now about what I perceived in the 1960s—so I feel comfortable describing what we thought the blues was then: the music of the neglected, the exploited Black residents of the South for whom the blues was a way to express unhappiness and dissatisfaction. Now, I know about the impact the blues had on jazz, classical music, popular music, literature, and theater. But I'm telling you what we thought in the late 1950s and through most of the '60s.

I still hear that in the music. But I also hear the joyousness and grace of songs such as 'Ain't No Grave Can Hold My Body Down,' sung by Bozie Sturdivant and heard on *Negro Religious Songs and Services*, a Library of Congress record, which still mesmerizes me every time I hear it; or 'Cocaine Blues,' a light-hearted romp about the drug written by a bluesman who probably never tried it (and which became one of the best-known songs Dave recorded). I also know now, as I didn't then, that many of the musicians we thought had been ignored had actually been professional entertainers, and some had been involved in vaudeville. That new knowledge doesn't change the music. It just puts it in a context that's different from the one that we imagined "back then."

Chapter 3
YOUNG SEX ... AND A WORD ABOUT ELDERLY SEX

I'm in my eighties, and I'm always surprised to hear women say, "I'm glad to be finished with that." Or "I stopped wanting sex years ago." I just don't get it.

In the 1940s and '50s, young people weren't taught about sex. I may have known even less than most children; my parents never mentioned it. In the fascinating Friday evening family gatherings I loved, the only references to it were allusions to my drinking uncle's mistress. And I had learned that one of my aunts had three abortions. "She was careless," they said. I never asked how she was careless and no one ever told me.

First Experiences

I remember discovering masturbation when I was very young. It relaxed me and helped me fall asleep.

My first experience with sexuality with someone else was with an elementary-school friend who talked me into feeling one another's chests. We were about 8 years old and I can't call them 'breasts,' because they weren't; we had flat, little-girl chests. But it felt good. I knew that what we were doing was 'wrong,' and that my parents would be angry if they knew about it—but I didn't know why.

That summer, my family went to the bungalow colony in the Catskills where we spent four consecutive summer vacations. There were three other girls my age there that year, and I suggested that we emulate my experience with my Brooklyn schoolmate. My summer friends were curious, and one afternoon, we exposed our chests and touched them. We played this game twice but we got scared of being found out so stopped.

How do kids know that sexual activity is wrong? We didn't even know that we were engaged in sexual activity. But we knew that what we were doing was socially unacceptable and certainly unacceptable to our parents. I'm sure a lot of research has been done on that, and I'm not about to read it … but it's a question.

So, sex again was a solitary activity until I was 17.

Before that, there were some forays into it, but they weren't pleasant.

When I was in high school, I became friendly with a girl who lived across the street. This story is about her father. I was about 14, tall and chubby, and in her family's kitchen, getting a glass of water. Her father walked up to me, put his arm around me, and kissed me. Really kissed me. It was a soul kiss … he put his tongue in my mouth.

I'd never heard of that. I was disgusted. And horrified. My friend's father did that. I knew he shouldn't have.

I didn't want to tell my parents what had happened. I knew they would be angry. I thought they might be angry with me as well as Mr. X. I thought they might ban me from going to my friend's house. I thought they might confront her father. So I kept it to myself—but I stayed away from her house for a long time, then made sure her father and I were never alone in a room.

The following summer, when I had just turned 15, my parents took my brother and me (my sister worked that summer) to a different bungalow colony. This one was in Rockland County, where I now live. One of my mother's sisters lived in Rockland, which, in 1954, was more rural than suburban. Our bungalow was on the road used to enter and leave the little summer community.

One of the bungalows was occupied by two brothers who did construction work nearby. I was taken with one of the men. He was in his twenties. I found him attractive. I watched him and his brother return from work every day. And I thought he looked at me with interest.

He probably did. At the start of the summer, I was tall and chubby. During the two months we were there, my excess weight disappeared. I didn't diet. I didn't exercise. I didn't do anything to lose weight. It simply went away. And I emerged with an incredibly attractive body.

I was still tall. But, now I was tall and slim. My stomach was concave; my hip bones jutted out; my ass was flat; and I had large breasts. I didn't realize that my body was similar to my mother's … except that I was

5'11" and 15, and my mother was 5'1" and 44. Back then, in 1954, that seemed old.

Every afternoon, I stood in front of our bungalow, and I guess the only term I can think of for what I did was 'posed' so this young man would notice me. It's embarrassing now to realize how obviously I was soliciting his interest. But this was 1954, and that's what many young girls did. Young girls probably still do it.

It worked. Sometimes, the young man would stop and we'd exchange a few words. One day, he asked me to go for a drink with him. I knew nothing about liquor. I'd never been in a bar. I had tasted wine and beer (just tasted, not drank), and occasionally, when my father drank a shot of Bell's Scotch from the bottle, he let me lick the cork.

The legal drinking age in New York State then was 18, but I suppose my height helped me look older than I was. We went to a bar, and I ordered soda. My companion had beer. Lots of beer. When we left the bar, he stopped the car on the side of the road and drank more beer. I don't remember how he convinced me to get into the back seat with him. It probably wasn't difficult. I didn't know what was going to happen.

The rest was predictable … but not to me. He tried to have sex. I protested. He held me down and tried to force me. I still didn't know the mechanics of what was happening. Luckily, he'd had too much beer to accomplish what he was trying to do.

A bit of luck: a police car pulled up next to his car and a police officer asked what was going on. The young man said something or other and the cop told us to move. Why didn't I yell for help? Because I was embarrassed? Because I was as afraid of the police officer as I was of him? Because I was afraid the police would take me home and tell my parents what had almost happened? Because I wanted whatever might happen to happen? Probably a bit of all.

I returned to my parents' bungalow very disheveled. That evening, my parents started to worry about me and sex.

Last night, I talked with a female friend who had a similar experience in her teens with a stranger who offered her a lift during a rainstorm, telling her that he was a friend of her mother's. He started to grope her, but stopped after a while. She also froze. She told me that during the incident, a song was playing on the car radio, and that for years afterward, every time she heard the song she was traumatized.

I wasn't traumatized, or even very scared. I felt that something I didn't understand was happening, and I didn't know how to figure it out.

It's been difficult to tell anyone about this experience during the years of the #MeToo movement. As a feminist, I have known for a long time that I should be enraged with him. I was only 15, didn't understand what I was doing, and, although I encouraged him to be sexually interested in me, I didn't understand the possible implications of that—and I didn't encourage him to try to rape me. And he wasn't a kid; he was an adult. But, I wasn't angry; I was upset. I was appalled at my own behavior: preening for some guy's attention, not consciously knowing that I was inadvertently encouraging him to approach me sexually, not struggling as hard as I could have to get away. Of course, none of those justify what he did. But in 1954, men weren't blamed for reacting aggressively to what seemed like a female's sexual invitations; and I grew up in a household in which if something unpleasant happened between me and someone else, I was usually asked, "What did you do to provoke it?"

Whatever Sex Was, I Was Interested

The next year, I learned that whatever sex was, I was interested.

In my senior year in high school, I still was 15. I hadn't ever been on a date; I was still taller than almost every male in my high school. A friend arranged a few blind dates for me. They were dreadful. A young man would take me to the movies, then we would go someplace for ice cream. Sometimes we would double date. But, I couldn't make small talk; I had no experience doing it and had nothing to say. None of the young men asked me out again.

Then I went on a date with Albert. We sort of connected. He attended Yeshiva University—I didn't know it was an Orthodox Jewish college—and studied accounting. He said he wanted to marry me. My parents were delighted.

Finally, a young man was interested in me. I knew I should be thrilled, but I wasn't. I felt that something was wrong. Albert and I would neck on my parents' couch. He would feel my breasts. When he left and we kissed and hugged goodnight, I could feel his erection through his clothes. I told him that petting, the term for what we were doing, wasn't enough. I couldn't even think, much less say, that I wanted to have sex, but I could think and say that I wanted something more than we were doing. He said we had to wait. "Wait for what?" I demanded. "Marriage"

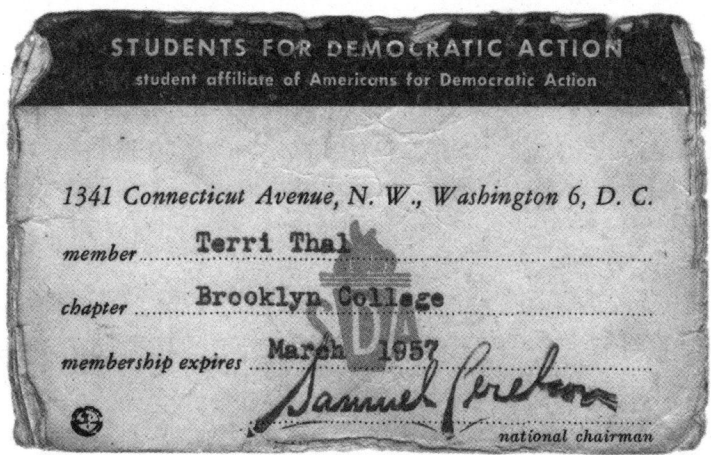

Membership Card for Students for Democratic Action, 1957

was the answer. But we couldn't get married for five years, when I would graduate from college.

That wasn't the only reason I broke up with him, but it was one of them. The other reasons involved my sense that marriage to Albert would mean housekeeping, babies, and no independence. I didn't know what I did want from life, but it certainly wasn't that.

Fast forward a year to spring 1956. I was a freshman in Brooklyn College, a few miles and a bus ride from home. I had joined Students for Democratic Action (SDA), the youth group of what was then considered the left wing of the Democratic Party.

At the SDA national convention, held at Sarah Lawrence College in Westchester, NY, just outside New York City, a group of attendees had a party. I'd never been to a party where people drank alcohol, and I'm sure this contravened college rules.

A socialist named Bogdan Denitch, who later became a noted sociologist, was at the conference to try to recruit SDA members to a socialist organization. As a group of SDA members swigged liquor that evening, I held up a bottle of vodka and asked, "What will happen if I mix it with beer?" Of course, the reply from someone was, "Try it and see." So I did.

The only other thing I remember from that night is lying in bed (fully clothed) with Bogdan beside me. I was oblivious to why he was there. He put his arm around me and, in his sexy Yugoslavian accent, asked, "How old are you?" "Sixteen," I said.

Bogdan drew away and firmly, but nicely, said, "The first time you do it, you should think you're in love."

I don't care whether he was being kind or avoiding a possible sexual assault charge; the legal age then for sexual intercourse in New York State was 17. Whichever his reason, I have been grateful ever since I realized what did not happen. I doubt that we would have had sex; I was befuddled, not interested, and probably wasn't awake enough; but it could have been an uncomfortable, unpleasant, confusing experience.

My virginity lasted another six months. And when I 'did it,' I didn't think I was in love.

A Word About …

This chapter originally was called *Young Sex*, but I started it by saying that when older women say, "I'm so glad I'm finished with that," I don't understand why. So I want to say something about "older sex." That quotation actually reflects what I hear from many women and what a large section of society believes about women; that they dry up and don't want sex when they hit middle age. The prevalence of that belief is astounding.

I think it's weird. Maybe our organs get dry, but there are a zillion ways to wet them. And there are a zillion gadgets to use on them if the partner can't do it with their body.

Several years ago, my gynecologist retired. I was only in my seventies. After more than a year of asking for recommendations, I tried a woman ob/gyn in Rockland. She was booked up for months, but I was OK about seeing her nurse-practitioner; NPs generally are wonderful. This NP carefully repeated my name, then recited the obviously scripted explanation for everything she did. Just before the physical vaginal examination, she said to me, "Of course, you're not sexually active." "Gulp," I thought. I remained polite. But—I found a new ob/gyn who would understand that I thrive on sex and that all I want to know from her is whether all the nodes and whatevers are OK or might be dangerous. If she thinks screwing is an inappropriate activity for an old lady, she's never said so.

Chapter 4
IT'S A SMALL WORLD

Small World Story 1: The Authors Guild

While in the first stages of writing this book, I joined a Zoom meeting of a group of writers. I saw the meeting listed on the website of The Authors Guild, an organization of writers that I had just joined, and thought it would help me learn how to tell stories better.

One of the first comments by the woman who was facilitating the group was that Marjorie Turner Hollman, a contributor to the group's success, wouldn't be participating in that day's meeting because she and her husband were going on a hike. I was fascinated to hear that; Marjorie's husband is my youngest nephew (who is well into his fifties). I know she's a successful writer of books about finding easy walking trails, which I find useful, but it was a surprise to have tumbled into her group.

It's another example of the 'small world' syndrome. I have found that there are circles within circles within circles, all occupied by people I know, or who know one another, or who have some point of contact.

Small World Story 2: Paul and Cynthia Gooding

Dave Van Ronk and I were very involved in the socialist movement. While we despised people who still were members of the American Communist Party, we understood why they had joined it. Before that organization became a tool of the Soviet Union, betrayed trade unions and other workers' movements during and after the Second World War, destroyed its own working-class base, and murdered political dissenters and Jews, it was a radical movement that posed an alternative to capitalism.

A year after Dave and I broke up, I met Paul Solomon Orentlich, a Village bartender, a sculptor, and a financial public relations practitioner, who was twenty years older than me, and we lived together for twenty-seven years until he died. Paul had been in the American Communist Party when he was in his teens but had left because of the Soviet betrayals and murders. He also had been in People's Songs, which was made up of people who either were in the Party or sympathized with it; he had created arrangements for folk singer Cisco Houston, who Dave and I knew slightly; and Pete Seeger had asked him to be part of the Weavers … all before the Second World War.

Later, but years before we met, Paul had roomed with—just roomed with, hadn't had an affair with—Cynthia Gooding, a folk singer. Dave and I both admired her and we were friends. Cynthia was younger than Paul but somewhat older than me, and the only women I knew then who was taller than me.

Small World Story 3: Martus and the Record Cover

Three years after Paul died, I went out with Martus Granirer, who lived near me in Rockland County, the area about 35 miles (56 km) from Manhattan where Paul and I had moved in the 1980s. Martus and I wound up living together for eighteen years, until he died in 1996.

When I met Martus, he was a well-known, land-protecting lawyer in Rockland. Turned out that years before, in the 1960s, he was a photographer in Manhattan. He photographed abstruse objects that he set up to show philosophical relationships of space and time. He became known in the world of photography and some of his photographs had been bought by museums, including the Museum of Modern Art. However, to earn a living, he had done commercial photography, specializing in books, and he also photographed records.

Dave had hated the record jacket artwork on his first solo record, for Folkways Records. It featured a large photograph of an espresso machine, with Dave's name in small type. Of course, you've guessed correctly, Martus had taken that photograph and designed the record jacket.

Martus' explanation: Moe Asch, the owner of Folkways Records, had told him to find a pretty girl and photograph her in a coffee shop for the record jacket cover. Martus thought that was trite, and instead juxtaposed a large espresso machine with small type. When they met and Martus told Dave the story of how the record jacket was designed, Dave agreed that an espresso machine was better than a strange young girl … though he still didn't like the cover.

Chapter 5
JESUS CHRIST, THE FBI

"Jesus Christ, the FBI," I thought as I shakily went to my class on eighteenth-century European history.

1957: First Threat

It was spring 1957. I was 17, a sophomore at Brooklyn College, and had been going to meetings of a socialist organization called the Young Socialist League (YSL), the youth group of one of the several American factions that called itself Trotskyist.

I didn't know what a Trotskyist was, and barely knew what a socialist was. But I believed that every person in the world is born with the right to food, shelter, and education; later I added healthcare. Clearly, not everyone was getting those things. There was racial and ethnic discrimination in the United States; on every continent, people lived in degrees of poverty I couldn't fathom; virtual slavery existed in American mining communities; the Soviet Union sent political dissenters to gulags. Clearly, the United States was class-driven (I didn't yet realize that it is also race-driven). Would socialism, whatever it was, be able to change all of this? I had to believe it would.

So, I went to meetings of the YSL, not really understanding the rhetoric. I listened to talks about obscure issues such as the different theories of how Russia changed after the revolution. Was it now a degenerated workers' state? Was it now an example of bureaucratic collectivism or state capitalism? The YSL adhered to the theory of bureaucratic collectivism, a theory I only fully understood many years later—2013 in fact—thanks to an article in the *New Yorker* by Louis Menand.

Back to 1957, and one morning, as I walked the three long blocks from my house in Brooklyn to the Avenue J bus that took me to Brooklyn

College, two men stood in front of the elementary school I passed. One was tall, large, blondish, and clean-cut; the other was shorter, older, and looked sort of Eastern European. They approached me, saying, "Terri?" I stopped and without thinking, said, "I won't name names." I had lived through the Army–McCarthy hearings and knew that people had gone to jail for not identifying Communists they knew or worked with. "I won't name names" was an automatic rejoinder.

The FBI agents showed me their ID, then asked me to talk about the YSL. I refused. After a while, they said, "You have a sister. Her name is Joyce." They proceeded to tell me about my sister's life at Brandeis University—her friends, and that she had taken a course with Herbert Marcuse, a German-American philosopher, sociologist, and political theorist who later, in the 1960s and '70s, became an icon to the New Left. It was terrifying to think that the FBI took my activities so seriously that they spent time and money digging up such detailed information on my family. My sister was not a socialist; she had, perhaps, explored it … but she didn't believe it was a solution to poverty and discrimination.

I pointed out to the agents that if they had all that information about me, they certainly knew much more about the YSL than I did. I wasn't a member, I noted, just a 'contact,' as the YSL called the non-members who were interested. I was in less of a position than they were to get such information … and if they knew that much about me, they certainly already had a lot of information about actual members.

Finally, they told me to think about what to do for two weeks, then they would return. Before they left, they made the biggest threat of all: they could tell my parents about my left-wing activities. My parents had some idea that I was involved with socialists—I went to socialist meetings in Manhattan every Friday evening, and I talked incessantly about socialism at home—but I knew that if they learned that the FBI had any interest in me, they would panic and try to prohibit me from having anything to do with my newly found interest.

The agents insisted that I promise not to tell anyone that they had visited me. And, since I was too naïve to realize that it was a bullshit promise, I kept it, telling only Roy, a folk singer I had met at YSL meetings and with whom I was now going out. Roy blanched and said, "Tell them anything they want to know. Then, get out of being near the YSL or any other group like it." I was horrified by his reaction; it seemed cowardly.

Two weeks later, I told the FBI agents that I didn't want to have anything to do with them. I was scared ... terrified ... but I couldn't do what they wanted. Thank goodness, they did not contact my parents.

1960: Phone Tapped

In the early 1960s, when Dave and I lived together and were involved with a different Trotskyist organization, the American Committee for the Fourth International, which later became the Workers League, we joked about our phone being tapped ... but I didn't believe it was. Who would take us that seriously? I was more afraid of being arrested for buying pot than I was by the FBI.

One afternoon, I had a long phone conversation with someone, hung up, then picked up the receiver to make another phone call. I was startled to hear my own previous conversation. I listened for a while, rapt and astounded. Had it been taped? I supposed it had—how else could I have heard it? I never wanted to become paranoid, but to this day I wonder what was going on.

As I became more active in left-wing organizations, my biggest fear was that I would harm my brother professionally. Leon was five years younger than me and planned to become a doctor, something he'd wanted to do since an uncle gave him a medical microscope as a Bar Mitzvah gift. I adored him; we were close friends as well as siblings, and I didn't want to screw up his career.

When he completed medical school, Leon applied to work with the federal Public Health Service. He was summoned to Washington, D.C., where he met with two public officials. He said their first question was, "How well do you know your sister?" He told them that we had grown up together, so he knew me pretty well. Then, of course, they wanted to know how much he knew about my political activity and whether he agreed with it. According to Leon, he told them that he knew a bit about it, thought I was crazy, and didn't share my views. (All of that was true.)

In the conversation, he said, they knew about everything I'd done: the benefit concerts for Congress of Racial Equality (CORE) and Student Non-Violent Coordinating Committee (SNCC) for which I'd gotten folk singers to perform; my later participation in socialist groups; my trips to England to political conventions or meetings. But, Leon said, they didn't know that Dave and I had separated. So, as he told me, "I brought them up to date."

1970: Fingerprints

I didn't hear from the FBI again until the early 1970s. When I stopped managing folk singers, I spent a few months working in a brokerage company—an odd place for a socialist, but I had accepted a job there. One day, staffers were told that the FBI would fingerprint all of us the next day. For me, this presented a dilemma. I had been fingerprinted when I got a teacher's license in the late '50s, but since then, I had become more concerned with civil liberties, and I objected to federal surveillance of citizens.

When I got home that evening, the nice, elderly superintendent of my building rang my bell. He wanted to tell me that the FBI had visited him to ask about me. "I told them you're a very nice girl," he said. Later, one of the women who lived below me knocked on my door to tell me the same thing.

I went to work the next day, not sure what to do. It turned out that I didn't have any choice: I was fired that morning. I guess the brokerage company didn't care whether or not I was nice; the FBI had told it what to do.

I know that since I considered myself a socialist, working in a brokerage house, a bastion of capitalism, contravened my own belief that I should be working for systemic political change, and I suspect that I would have ended up resigning. But, that was a decision for me to make. I wasn't fired for incompetence. I was fired for political activity outside of my workplace. Would that have harmed the company I worked for, or any of its employees, or any of its clients? Would it have harmed the security of the United States? Was I doing anything illegal? Obviously not, since I never was arrested nor even interrogated by the police or by any federal agency.

Oddly, neither Dave—who had been in the same political groups as me—nor I ever felt that the government made any effort to impede his performing.

Years later, in the mid-1970s, I was summoned to grand jury duty, where people were routinely fingerprinted. I refused to be fingerprinted. After an argument from public officials, I was told to go home and think about what to do for one week. By then, I was living with Paul Solomon Orentlich and had become friendly with Leonard Boudin, a noted civil liberties lawyer. I called Leonard and asked him what to do.

"Get fingerprinted", he advised. "We will fight grand jury fingerpicking and we will win, but not now. If you refuse to be fingerprinted now, you'll go to jail."

When I went back to the court and acceded to being fingerprinted, the person doing it banged my hand down so hard I thought it might break.

I didn't try to get my FBI record until 2019, when Aaron J. Leonard wrote first a book about folk music and the FBI from 1939 through 1956, and then an article about the FBI's interest in Dave during the 1950s. I'm not sure I filled out the application properly, and I specified that I only wanted the record that I didn't have to pay for. Months later, I received a form saying that my FBI record had been destroyed.

That may be true. If so, it's almost insulting. The FBI says it destroys the records of people who no longer are perceived as a possible threat. How do I want to be perceived?

I know that last question is odd. There's almost a hierarchy of status among people on the Left: "I was more persecuted by the government than you were." So, part of me wants to have an FBI record still extant. It wants me to have been considered a threat to the government, but without having to suffer for it. That attitude holds for so many people I know who were or still are around left-wing politics. It's almost as though our work, the time we gave to some movement, our efforts to create change in society, are partly validated by having been recognized by the U.S. government as a threat.

Why do we need that? Perhaps because the years we spent trying to foster civil rights, build a labor movement that would embrace our socialist ideals, convince others that they should join us to try to create a socialist world, didn't produce enough results. Having an FBI record shows that we tried. People who were persecuted by the FBI or by the House Un-American Activities Committee (HUAC), people who went to jail or lost their jobs and couldn't get hired anywhere because of their political actions, are noted and remembered and honored by left-wingers in this country. We want to be remembered as one of them.

1981: Under Surveillance

Recently, I learned that I had been under surveillance by a local police force because I had allowed the lawyers for Kathy Boudin, who was convicted for felony murder based on her participation in a major robbery in Rockland County, where I now live, to make phone calls from my house. In 1981, Kathy Boudin acted as a decoy in the escape vehicle of a group that robbed a Brink's armored car in a mall about 5 miles (8 km) from my house. Two police officers and a security guard were killed, and another security guard was injured.

Earlier, Boudin had been part of the Weather Underground group that in 1970 was crafting a bomb intended to be used against U.S. Army personnel when the explosive unexpectedly went off, killing three of the people who were making it and destroying the building. She and another woman who were in the building, but who were not involved with the bomb, lived, but went into hiding for ten years.

Paul, with whom I moved to Rockland County in 1981, had been a friend of Jean and Leonard Boudin, Kathy's parents, for many years. He had known Kathy when she was a baby. I never met her—I met her parents after the bomb accident. We assumed that her father and she were in touch, but no one ever talked about it.

I had met and liked the Boudins when Paul and I started to live together in the early 1970s. Jean was a poet. Leonard, as I wrote earlier, was a noted civil liberties lawyer. I was interested in becoming a lawyer, and was flattered when he said if I went to law school, I could clerk at his office. He also brought me onto the board of directors of the New York Emergency Civil Liberties Committee, the organization Bob Dylan later insulted publicly when it gave him an award.

After the Brink's robbery, Paul called his friends to tell them how sorry he was about the incident, and they asked that I visit Kathy in jail and try to find an optometrist and a hairdresser for her. I refused to visit; I couldn't think of what I would say to someone who had engaged in such a destructive, adventurist activity. I did try to enlist eye and hair practitioners for her, but I still went to Manhattan for those services for myself, so I found myself approaching strangers in Rockland County. Even if I'd known them well, I doubt that they would have helped Boudin.

She was so hated in Rockland County that speaking her name literally caused at least one person I approached to spit. Another, an orthodontist I knew slightly, hissed, "I wouldn't go near that fucking bitch." Boudin was treated abysmally by the Rockland County criminal justice system. People who visited her in jail, including those who brought her baby son with them, were strip-searched. A special cage was built to hold her during her trial.

Although I was disgusted by her actions, I was appalled by the way she was treated by the criminal justice system; I thought she deserved the fair treatment the U.S. promises people who are arrested. When her parents asked if her lawyer could use our phone, I said "Sure." I believe that everyone deserves a fair trial, and her legal team needed to communicate with whomever.

Several years later, a policeman who lives in my community told me that because I allowed her lawyers into my house (and who was watching them closely enough to know that?) it was under a police watch for months afterward.

I want to note that Kathy Boudin regretted being involved in violent actions. She became a model prisoner, earned a master's degree in adult education and literacy while in prison and then, five years after her release, earned a doctorate from Teachers College at Columbia University. She became concerned with the social consequences of mass incarceration, and was deeply involved with organizations that try to help people in prison restore their lives.

I know that many people believe that no degree of remorse or changed behavior should allow someone who kills or helps in the killing of a police officer to have their prison sentence reduced. While I disagree, I understand the feelings behind that. My own concern is, what happens to people in prison who have changed as much as Kathy Boudin but who don't have networks of activists pushing for their release as she did? I believe that, regardless of their crime, they, too, deserve a fair parole hearing.

Over the years, I've wrestled with the question of government oversight of citizens, government surveillance of citizens, the responsibilities of government, and how they intersect with those of citizens. Would it be different in a truly democratic socialist society? In such a society, would the lines between government and citizens be diminished? Diminished, perhaps … but not eliminated. I think that except in utopian communities, one group has the ability to exercise power, and there's always a tension between power and lack of it. I can't predict how that might be resolved.

Chapter 6
ELEVEN YEARS AND ONE MONTH

Where Dave and I first met: I was 17 and at a party in a huge apartment on Riverside Drive with a zillion large rooms. Most of the people there were science fiction fans—this was my first experience with 'sci fi fandom.' A young man named Shel had been patting my hand, insisting that we go to a bedroom to "experiment." It was clear to me that Shel wasn't looking for sex but wanted me to smoke grass.

To this young woman from Brooklyn, marijuana was that awful stuff growing in the fields near Lafayette High School, which I had attended. Each spring, the police would burn down the weeds.

Shel pushed hard. I was becoming annoyed. Suddenly, a tall, scruffy guy appeared and said, "Shel, leave her alone." Then, to me: "You don't have to do anything you don't want to." This tall, scruffy guy was Dave Van Ronk, and we spent the rest of the evening holding hands. Of course, I was impressed. A long time later, he told me that he'd been stoned on grass that evening but didn't want Shel to drive away an attractive woman. I never thought that was insulting; I was flattered.

That was sometime in winter 1956–57. Months later, in early September 1957, I was in the Figaro, a Greenwich Village coffee house, with several members of my bohemian crowd from Brooklyn College. Marty, a mathematician who was teaching for the first time at NYU the next morning, was trying to figure out how to open his class. With sarcasm? Wit? What to say? Inspire them? Impress them?

Dave was sitting nearby. We wound up in conversation and he offered to take me home. Home wasn't a short walk from the Village. It involved a one-hour subway ride to the depths of Brooklyn, then a nine-block walk. That would deposit me at my parents' home—not a place that would welcome a poor, non-Jewish folk singer. He schlepped out to Brooklyn with me, and we were together for the next eleven years (and one month).

I had been going to socialist meetings on Friday evenings, and continued to, with Dave often meeting me, and we hung out together Saturdays, either at the Figaro or the Caricature, at other coffee houses on MacDougal Street, or at his loft.

When we met, Dave didn't have an apartment. He was staying at the home of Lee Hoffman and Larry Shaw. Lee was a science fiction fan, an editor of early folk music fanzines, and an author of science fiction, Western, and romance novels. In 1957, she started a mimeographed folk music fanzine called *Caravan*, which was produced "on the cheapest paper imaginable," then distributed "FREE FOR THE ASKING." It quickly became the paper of record for the burgeoning folk music revival.

A month later, Dave and a friend from Richmond Hill, Queens, where he had grown up, got a huge loft on Monroe Street, way downtown. The loft was on the fifth floor, and we got there either on a large, difficult-to-use freight elevator or by walking up a lot of stairs. It was about 100 feet long and 25 feet wide (30 × 8 m), and divided into two rooms. One room had a fireplace; the other had a gas heater, although it didn't work well. Toilet in the hall, of course. Cold water; the gas heater wasn't connected to the water supply.

Dave said it once had been Norman Mailer's loft—if so, Mailer, too, had had a lot of cold sex.

Dave and me in my parents' house—before I got contact lenses.
But, why am I wearing a shower cap?

Christmas 1957. Dave, Judy Isquith, a friend from folk music; some friends of his from Queens; myself, and enough others to make about a dozen people gathered at the loft for dinner. There was an undecorated Christmas tree. Where did Judy cook the turkey? I don't remember whether the stove worked, so I don't know where she roasted it. We used paper plates. Tableware? There wasn't any, so I led a raid on the Garden Cafeteria on East Broadway. A few coffees to justify our presence, a visit to the tableware counter under my instruction, and we emerged with enough forks, spoons, and knives for twelve. Later that winter, as my train from Brooklyn crossed the East River on the Manhattan Bridge and reached the Manhattan side, I could see the Christmas tree we had put out on the fire escape.

I was an accomplished thief. I didn't have any compunctions about stealing. This wasn't a political statement of opposition to the oppressive ruling class. It was simply stealing. Stuff I wanted or could not afford, stuff that I thought showed me off as some kind of intellectual. At Brooklyn College, among my friends and political colleagues, I was known as a first-class book thief.

As a kid, I stole a china reindeer from a Woolworth's when I was about 9. And a paperback of *Sue Barton: Student Nurse* when I was in third grade. A dress from the tall girls' department at Lane Bryant when I was 16. Two fat volumes of Spengler's *The Decline of the West* from the bookstore behind Brooklyn College. (Yes, I read them.)

When I got caught stealing the *Sue Barton* book, and the candy-store owner called my mother, I explained to her that we were only allowed to take four books at a time from the public library, that I usually read them within a week, and that I then didn't have anything to read until she took me to the library again. Oddly, my very strict mother did not make a huge fuss about what I'd done. I asked her not to tell my father what had happened. Of course, she told him—but oddly, he never said anything about it to me.

Dave was both dismayed at and amused by my kleptomania, but he forgave it. I think he was mostly afraid that I'd get caught. When we moved in together in summer 1959, I noticed that he didn't object to the roast beefs and coffee I copped from the supermarket. And, although he was appalled by my occasionally stealing from libraries, he was excited when I came home with a complete, hard-bound set of the *Child Ballads*. He even took them with him when we broke up. I was more pleased with

Leon Trotsky's *Between Red & White*, which I found witty. My excuse for the thefts: no one had checked any of those books out for more than 20 years, and we would appreciate them. Which we did.

I stopped stealing in the early 1960s, partly because I started to feel guilty about it, partly because I was afraid of getting caught.

A few months after the Christmas dinner, Dave and his friend gave up the loft, and he rented an apartment on MacDougal Street, above what later became the Gaslight Cafe, with Sam Charters—who made field recordings of Black blues musicians in the south in the 1950s and '60s, and also produced records and wrote books about the blues. This was another cold-water flat. There was no way for a young, would-be folk singer to earn a living in New York then, and Dave's financial situation was precarious, but I disliked using newspaper as toilet tissue and so, each weekend, before I went to the apartment, I first visited Rienzi, a coffee house across the street, to swipe one roll for my visit. It wasn't a very glamorous life.

Not glamorous, but fun. We developed sort of a routine. Friday evenings, we would meet at the headquarters of the Young People's Socialist League (YPSL), the youth group of the Socialist Party, which Dave and I had both joined in 1958.

Dave had learned about the philosophies of the left from anarchists, and I had been introduced to them by Trotskyists. I've occasionally wondered whether we would have lasted as a couple if we hadn't had a shared political perspective and an interest in furthering it. We were young—I was 18 and he was 21. We had other interests—I was in college and he was trying to develop a career as a musician. Our backgrounds were different—he came from a devout Irish-Catholic family, while I grew up in a Jewish family that honored religious customs; he considered himself an atheist, and despised the Catholic hierarchy, while I felt Jewish, liked Jewish culture, spent Jewish holidays with my family, but knew little about the Torah. In the 1950s, girls did not have bat mitzvahs, and were given little, if any, Jewish education. I had none.

There was no place for a young folk singer to work then, so Dave had time to dedicate to left-wing politics; and I spent probably too much time on them, to the detriment of some of my studies.

I reveled in anything that helped me understand the dynamics of social disparities. In my senior year at Brooklyn College, I took a seminar with John Hope Franklin (the first person of color to head a major college history department and read W.E.B. Du Bois' *Black Reconstruction in America*, (which I've recently reread, and recommend to anyone concerned with racial inequality), as well as books by Vernon Parrington, James Bryce, W.J. Cash, and Alexis de Tocqueville (I still have them, of course). I did well in classes like that. However, at the end of a required course in biology, I received a postcard in the mail with my grade circled in red: it was "F." Next to it was a note from my teacher: "If you had spent on biology a fraction of the time you spent trying to make the socialist revolution, you probably would have gotten an A." I had to repeat the class and cut up a pig again. Not fun, —and embarrassing.

We went to socialist meetings, but did little else to change the social order. We didn't yet sell the organization's newspaper, an activity all socialist groups insisted their members participate in … that happened later.

Saturday evenings, we went to parties, to political meetings, to folk music sessions; and when Dave had an apartment, we had sex. I didn't call it "making love" until, close to a year after we met at the Figaro, he told me he loved me and I responded enthusiastically. We were in Tompkins Square Park, which was unusual; we were much more likely to be further west in Washington Square. Then we went to his apartment and made love.

How to describe first love, especially being in love with someone whom you equate with God? It wasn't glorious bells or music or visuals. It was more a feeling of profound satisfaction. Warmth. Yes, sometimes my heart beat faster. Sometimes, I was so proud of him that I felt as though I were glowing.

My parents were less happy. They wanted their kids to marry Jews; intelligent ones, of course, but anyone other than a Jew was not acceptable. Certainly not a poor, scruffy folk singer with an Irish nose. They weren't intolerant of other religions; their objection to Dave was founded on what he wasn't, not what he was. Not Jewish equaled not for their daughter.

Meanwhile, I had college classes, term papers, exams, and socialist activities. I remained friendly with the people in my "bohemian" crowd when they showed up at Brooklyn College … but they had graduated, were teaching, or were in doctoral programs. The group simply didn't exist anymore. In retrospect, being accepted into that group was one of the best things that ever happened to me. My ego (now generally called self-esteem) was boosted; because people I considered intelligent, creative, insightful, seemed to think that I was one of them. I wasn't accepted because I had a great figure, or because they were being nice to me, or for any reason other than that they thought I was like them.

With the demise of that group, I spent more of my time at school with the socialists. The Brooklyn College cafeteria was where many of us hung out, drinking execrable coffee. Most cafeteria tables were occupied by students who were related by friendship or house plan membership (a house plan is the equivalent of a sorority or fraternity at the City of New York colleges). Other groups: one table comprised Blacks; one was taken by the eight young Communist Party members who attended the college; one was for the people who worked on the school newspaper; one was for us four socialists.

When I was able to convince my parents that I was spending Saturday night with a female friend, I stayed with Dave, but I always worried that they would call me at a non-existent phone number. Of course, they did find out we were sleeping together. In summer 1958, Dave and I went with Luke Faust and his girlfriend Sylvia to the Catskills, to a camp that had been in my father's family longer than I had. Leisure Lodge comprised two small, unheated cabins with no running water; there was an outhouse between them, with walls decorated with articles from the *Saturday Evening Post*. It had electricity and a wonderful old electric stove. I told my parents we were going there, but I also told them there would be other people with us and that the males and females would sleep separately.

We had no car, so we went there by bus. I cooked for the first time in my life. I bought one pound of stewing beef and a lot of onions and vegetables, trying to emulate what I had seen my mother do to make a stew. I guess it was good, and everyone was hungry, because when I served it, everyone else dug in before me and there was no meat left for me. Later, I realized that one pound of meat, which shrank while cooking, was very little for four people in their 20s, but I had never cooked before and had guessed at the ingredients and amounts.

Luke and Sylvia left early Sunday, and Dave and I stayed to clean up. We had told our friends that the place belonged to my family and that we had to be neat, but we found several very full condoms next to the bed our friends had slept in, which did not amuse me.

In the early afternoon, a car pulled up. My parents had visited my brother, who was at a Boy Scout camp about 30 miles (48 km) away, and had decided to come to Leisure Lodge. Did they really expect to find a bunch of people with us? I never knew. When Dave called out that my parents were outside, I simply sat down on the floor and wished I were someplace else. I pointed out to them that the other guests had left early, but my parents didn't believe that Dave and I hadn't slept together. They wanted me to leave with them, which I wouldn't do. "I came with him and I'll leave with him," I said bravely. Dave and I took a bus back to Manhattan, and I mentally—and perhaps physically—shook all the way home. *Would they disown me? Would they force me to choose between living at home and going with Dave?* He said that if my parents threw me out, we'd live together and he'd put me through my last year in college, but we both knew he wouldn't be able to do that.

No one disowned me, but my parents made their displeasure and unhappiness known to me very clearly. They didn't talk to Dave until we got married three years later, except for once when they were worried about a facial tic I had developed.

Several months later, in midwinter, Dave took me home from the Village in a snowstorm because he was concerned about my safety. It was sweet of him, but there he was in Brooklyn, nine blocks from the subway, and I knew he shouldn't trudge back to the subway (which ran aboveground in that part of Brooklyn) in the heavy snow to wait for a train that might not even arrive. I woke my parents and asked if he could sleep on a cot in another room. They may have not wanted him to be my boyfriend, but they said yes. So he did. The next morning, they left the house early to visit people, so everyone was spared what would have been a very uncomfortable encounter.

Sundays were folk music days. On warm afternoons through spring, summer, and fall, folk singers gathered in Washington Square. Bluegrass and country groups predominated. Roger Sprung's group, the Shanty Boys, with Roger, Lionel Kilberg, and Mike Cohen, were always there. Roger had been a member of a group that recorded four tracks on the ten-inch *Folksay* albums, one of my introductions to folk music. The New Lost City Ramblers—Mike Seeger, John Cohen, and Tom Paley (replaced in 1962 by Tracy Schwarz)—introduced northern urban audiences to "authentic" southern folk traditions. The Greenbriar Boys—Bob Yellin, John Herald, and Eric Weissberg (later replaced by Paul

Prestopino, who was in turn replaced by Ralph Rinzler)—were in Washington Square every week. Non-bluegrass or country musicians were there, too. Dave played there, sometimes with Roy Berkeley. So did Luke Faust, Happy Traum, Ben Rifkin, Erik Darling, Barry Kornfeld, Gil Turner, Dick Rosmini, Ramblin' Jack Elliott, Irene Kossoy and Ellen Kossoy, Bob Brill, and many people who did or didn't go on to become part of the Folk Music revival.

Later in the afternoon, we'd head over to the American Youth Hostel building on West 8th Street, where there was more folk music. Dave and I had a slightly snide attitude toward the scene at AYH. People there hiked, square-danced, and generally seemed to be healthy, outdoor types. We, on the other hand, were city-dwellers who liked left-wing politics and science fiction, smoked unfiltered cigarettes, and didn't relate to outdoor activities. Dave called the AYH denizens the "wee people." But the music was good and Dave wouldn't miss a chance to make music.

The day would continue at 190 Spring Street, in Roger Abrahams' or Roger Sprung's apartment. A lot of bluegrass and other folk musicians, many the same people we'd seen and heard in the afternoon at Washington Square, would gather and play music. One man who had an apartment in that building owned a monkey, which had free rein of the place. I wasn't and never have been a fan of pets, and I didn't take to the simian, but that didn't matter—he roamed through the apartment and approached whomever he chose.

Date Night

Dave and I had been seeing one another for several months. I'd meet him in the little diner next to the Waverly Theatre, or in Figaro, or at the loft he then lived in on Monroe Street, or, when he moved there, at his MacDougal Street apartment. We'd go someplace to listen to folk music, or hang out in a coffee house, or have glorious, fun sex. He usually escorted me home—an hour-long subway ride to Flatbush (in Brooklyn) until I said it wasn't necessary; I felt safe going home alone and there was no need for him to travel for two hours.

Before I met Dave, I had almost never gone on the kinds of dates most young women had—to movies or parties. Finally, after Dave and I had been seeing one another for several months, I said, "I want to go on a date. I want to be picked up, taken someplace, then taken home. I love having sex with you, and picking sessions are fun for you, but I'm not a musician and I don't have a real role at them. I want a date." "OK," Dave said. The following weekend, he said he was coming to Brooklyn to pick me up. "Why?" I asked. "Because," he explained.

Friday night, Dave rang the bell of my parents' home. I left with him, and we got on the subway. We didn't go to the Village; we went someplace in Queens and saw the movie *Some Like It Hot*. Then we went to Jahn's for ice cream. I didn't even know what neighborhood we were in. I knew what Jahn's was, but had never before been there. It was an ice cream parlor known for its huge servings, and was a popular place for young couples on dates. We did not have its noted kitchen sink sundae. We left Jahn's, got back on the subway and went back to my parents' home. Dave kissed me goodnight, saying, "You wanted a date, you got your goddamned date. Don't ever ask for another one."

That was our last date. We went back to meeting in the Village, going to concerts or picking sessions, and having sex.

California

The following winter, Dave heard that there was work for folk singers in Hermosa Beach, California. There was none in New York. Dave, who had strong opinions and strong prejudices, hated the idea of California, which people on the East Coast considered "woo woo land," and I wanted him to stay near me. But the promise of both an income and a chance to perform regularly was enticing, and we agreed that he would go but would return in time for my 20th birthday the first week of June and my college graduation two weeks later.

I was on the New York City steering committee of YPSL, and Dave was a member of YPSL. I was able to get both of us elected as delegates to the forthcoming national conference in Chicago. Neither of us New York City-born denizens could drive, but we knew we would be driven to Chicago by a comrade, and we knew someone else who planned to drive from Chicago to California after the conference, so Dave arranged to go west with him.

I remember nothing of the long ride to Chicago. When we got there, we walked into the apartment of a comrade named Dale Drews, who was putting us up for the duration of the conference. In the bedroom, we saw a polka-dotted wall. Then I realized the polka dots were moving. They were cockroaches. I'd never seen anything like it. I was physically disgusted, and the thought of spending several nights there was scary, but we had no place else to go. I was reluctant to take my clothes off, not knowing what might crawl all over me, and although we knew we wouldn't see one another for five months, the atmosphere played havoc with our sex life.

The only thing I remember about the conference itself is a discussion in the steering committee about expelling Dave from YPSL. He had committed some dreadful sin, but I no longer recall what it was. All steering committee members were told not to tell him what was being considered; I asked whether they were kidding. They sheepishly said that I shouldn't tell him, but that if I did I wouldn't be penalized for it. Jerks.

Dave wasn't expelled, and a few days later he, our friend from California, and another young man took off for the West Coast. Dave tells of that trip in his book, *The Mayor of MacDougal Street,* which he started to write and Elijah Wald completed in Dave's voice after he died. It's very good, and I urge you to read it.

I went back to New York. Dave and I corresponded—I still have his letters—and occasionally, he had enough money to call me. I could call him very infrequently; he didn't have an apartment, so he didn't have a phone. Also, back then, all long-distance calls were billed individually and showed on the phone bill, and I didn't want to ask my parents to pay for calls to someone they didn't want me to be involved with. I didn't even want them to know that we talked.

It's odd now to realize that Dave had so little money that sometimes he couldn't make calls from payphones, or that he didn't have a phone in his apartment in Manhattan because it cost too much, or that he often ate soup for dinner because it was cheap. In the 1950s, a young person could live on very little, but even if prices were much lower than they are now, you had to have some money to survive. I realize now that I don't know how he got by during the first year in which I knew him. He occasionally got a 9 to 5 job working as a messenger for a printer, but that happened infrequently and the jobs never lasted for more than a few days. Clearly, Dave lacked something that was needed to hold down a job.

While he was in California, I continued to go to socialist meetings and to folk music events, where I was pleased to find that I was welcome in the social scenes we frequented; I didn't need his presence to justify mine. I found the year-long American Studies seminar I took in my last year of college stimulating, and I read voraciously. I spent a lot of time with Stu Ritterman, who would be graduating from NYU; I had a sense that the following year, after we both had graduated from college, we probably wouldn't be as close as we had been.

I completed college, but didn't want to go to a huge graduation where I'd be one of 900 people walking across a stage. That was massively unfair to my parents, who had put me through college and had tolerated my socialist ranting and my insistence on falling in love with a poor non-Jew with not especially good financial prospects. They would have enjoyed seeing me get my diploma, and I regret that I deprived them of that. In late May, Dave wrote that he was leaving California so he could be back for my birthday. Then, one day in early June, just before my birthday, I was in the Village, and lo and behold, Dave was coming down the street. I ran down the block and into his arms, just like in a movie scene; I felt tremors of happiness. He didn't have an apartment to go to, but wherever he stayed that night, I was with him.

219 West 15th Street

Two weeks later, I graduated from Brooklyn College and we moved into an apartment at 219 West 15th Street that some friends were leaving.

We settled into our fifth-floor railroad flat walkup, with a tub that had a flip-down enamel cover in the kitchen and a toilet in a tiny room in the hall outside the apartment. Having one toilet per apartment was unusual for railroad flats in Manhattan; usually, toilets were shared by a few residents. A railroad flat was an apartment in which the rooms were lined up one after another; none was at an angle. We paid $70 a month rent, which was twenty-five percent of my salary—the exact percentage financial experts recommended. The apartment was 'furnished' with an enamel-topped table and some chairs in the kitchen, a three-quarter sized bed (bigger than a single bed, smaller than a double, and yes, sheets were made specifically for that size mattress), some sort of hard, couch-like thing and an ancient armchair in the living room, and a lot of cockroaches that we killed to the best of our ability.

We were young and walking up five flights of stairs didn't bother us, except sometimes. When Robert Shelton wrote a very positive review of Dave in the Sunday edition of the *New York Times*, I bought five copies. It didn't occur to me that I could pull the article out of four of those newspapers, throw the unneeded newspapers into a trash can on the street, and not schlep them up five flights of stairs. They became heavier and heavier as I ascended. Later, we had to take all but the page with the review back down those five flights of stairs. I hope I've thought through other activities more carefully over the years.

When my parents visited to see my new home, we hid Dave's belongings and he left for the afternoon. My mother's comment was, "We spent years trying to get out of this kind of place." The apartment was just like the ones they had lived in on East 9th Street between Avenues C and D on Manhattan's Lower East Side as immigrants to the United States in the 1920s.

I insisted to my parents that I lived alone. They may have believed me—for a while. Dave and I established a rule that only I answered the phone; Dave didn't like answering it, and we insisted that guests shouldn't. That worked until one evening, when some idiot guest picked up the ringing phone and said, "Van Ronk residence." My mother said, "Put Terri on the phone." We didn't kill the idiot; the harm was done.

Teaching

During my last semester in college, anticipating that we would live together and realizing that someone had to earn money and that Dave couldn't, I had crashed in two courses in education and passed an exam to become a substitute history teacher in NYC junior high and high schools. I was even fingerprinted, something that we considered a huge invasion of civil liberties but which was mandated for a teaching license.

I went to two job interviews. One was in a junior high school on Manhattan's Lower East Side. I wasn't even interviewed; I just filled out an application and was told, "We'll get back to you." As I left, a group of girls from the school walked up to me and asked, "Will you teach here next year?" I said I didn't know. "You don't want to teach in this shithole," one of the girls said firmly. "You get out of here and get yourself a job in a decent school." Ouch! *Note*: I was offered a job there.

I was also offered a job in Charles Evan Hughes High School on West 18 Street, between Eighth and Ninth Avenues (now the Bayard Rustin Educational Complex). Our apartment was on West 15 Street, between Seventh and Eighth Avenues, so it was a short walk away. I liked the department chairperson, and teaching in high school was preferable to teaching younger people in a junior high. In my interview, I'm sure I articulated typical youthful, idealistic intentions—opening up young minds, expanding horizons, bringing current reality to history lessons. None of that was possible, I learned.

Teaching history in a high school—it wasn't yet called social studies—was an adventure for a socialist. I was 20, only two years older than most of the students in my American History classes, but I'd graduated from college, lived with my boyfriend, and supported us financially—and that made a world of difference between my students and me.

I bought comfortable, teacher-looking, lace-up shoes and, luckily, most of my sweaters were large and didn't emphasize my big breasts. Every evening, I reviewed the material to be taught the next day, and each week I prepared lesson plans carefully; what I would cover, what I would emphasize, what examples I might use, what key facts the students should remember. I was acting professionally, but that last now strikes me as a bit ludicrous. One of the objections of educators to history as it's been taught in school is that for many years, all that was presented was facts: dates, wars, territorial acquisitions, epochs marked by sometimes irrelevant details, but with no perspective and no attempt to meld those factors with the lives of people.

The school I taught in was mixed ethnically. It included students from the Village and from Chelsea, which was not yet a neighborhood for professionals but comprised a mix of people of Irish or Italian descent, enough Latino families to see the start of inexpensive Hispanic restaurants, very few Blacks, and very few Jews. I liked a lot of my students, and I still believe that they were not allowed to try to succeed. It made me angry then and makes me angry now.

Bianca was in my home room class—home room was where students started and ended their day, and where they spent one period (a 50-minute time segment) each day. She was 16, chubby and sweet, and wanted to enroll in an academic program. High school students were ranked into 'academic programs' for kids considered smart enough to work toward going to college; 'commercial programs' for those who weren't considered 'college material' but who could be trained for office jobs that needed secretarial or low-level arithmetic skills; and 'general programs' for the rest. Neither the students nor their parents had any choice about the kind of program the youngster was in. That was determined in some administrative office. I realize now that I didn't know who made those decisions.

Bianca was in a commercial program, but she wanted to be able to go to college. She was fairly smart but didn't have a good academic background. Her grades were OK—in the 70s and low 80s, meaning that she earned Cs and Bs. Not quite good enough for college, the administrative gods ruled. So she wasn't allowed to try.

Miguel also was in my homeroom class. He was Latino, slim, smart, and passionately interested in geography and maps. I thought he could grow up to be a cartographer. But, he, too, was not considered capable of being in an academic program. His plight broke my heart. Confession: students sometimes gave teachers end-of-the-year gifts, and I still have a little leather purse Miguel gave me. I wonder what happened to him; I hope he found work that made him happy.

John was in my American history class. He was Italian, had black hair and very fair skin, and could have been in *Saturday Night Fever*. He lived in the Village, and was somewhere between having a big mouth and being charming. John told me that he knew I lived with my boyfriend, knew we smoked pot, and hinted that if I didn't give him a decent grade, he'd tell other students and administrators. I was scared—accusations like those could have gotten me fired. But we got through the year with no fireworks, and John earned his 'B.'

Jackie was my favorite student. She was a very light-skinned Black teenager, which then was considered a mark of distinction, since this was before Black Pride allowed women of color to revel in their own skin shade. Jackie was intelligent, passionate, a rebel, ran away from what she said was a broken home where she was mistreated by her parents, smoked pot, and I adored her. Once, when she had left home for a while, I brought her to our apartment and fed her; I didn't let her spend the night there, but I probably could have been fired for socializing with a student. I wanted so much for her to become a secure woman with a future. I still get angry when I remember how much she wanted to get away from her home and her past, how much she longed for a future as an educated woman, and how little I could help her.

Her plight broke my heart.

Dave was entertained by my job. He was incredibly smart and well-read; he knew more about anthropology and poetry than most college graduates, and was steeped in American labor and left-wing history, but he had been thrown out of Richmond Hill High School in Queens, NY, for truancy. As he told the story, the principal called Dave into his office when he became 16, stridently announced, "Van Ronk, you're ineducable," and, in essence, told Dave he was expelled. Dave delighted in helping me mark quizzes and tests. I was surprised by his attitude toward the students; I thought he'd be supportive of them. Instead, he'd review the tests, yelling "Got'cha. You get 'F' for that, you dirty little kid," as he scrawled a grade on the student's paper in red. Several years later, he was invited by Richmond Hill High School students to perform there, and did so with great panache.

In June 1960, the school's population diminished, and the department chair retained one of the five new teachers he had hired the previous fall. I wasn't the teacher he kept. I was young and inexperienced, and, although I think I could have become a good teacher, I needed training and time to get there.

For a short while, I did day-to-day substitute teaching, which was awful: The kids regarded substitute teachers as unwelcome intruders. I quickly learned that at the start of each fifty-minute teaching period, I had to send for an administrative staffer to coerce the students to stay in their seats and not torture me. Luckily, new coffee houses in the Village started to hire folk singers, and soon I was able to retire from my short teaching career.

That year, I developed what we realized was a psychosomatic twitch. It was unpleasant, being visible and making my neck and jaw hurt. It was curious; I twitched only to the left, which was a harbinger of medical issues to come. Years later, I realized that the left and right side of my body feel different; and the left and right sides of my face feel different. The right feels 'normal,' meaning it has little feeling. The left is tense and feels odd. No doctor has ever come up with an explanation, not even my very good neurologist—and I specify my 'good' one because I saw several who seemed fairly incompetent before I found Dr. Sweeta Goel.

Both Dave and my parents were concerned about the twitch, and my parents broke their rule of not speaking to him long enough to call him and ask what he thought they could do to help. I don't know what he said. They told me they thought I felt guilty because of my sexual activity and my living arrangement. Then they offered to pay for a psychiatrist.

I saw him weekly. Our fifty-minute sessions ran about forty minutes, and got even shorter as I continued to see him. He used sodium pentothal (truth serum, never proved to be effective) to try to help me talk about my memories, including whether my father sexually abused me. He constantly inserted questions about how my father acted toward me into his conversations with me; his attempts to find out whether my father had abused me were obvious and, I thought, obnoxious. He didn't want to accept that my father never touched me sexually. He told me I was paranoid—but one day, when his sodium pentothal wasn't delivered on time, I heard him on the phone in his office saying to someone, "Why is it that of all the people whose sodium pentothal wasn't delivered, you chose to not send me mine? Why is my delivery late? Are other deliveries late, or just mine?" The conversation made me wonder who was paranoid.

Dr. V. also told me I should have children because if intelligent people like me didn't have kids, the unintelligent people would flood the world with stupid people. Even then, I wondered whether a shrink was supposed to give a patient that kind of advice. I'd never yet heard of eugenics, but I was appalled.

After about a year, I complained about the short sessions, and he offered me a long make-up meeting. I went to his office, waited for him for about forty-five minutes, then left. I called my parents and told them not to pay any bills they received from him. I never called or saw him again.

'Tell Old Bill'

Meanwhile, Dave was developing a roster of guitar students. I didn't realize how good a teacher he was, or was becoming. Dave couldn't read music, but he created a notational system that showed the chords and fingering for his versions of many of the songs that became legendary among the people who studied with him. In those early years, he was just starting to think that system through.

I heard his students play certain songs over and over, some interminably. For years, I swore I never again would listen to 'Tell Old Bill' voluntarily; it was one of the stalwarts of Dave's guitar instruction.

A few people who took lessons from Dave when we were together are still friends of mine. Both Danny Kalb and Steve Katz became professional and superb musicians. Danny, who died in 2022, was a brilliant, creative guitar player who later amalgamated his blues guitar style with jazz. Steve became a blues-rock guitarist. Both were in the Blues Project, one of the first and best blues-rock bands of the 1960s. In his memoir *Blood, Sweat, and My Rock 'n' Roll Years: Is Steve Katz a Rock Star?*, Steve wrote that sometimes, when he came to the apartment for his guitar lesson, Dave and I clearly had been having sex; he says he sometimes had to bang on the door to get us out of bed. It's a great story and I love it, but I don't remember that ever happening. Jerry Rasmussen is playing again; we're Facebook friends. Dan Lauffer, who I associate with H. P. Lovecraft as much as with folk music, lived nearby and we ran into one another occasionally until his death in 2023.

Dave himself was improving as a musician. His own later assessment of his playing in 1959 was harsher than most other people's, which I think is good. He was able to look at his early music from a distance and see its weaknesses and how he had been able to change. In the very early 1960s, he was immersed in the blues. He was learning and interpreting the music of a number of blues players, but I mostly remember hearing Lightnin' Hopkins riffs. I heard Lightnin' Hopkins so often, day after day, that I could conjure the chord changes in my head. Of course, that was the same 12-bar blues that 'Blind Lemon' Jefferson, Lead Belly, Charlie Patton, and others used, but Lightnin' was my way of identifying it.

He was beginning to work on ragtime music. His jazz background was useful for that, but Dave worked assiduously to play ragtime as though it was written for the guitar. I still meet musicians who tell me how difficult it is to play his ragtime arrangements—which I think would amuse Dave, who would figuratively wipe his brow while explaining how he experimented while developing guitar arrangements for music written for piano or recorded by a traditional jazz band such as 'Bunk' Johnson's.

Tip: When you listen to Dave's records, note how many songs recorded by Jelly Roll Morton he adapted for guitar.

I have to write about *The Bosses' Songbook*. Roy Berkeley wrote some parodies of songs that had been sung by members of People's Songs, which mostly represented folk singers who were members of or associated with the Communist Party. Dave and Barry Kornfeld added some songs, and a printer friend of Dave's from the anarchist and science fiction movements published two editions of the little paper-bound booklet. The publication became a hit among folk fans and some left-wingers (which meant a distribution of about 100), and is still remembered fondly by folk music people of the 1950s. I have one copy of each edition.

During the summer of 1959, we went to the Newport Folk Festival. We were comped and stayed at the hotel where performers were put up. My major memory of it: I walked into the elevator, and lo and

Words and melody line to Dave's song 'Gaslight Rag'

behold—there was a tall, splendid-looking woman, the first woman I'd met who was taller than me. Because she was older than me, I was awestruck; in those years, ten or more years made a difference. It was a treat to then become Cynthia Gooding's friend.

Cynthia started to perform in the 1940s, singing songs from Mexico (where she had lived as a teenager), Turkey, and Italy, and accompanying herself on guitar. When she traveled, she often collected and archived songs. By the early '60s, she was considered one of the older musicians in folk music, along with Ed McCurdy and Theo Bikel, and never became one of the Village coffee-house acts. Dave and I both liked her, and occasionally we went to parties in her Village apartment.

Years later, when I lived with Paul Orentlich, who had been a member of People's Songs many years earlier, I learned that he and Cynthia had been roommates—not lovers, he emphasized—for a while in the 1950s, when he had a sculpture gallery and she was a working folk singer.

190 Waverly Place

My student John was wrong about one thing; I didn't smoke pot—yet. Dave did, and at first I wouldn't let him bring any into the apartment. I was terrified of it. I considered it dope, with all that that implies, and it was illegal. Dave worked on me slowly. First, he convinced me to let him smoke it at home. Then, he convinced me to allow friends to smoke it in the apartment. Finally, by the end of the first year we lived together, I tried it.

Marijuana was amazing. Normally, I was so twitchy I found it difficult to relax and listen to music; but when I was high, my twitch diminished, my body became calm, and I could sink into music. For the next four years, our lives included pot.

We were careful. We seldom smoked pot during the day. We never carried any when we left the apartment. We bought what were called 'nickel bags' for a while, each containing about an ounce and costing about $10. After Dave started to earn enough money to support us, we started to buy a kilo, which Carmine, an acquaintance of Dave's, delivered and we tested before buying. A kilo is 2 lb 4 oz and we paid $250 per package; it lasted us a year or more.

That was a lot of marijuana to keep in the apartment. If the police had come for any reason, we knew we'd be put in jail. By the time we were buying that amount, we lived at 190 Waverly Place. There was a large area in the building's basement where residents stored stuff: furniture, suitcases, and cartons of things. We stashed our pot in the drawer of an old dresser someone kept there. It worked well for several years; then, one day, I went to the basement to bring up our package of marijuana to take out enough for a month—but it was gone. The dresser was there; the pot wasn't. We were furious. Someone had copped our pot, but we couldn't complain to the building's superintendent, and, for all we knew, he had taken it. So ended our storage place.

We picked up a kilo from Carmine once. With Jimmy Herman, a good friend, we went to Carmine's apartment far over on the east side, tried and bought the marijuana. We put it in a shopping bag, which I, who was the most respectable-looking of the three of us, carried. As we crossed Avenue C, a police car cruised by and slowed down. Luckily, we saw an empty taxi and hailed it without being stopped by the police. I shook for hours after that.

Neither Dave nor I ever carried grass again. A few decades later, young white people were often able to get out of marijuana charges with few penalties, although brown and Black people did serious jail time for dealing. But in the early '60s, anyone caught with a substantial amount went to jail—and a kilo was a substantial amount. I would not have been able to claim personal use.

Although Dave and I were discreet about using marijuana, it became a more important part of our lives than we would have admitted then. Each of us smoked several packs of unfiltered Camels a day (I got up to four) and some acrid marijuana at night. I switched to filtered cigarettes in the 1970s, then quit smoking. My doctors have said I was lucky I didn't harm my lungs. Dave, who never stopped smoking, developed voice and lung problems.

We would have said that our social life didn't revolve around pot, but it did. After a while, everyone who came to the apartment smoked it, folk singers and socialists alike. One reason why we purchased it in such a large amount was because we supplied our guests; people occasionally brought some to the apartment, but Dave and I never expected nor asked anyone to bring it. We smoked it every night and anyone who visited joined us.

One exception—Jack Arnold, our Trotskyist friend, didn't smoke either cigarettes or pot. After I started to use marijuana, I talked him into trying it. He did once, and kept saying, "It's not affecting me. I don't feel any different," as he stood up and walked into a wall. "Well," he said later, "it made my fingers feel odd." But other than that, he never admitted that anything had happened when he smoked it, and he never again touched it.

After my brother graduated from high school and went to Tufts University, he visited us whenever he was on vacation or on semester breaks, and later, he went to NYU for one semester and lived in the Village. Dave liked Leon a lot, and I loved and respected him, but he was my younger brother and I felt responsible for him. I was afraid that he'd learn that we smoked grass, and Dave and I discussed at length how to socialize with him without his discovering it. Could we smoke it before we saw him? What would happen if he was in the apartment with other friends of ours who wanted to turn on? It was a dilemma, until Leon called and asked me, "Do you know where I can get some grass?" I took the proverbial deep breath of relief and said, "Yes." And I was the person who turned him on for the first time.

Years later, after Leon had graduated from college and medical school, was interning at a hospital in Brooklyn and lived near there with Donna, whom he soon married, I worried whenever they left us, stoned. Especially when it was raining, and they were driving back to Brooklyn on Leon's motor scooter, crossing the slippery metal grating on the roadway of the Brooklyn Bridge. I always wanted to ask him to call me when they got home to tell me they were safe, but I thought that if I did that, he'd think I was acting like our mother.

Leon was unfailingly welcome, as were the many folk singers and socialists who came to visit most evenings. Dave and I didn't throw parties or invite people. We just stayed home and people arrived. Tom Paxton. Phil Ochs. Alix Dobkin, who lived in the building. Bob Dylan. Barry Kornfeld, who lived in the building. John Winn. Pat Sky, who lived in the next apartment. Dick Rosmini. Danny Kalb. Peter Stampfel. Jerry Rasmussen. Paul Geremia, when he was in New York. Tom Paley. Dave Woods. Alex Lukeman. Eliot Lerman, when he lived in the next apartment. Harry Jackson, if he was in New York. Joni Mitchell usually visited when she was in New York. Occasionally, Paul Simon, who was a friend of Barry Kornfeld's. Social democrats Jimmy Herman, Tom Condit, and Lenny Glazer; and Trotskyist Jack Arnold were there almost every evening.

I generally wore panties and a bra because the apartment was overheated. Occasionally, Albert Grossman, who managed Peter, Paul and Mary and later took Bob Dylan away from me, rang the bell and came up. Whenever that happened, I quickly put on a slip—something I didn't do for anyone else; but as I say elsewhere, when Albert was around, I froze.

Bob Dylan sometimes commented on my odd clothing. "Why do you wear droopy drawers?" he would ask. The answer was embarrassing. Before I left home to live with Dave, my mother had bought my panties, and, after I lost weight at age 15, she continued to buy the same size for me that she had bought before. So my white cotton underpants were huge on me. I don't know why I never asked her to get a smaller size. When I moved in with Dave, she continued to buy them for me and I continued to wear them, although they still were too big. By then, I had a concave stomach, my hip bones jutted out, and I had no ass, so the underpants were, indeed, droopy in the back. At least, when I wore them, it didn't look as though I was trying to appear sexy; if I had been, I would have worn undergarments that fit. Years later, Bob pointed out that I had looked very sexy. I probably knew it, but I really don't remember thinking about that back then.

Barry Kornfeld and Tom Paxton remember that we'd sit around and smoke grass. Dave would sit on the couch and put records on the phonograph. We had bought a single-play record player rather than one with a changer because it was better for the records; they were less likely to get scratched. But, as Dave took a record off the single-play phonograph, he'd throw it on a pile on the floor; he wouldn't put it in the record jacket first, just toss it on the pile. So much for taking care of our records.

I wonder whether we ever bored our guests with our presumably deep and, I suppose, interminable Marxist analyses. Like everyone who smoked grass, we thought we had brilliant conversations. Often, the next morning, we'd wish we had taped the last evening's witty discourses, but, of course, we never did. I suspect a replay would have shown us that we hadn't been as scintillating as we thought.

I stopped smoking marijuana in 1965. Suddenly, when I used it, I got scared: I was afraid the smell was wafting out of the apartment; I was afraid the police would come; I was afraid our neighbors would call the police. After a few months of this, I decided that I smoked grass because it made me feel good, and that if it made me feel lousy, I shouldn't smoke it. So I quit. A short time later, Dave stopped, too. We started to drink whiskey instead. My penchant for being treated just like a man kicked in, and I matched Dave drink for drink for several years, until I couldn't any more. Reality was that he was taller than me, bigger than me, weighed more than I did, and could hold more alcohol than I could.

Having friends who lived in the building was fun. In addition to Barry, Pat, Alix, and Eliot, 190 Waverly Place housed Elmer Gordon, a performance coach who played a lot of opera (which I now enjoy, but then couldn't listen to), and Caroline and Varda, whose last names

I forget. Opposite our apartment, at 191 Waverly Place, lived Robert Shelton, music reviewer for the *New York Times*.

Dave and I first met Bob Shelton when we lived in Chelsea. He wrote an article about Dave for the *NY Times* and I write elsewhere about carrying five *NY Times*' up five flights of stairs! We were not close friends. Bob was somewhat reserved and, I think, careful to separate his role as a reporter from his personal friendships. But he visited our Waverly Place apartment occasionally, and we went to a few gatherings at his place.

I admired him. During the McCarthy repression of the 1950s, he had been subpoenaed by the Senate Internal Security Subcommittee, refused to answer questions about his purported membership in the Communist Party, and was convicted and had the conviction overturned by a technicality several times. He never gave in.

Meeting Pat was awkward at first. He'd knock on the door and, when I answered, as I always did, he wouldn't say "Hello" but would ask in his southern accent, "Where's Dave?" After this happened about six times, I was angry. The next time he appeared, I asked him, I'm sure with some visible annoyance, why he didn't speak to me. Pat was startled and then explained that where he grew up, mostly in Georgia and Louisiana, a man doesn't speak with a married woman whose husband is not present. We drank some Scotch to seal our new friendship, and Pat remained one of my closest friends for the rest of his life.

I especially liked socializing with Ann and Sam Charters. Sam had a huge collection of blues records, and during the 1950s, he traveled to the south to get information about and to record blues musicians such as Lightnin' Hopkins. His book, *The Country Blues*, published in 1959, brought his search and the music to a larger audience and became a bible for blues fans. Dave and Sam had met before Dave and I got together, and had made some records together. By the time Dave and I started to live together, Sam had married Ann Danberg, who I first knew as the pianist on *A Joplin Bouquet*, the first recorded collection of music by Scott Joplin. I still play it; it's a lovely album. Ann became a writer and editor, especially of Beat generation poets and writers. Sam broadened his work to record production; he produced early recordings of the Holy Modal Rounders and Country Joe and the Fish, as well as Bahamian music (listen to *Music of the Bahamas, Volume One: Bahamian Folk Guitar*, 1959, Folkways Records FS 3844). When they moved to Sweden in the early '70s, he produced recordings of several

Swedish groups. Ann later returned to the United States, and taught at the University of Connecticut in Storrs, Connecticut. Sam was and Ann is incredibly smart, talented, and capable.

The four of us talked about possibly buying a brownstone way over in the west side of Chelsea, but even then, I doubt that we could have afforded it. Also, one day Dave looked at me and said, "We can't buy a house." "Why not?" I asked. "Because I can't even hammer a nail into a wall," he reminded me. Ah, that was true. Perhaps other guitarists are careful of their hands, but Dave was just ruefully admitting that he was a klutz. Barry, who came upstairs from his apartment to ours frequently, often wondered how Dave was able to play guitar so well when he was so inept at simpler things, like handling safety pins or painting. To his credit, Dave never tried to learn to drive, insisting that he was saving the public from another predator.

Dave and I didn't restrict ourselves to the Village, although we didn't have many reasons to go uptown. Two important ones: first, the Jazz Record Center, on West 46 Street. In the early 1960s, it was one of the few places (maybe the only place) selling British imports and blues records as well as jazz. It also was one of the first stores in New York City to sell classical Indian records, which we bought avidly. It was run by a large man named Big Joe, who knew a ton about blues and jazz. For a few years, Dave and I went there at least once a month and scored great music every time. On the same block there were a Philippine restaurant and a Mexican one that served large, soft tortillas covered with sauce and beans and eggs—inexpensive, filling, and wonderful.

The other reason: Times Square, to go to the movies. Times Square was still pretty squalid, which didn't bother us at all; we took it for granted and it never occurred to us that it might not be a safe place. It housed a lot of movie theaters that were open 24 hours a day, including one that featured Vincent Price horror movies, which were in bright, rich, stunning color. I never look at horror films now, but Dave and I gorged on them then.

We went to 'good' movies too, but we weren't avid film fans. A few movie theaters in the Village showed art movies, and we saw Bergman films (I was mesmerized by *The Seventh Seal*, which we saw before we lived together), independent movies such as *The 400 Blows*, a story about adolescence that remained Dave's favorite movie well into his older age, and *Les Enfants du Paradis (Children of Paradise)*, a love story set in the theatrical world of 1830s Paris. We were not sensitive people; we walked out of *West Side Story* in disgust, after what we thought was a stupid dance scene.

At home, we devoted a lot of time to Corporate Monopoly, which Jimmy Herman had invented. It was a more complex form of Monopoly; you put up companies rather than houses, and corporations bought out smaller corporations. There were written rules; I still have an old, typewritten set. Dave became a master Corporate Monopoly player and won pretty consistently. He loved winning, and grandly gloated over the other players. I never won.

Corporate Monopoly required at least four players, and by the mid '60s, there were fewer people around who wanted to take the time to play the game. During the last two years of our marriage, Dave and I played Russian Rummy fairly often. I was better at it than he was, and I almost always won. I used to say ruefully that I beat him at Russian Rummy until we broke up.

Dave wouldn't play in the poker games that went on in the Gaslight; he said they were too expensive for his blood. But we did play poker. In 1964, Dave and I started to play in a monthly poker game with the writer Larry Block, writer Donald Westlake, their agent, and a few others. I was the only woman at the table, and was pleased that I usually came out ahead. If Dave was working, I played anyway. Tradition was that winner bought drinks, and Larry, Don, and I consumed a lot of St. James at our apartment while Dave knocked back Irish whiskey. One night, when Dave was out of town performing, Larry, Don, and I went to my apartment after a game, where we drank and drank and drank, and Don stayed after Larry left. It was the first time I almost had sex with someone other than Dave—there was some heavy groping, and I reluctantly told him, "Nope. I can't." Neither of us let it affect our future poker games. We just pretended it hadn't happened.

I later learned that originally, I hadn't been invited to play in the monthly poker game. Dave had been invited. He lied to me, telling me that I had been, too. The slightly odd reactions to me the first time we joined the group had led me to wonder whether I was an intruder, but I won that evening, and was officially declared a regular participant.

My other at-home specialty was cooking. Sometimes Dave and I would have dinner before anyone showed up, but frequently, I found myself cooking for six or eight people, or more. I did a lot of big pot cooking and a lot of very good Chinese cooking. One evening in 1965, I was in a taxi on my way to Mott Street to buy three cakes of tofu—which cost 15 cents each. When we got to Chinatown, the street lights and store lights went out. I had enough presence of mind to ask the cabdriver to take me back to the Village, where I stopped to buy candles. Later that evening, Dave and I took candles to all the older people who lived in our building, and brought several people to our apartment to hang out together.

The meals I remember best were a Chinese steamed fish with black beans and stir-fried greens that took me two hours to make and which we and two guests consumed in about fifteen minutes, and a superb cassoulet that I produced for Dave, me, my brother, and my sister-in-law. It was midwinter, right after Christmas, and I had leftover leg of lamb and leftover goose and rendered grease from a goose I had roasted. I cooked the beans in the goose grease—they were superb, and the meal had enough fat to kill a person with a cardiac problem. But, it was a great dinner.

The weirdest visits were when Gershon Legman discovered me—and us. Gershon was a cultural critic and folklorist who was interested in sexuality, erotic folklore, and origami. He was especially known for his books on bawdy humor, including limericks. He knew my uncle, Harvey Swados, and when I met him in Manhattan sometime around 1966, after he'd had two books published, he apparently decided to be our friend. He admired me—it wasn't sexual interest; perhaps he was lonely. Gershon became one of our evening visitors. But, he talked and talked, and talked and talked. We couldn't follow much of what he said and found the rest to be a rant. Finally, one evening, as he came in, I hurriedly called our answering service and asked the wonderful operator there to call me. She did, and I loudly said, "Oh, my god, how awful. We'll get there as soon as we can." I rushed to falsely tell Dave that his mother had been in an accident and we had to go to Queens, and we went to the 8th Avenue subway—accompanied by Gershon. I was terrified that he'd follow us onto a train, and we'd have to take a subway ride to somewhere. Luckily, he didn't go into the train station with us. We waited on a platform until an A-train had pulled out, went back up to the street, and sneaked home. However, Gershon's limerick collections are wonderful.

One evening, Dave and I turned to one another at about 10 o'clock, saying, "There are twelve people here. We didn't invite any of them." And we left and went to a movie. I don't remember whether anyone still was in the apartment when we got home.

We Get Married

When Dave and I started to live together in the summer of 1959, we agreed that if we lasted as a couple for two years, we would get married. But, we kept postponing, and in the summer of 1961, we were too busy to pay attention to marriage. We were trying to organize the people who worked in basket houses—places where someone passed a basket to collect cash from attendees to pay the performers—to demand salaries instead. Finally, we said, "Let's do it." Dave asked Tom Paxton to be his best man, and I asked Doris Honig, a woman who had taught English in the high school where I had taught social studies, to be my "something of honor." We booked a date early in August at City Hall.

The day we had our blood tests (are they still required in New York State for marriage?), I said I needed to celebrate, and we bought coloring books and crayons. I have no idea what the relationship between them and marriage was, but it seemed to be the right thing to do then. I still have one coloring book with (mostly unsigned) art by Dave, me, Bob Dylan, and a few other friends.

We didn't tell many people that we were getting married; I think we were a bit embarrassed to be doing it. I told my parents, although since they didn't speak to Dave, I didn't ask them to come; and I told my brother. The night before the eventful day, my brother called and asked, "How do I get to City Hall?" I was delighted that Leon wanted to be there; I hadn't asked him. Since my parents weren't coming, I thought it would be rude to invite any other family members. I gave Leon subway directions, then my mother got on the phone. I don't think I'd ever known my mother to cry, except when she learned that relatives had been slaughtered in Russia. But she was crying. Of course, I got off the phone in tears. Dave looked at me and said, "Call your parents and ask them to come." I was stunned. Then, I said, "You do it." And he did. To this day, I'm amazed at his graciousness.

We got married in City Hall. We had decided to dress up a bit. Dave wore his only suit, a Harris tweed that was unbearably hot for an August day in New York. I wore a dress I didn't feel attractive in, but I didn't have time to iron anything else. My wedding band was a silver ring my cousin, Dorene Beller, had given me to wear when Dave and I checked into hotels on out-of-New York City gigs. That was needed back then.

I remember two things about the ceremony. The first is my saying to Dave, "I believe you. You love me. Let's get the hell out of here." The second is the effort it took to keep from laughing hysterically. The man who married us intoned the brief, required questions on a scale of what sounded like an octave. "Do you…" he started, and when he asked Dave, "Do you, David…" he went from lower something to upper something; and when he asked me, "Do you, Terri…" he went back down. Dave, Tom, Doris, my brother, and I could not keep straight faces. I don't know whether my parents were amused.

Later that day, we went to my parents' summer house with them. I'm still pleased that they established a cordial relationship with Dave.

A few nights after we got married, Dave and I wandered over to the White Horse Tavern, one of our occasional hang-outs. The Clancy Brothers and a few other folk singers were there, cheered us and bought us repeated rounds of drinks. We were sort of embarrassed. I still have the heavy china mugs, one with the White Horse logo on it, that one of the managers gave us that night.

Dave's mother wasn't any more thrilled about our marriage than my parents were. Grace was a devout Catholic, and while she wasn't supposed to know that we were living together, she called me occasionally to ask me to encourage Dave to go to church. Dave despised the Catholic hierarchy in New York, but I always told his mother that I'd try. A few weeks after the ceremony, he told her we were married. She phoned to tell me that while she liked me, she couldn't condone our marriage because by marrying a non-Catholic, Dave was ensuring that he would go to Hell. I didn't know what to say.

If you wonder whether we thought about having children, we did and we didn't. When we started to live together, we agreed that we'd have a lot of kids. Someday, Dave suggested, we could have "a football team." I said, "OK." I don't know whether he knew what a football team was, or how many people it comprised. I didn't, and still don't. We joked about it a few times, but never discussed it seriously. It was pretty clear that neither of us was interested.

It's good that we weren't. I think he would have been the world's worst father, and I was turned off by the thought of being pregnant, of having a huge tummy and breasts that were larger than the ones I already had. I was appalled at the idea of walking as awkwardly as pregnant women did. I was horrified by the prospect of giving birth. I couldn't fathom what I possibly would do with a creature that wouldn't be able to communicate intelligently for many years.

Eventually, I said that I would consider having a child if I was guaranteed that it would be a girl who would emerge from my body at age 15, able to discuss Isaac Deutscher's excellent three-volume biography of Leon Trotsky.

I never became pregnant; I used a diaphragm for several years, then took a pill and was fairly religious about it. I have no idea whether I'd have been able to conceive. It wasn't an issue—later, a year after Paul Solomon Orentlich and I started to live together, I had a tubal ligation.

I Was—and Am—Pro-Choice

I didn't become involved in the feminist movement. I read a bit about it and was very skeptical.

Women getting together to look at their vaginas? No, thanks. I insisted that to be considered equal to men, women needed the comprehensive social change that only a socialist movement could bring about. Now, I realize that my own antipathy toward most women, my sense that they were primarily interested in things that attracted men, and my own need to be treated "like a man, not like a woman," colored my thinking and ensured that I criticized that movement. I also realize that I knew only what the press chose to publish about it, which probably was as misleading as the information they published about the war in Vietnam. But at the time, I was unnecessarily nasty about the feminist movement.

However, I was very pro-choice. When a good friend became pregnant and needed an abortion, she couldn't reach Dr. Robert Douglas Spencer, an abortion provider in Pennsylvania whose name was on the bulletin board of every female dormitory in the northeast.

I helped her locate an abortion provider—he presumably was a medical doctor. When she called, he wouldn't see her. I then called him; I have no idea why, after talking with me, he agreed to perform an abortion. She schlepped up to Harlem to what she later described as a dirty apartment; she paid him $400 in cash, and she had no problems later.

I was appalled. We knew that women could do destructive things to themselves trying to self-abort. Several years before we met, Dave had gone out with a young woman who, after a short time, told him she was pregnant. They didn't know of any abortionists and neither of them would have been able to pay one. Instead, the 16-year-old girl rode a bicycle down several flights of stairs in a loft building. She may not have been pregnant, but she thought she was, and thought she had no recourse other than one that could have harmed her seriously.

Dave and I decided that we could offer to help women find abortionists and then help pay for the procedure, if they couldn't. We patched together $300, put it in an envelope, stashed it in our dirty laundry basket, and told friends it was available. It was used three times. In fact, in the year 2015, when I posted on Facebook about having done that back in the early '60s, someone I hadn't seen in many years wrote to remind me that he and a girlfriend had used our fund.

Back to School

By 1961, Dave was earning enough as a musician for me to be able to stop teaching. I wanted to earn a PhD, and he offered to support me while I went to school. His one requirement: that I use his name. He had been thrown out of Richmond Hill High School for truancy and didn't regret it, but said if I earned a doctorate, he wanted to see 'Terri Van Ronk' on my diploma. I acceded.

The City University of New York colleges didn't charge tuition, so expenses were for books and photocopying materials for research papers, which added up—this was before computers, and copying was done on microfilm and microfiche.

Although I wanted to major in American Studies, I couldn't even find a graduate history program at City College, so I settled for political science. I hated it. It seemed to me that the focus was on statistical analyses, while I wanted to learn about theories on power or perspectives on how political systems worked. I thought most of the courses were bullshit. One typical analysis we had to review was a study of whether U.S. Congressional Representatives and Senators tended to come from wealthier homes than most Americans. Duh? Some researcher got funded for that. It infuriated me. Someone got a grant to do research that would document something I already knew, and I had to read it ... what garbage.

This was not long after the McCarthy scare had ended. Although I had learned the basic differences between socialism and communism from my high school American History teacher, some of my graduate school professors needed that lesson. One of them spent so much time telling me I was a dupe of the Communist Party, refusing to accept that I was a socialist who despised the Communist Party, that I dropped his class. I hated going to his classes, and I figured his attitude preordained a lousy grade.

One professor who had emigrated from Czechoslovakia and understood my political proclivity became my thesis advisor. Ivo Duchacek had been a member of Czechoslovakia's Parliament. After the Soviet-sponsored takeover by Czech Communists in February 1948, he fled through the forests of Bavaria and to London, coming to the United States in 1949. When he became my advisor, I didn't know that, nor did I realize that he was editor of the Czech desk at Voice of America. I just knew that he understood what I was trying to do.

I wanted to write a Marxist analysis of why the Independent Socialist League, the adult organization of the YSL that I had been around while I was in college, was turning to the right and becoming part of the Democratic Party. I did intensive research at the home of Jim Robertson, who had left the Socialist Workers Party with a small group of people shortly before the small group that I had become part of left. Although the two small groups came out of the same Trotskyist organization, their differences meant that they couldn't work together, and generally, people in them didn't even talk to one another. But Jim and I got along, and he allowed me to go through his huge collection of papers and files.

I wrote one chapter, then Dave asked me to become his manager and I stopped working on my thesis. Years later, I found my notes and read that chapter; I had been writing a history of the Independent Socialist League, not a Marxist analysis.

I never got my PhD. Eventually, I lost all the credits I had earned toward a Master's Degree at City College, and in the 1980s I had to take new classes and pay tuition at Pace University to earn a Master of Public Administration. Again, I thought the program was not a good one. I hoped it would help me understand the administrative aspects of not-for-profit organizations. It didn't, but a few years later, having an MPA helped me become executive director of a small organization.

And Out of School

When Dave started earning a living as a performer and gigs out of New York City opened up, I traveled with him. I did that for one or two years, then decided that I didn't want to make being Dave's girlfriend or wife my career. I told him that I didn't have to eat club sandwiches in some diner at 1 a.m. because nothing else was open after the performer left work. I stopped going to out-of-town gigs with him unless there was a special reason to do so—I often went to Boston because my sister and her family lived near there, and it gave me an opportunity to see them.

I remember my sister and brother-in-law coming to the Café Yana in Boston in the early 1960s with my oldest nephew, Aram, in her arms. Aram's a good guitarist and a better fiddler, and while he never became a professional musician, he's always played with a group. Now, he's part of a klezmer band. My middle nephew, Eric, is a caller in a contra dance band and joins it playing flute, tin whistle, hand percussion (spoons, guiro, maracas), and Quebecois foot percussion.

During one of those out-of-town gigs, Dave fired his manager and hired me.

Shifting my attention from graduate school to managing a folk singer wasn't very difficult. I'd been traveling with Dave when he worked outside of New York City, and had a sense of the coffee houses and clubs and many of the owners.

At that time, there were clubs on the East Coast and the West Coast, and few in between. The first in the New York area was Caffè Lena in Saratoga Springs. It was started by Bill and Lena Spencer. They broke up after running the cafe for two years, and Lena kept the club; she loved the music and adored the musicians. Caffè Lena has become a legend. It still exists. It's managed by a not-for-profit foundation that also runs a school of music and hosts community forums.

One out-of-New York City gig was memorable—although not for the right reasons. It was in Lake George, NY, which is in the Adirondacks Mountains, about 200 miles (320 km) north of Manhattan. In the early 1960s, Lake George was far enough away from New York City to not yet be a well-known vacation resort. Someone from a new coffee house there called me, and I booked Dave into it. I knew nothing about it; when the woman got in touch, I got an advance on his salary and the contract stipulated that his motel room would be next to the club and that he wouldn't be charged for it. I thought Lake George would be nice place to visit, so I went there with him.

First thing we noticed: a sign on the front of the building with a notice about a church service on top and a notice about Dave's appearance below. That didn't sound auspicious. The first night's performance went well, though; there was a decent crowd, a good microphone, and Dave felt good afterward. We went to our motel room and found our grass—we had brought a small stash with us. We smoked some, then we heard the siren. It was very loud. It wailed and wailed, and came closer and closer. We lay in bed shaking, waiting for the police to surround the motel and yell, "Van Ronk, come out with your hands up." I don't know how long we waited, but it was one of the scariest times of my life. I flushed the unused marijuana down the toilet, and realized later that we had unnecessarily thrown it out; the police weren't after us.

The next day, we started to walk to the lake, which is known as a gorgeous spot in the Adirondacks. One of the reasons I had gone there with Dave was to take a boat ride on Lake George. We left the motel and saw a gaggle of children following us, whispering to one another about Dave's beard. We felt like the Pied Piper of Hamlin. We turned around, went back to the motel, and hid in our room.

Undaunted, the following morning, I said I had come all the way to Lake George to see the damned lake, and wanted Dave to go there with me. Dave held back, but I remonstrated that he was missing out on something he might enjoy. Finally, he marched me to the shore of Lake George, and asked, "Do you see it?" I said "Yes." "Good," Dave said, and he turned me around and marched me back to the motel. I've never been in a boat on Lake George.

Visiting England and Ireland

In the summer of 1965, we went to England for six weeks. By then, Dave was working as a performer fairly steadily, and my parents had realized that our relationship was not injurious to me. My father arranged for us to stay in the extra London apartment of someone he knew through his work in the textile industry. I'm sure my father didn't realize the 'extra' apartment really meant extra-paramour; Dave and I didn't until we returned to the place one afternoon and found the textile executive and a young woman almost dressed and ready to leave. We were uncomfortable; I wondered if my father's business acquaintance was.

I hadn't booked Dave any gigs in England, but we visited clubs, met a lot of folk musicians, and he was spontaneously invited to play in several places, including the Troubadour, probably the best-known folk club in England, and Les Cousins. We met Derroll Adams, a legendary folk musician who was a friend of Ramblin' Jack Elliott's. Like Jack, Derroll was well known for the people he influenced, including Donovan. We met Ewan MacColl, a folk singer-songwriter, folk song collector, labor activist, actor, and communist, who collected hundreds of traditional folk songs and recorded more than one hundred albums, many with English folk song collector and singer A. L. Lloyd. We met Anthea Joseph, who ran the Troubadour. Anthea was a bit taller than me, which was unusual for a woman, a no-nonsense person, and we became friends very quickly. She and I kept in touch via expensive international phone calls for several years, and I still have a knitted tea cozy (teapot cover) she gave me.

We spent a few days wandering around with Paul Simon, who was recording in London and had good contacts for grass and hashish, a concentrated form of grass, which we'd never smoked before; it wasn't part of the NYC folk scene culture. We also discovered London pubs, and I fell in love with single malt Scotch, which then was barely known in the United States. It was thick and smoky, and rolled around in your mouth. It was the alcoholic equivalent of Häagen-Dazs ice cream, the first thick ice cream easily available in the United States.

I remember one conversation with Paul Simon. Socially, being a short teenaged boy or a tall teenaged girl in the 1950s had been difficult. We were trying to figure out which was worse. We finally decided that it was worse to have been a boy of 5'3" (1.6 m) than a girl of 5'11" (1.8 m) if the boy never grew to be any taller. As an adult, his height still bothered Paul, whereas I had gotten to like mine.

After a few weeks of getting a feel of London and nearby cities, we went off to Ireland. Dave's mother's family was Irish, and the visit was partly an homage to the culture he had inherited and partly to hear Irish music that hadn't been transformed by record companies. We wound up seeing a country that, in the 1960s, we considered prudish and almost barbaric in its politics.

I was disgusted by its treatment of women. Liam Clancy (of the Clancy Brothers) had given us a list of pubs to go to in Dublin, and while the music was good, I found all of them horrifying. I was expected to smile and be polite and nice. I was expected to drink beer or ale; whiskey was a man's drink, and people we met (all male) thought it was odd—even untoward—that I liked it. If Dave had carried a guitar, I was sure I would have been expected to carry it while walking several feet behind him. At least the stout and the porter were good, and we both enjoyed them. At night, I went into a closet in our hotel room and banged on the walls, screaming "Fuck, fuck, fuck," just to get it out.

We spent several days on the Aran Islands, three small islands at the mouth of Galway Bay, off the west coast of Ireland. They were amazing: green had so many shades that the very, very green countryside wasn't monotonous. The islands featured cottages with thatched roofs, which will last 25 years before needing replacing.

The islands are made up of carboniferous limestone and do not have naturally occurring topsoil. Early settlers augmented the soil with seaweed and sand from the shore. It must have taken a massive amount of time and work.

I was intrigued by the ancient stone walls that crisscross the islands. These are drystone walls, built to protect the soil, and they enclose small fields where cattle and sheep once grazed. A drystone wall is two separate but interlocking walls, tied at regular intervals by longer through- or tie-stones, and a middle filled with a mass of smaller rocks and pebbles. The animals were essential in an economy in which people relied on subsistence, or near-subsistence farming and fishing. I noted that there were no communal grazing or farm fields; only small, apparently privately owned parcels. That was unusual in pre-industrial societies.

There were no clubs, no movies, no concert venues on the Aran Islands in the 1960s. There were pubs, and of course Dave and I hit the nearest one. Since we were in Ireland, we properly ordered Irish stout, which is black beer with a dry-roasted character that comes from coffee-like roasted barley. Stout is dark and creamy, with an aroma of roasted malt. I drank a lot of it in the pub; Dave later told me that the owner of the house we stayed in wryly congratulated him on my ability to consume as much as I did and still walk.

My World Changed

Recently, a friend turned 30. His birthday reminded me of the months preceding Dave's 30th. They were like something out of a cheesy movie. Dave had decided that all good things would end when he turned 30. It all would be over. No more career, no more music, no more great sex, his brain would rot ... I don't even remember what else was supposed to end. It was nutty. Here was a brilliant, talented man accepting some of the garbage the kids were shoving at us, that life would end at 30.

Several years before, Dave had started to use the *I Ching*, also known as the *Book of Changes*, an ancient Chinese book of divination. It's traditionally done by tossing yarrow stalks and comparing how they land with a corresponding hexagram in the book, although Dave used coins instead of stalks. They are used to make or to ratify decisions—often ethical ones. I recently found an old copy of the book, *I Ching*, in my house in perfect condition, although I'm pretty sure Dave took his copy when we separated. I hope it helped him find direction and assuage his later concerns.

By about 1966, the New York scene had changed. Our folk singer friends no longer were in New York very much: there was a lot of work in other places and they were on the road a lot. So was Dave. There had been other changes: Bob Dylan and Suze Rotolo had broken up years before; Bob had moved into another world and Suze wasn't around very much. Tom Paxton had gotten married and spent his non-working time with Midge. John Winn had moved to Maine. Pat Sky had moved to Rhode Island. Our Trotskyist friend Jack Arnold had moved to North Carolina. Tom Condit had moved to California. Lenny Glazer had joined some weird movement...I once saw him marching with a group of Holocaust deniers; Dave and I were appalled. Fewer people hung out in our apartment every night.

I started to spend time with women friends. For me, that was new.

When Dave and I first lived together, the only female friend I had was Sylvia Brill—who went to Tangiers with her husband Bob, a good blues guitarist, and stayed there for several years, while Bob bought and sold cannabis and hashish.

So, here I was in the mid '60s. Naomi Fein had moved in with Barry Kornfeld, who lived in our building on Waverly Place. Carla Rotolo, Suze Rotolo's older sister, who worked in theatrical groups, had taken an apartment around the corner. When Dave was away, the three of us spent evenings in our apartment, listening to some folk music, jazz, and music such as the superb Koutev Bulgarian National Ensemble, drinking white wine, and sautéeing artichoke hearts dipped in pancake mix in olive oil. I also listened to more classical music when I was alone, exploring the works of such dissimilar composers as Krzystof Penderecki and Johannes Brahms.

Someone had given me an Ouija board, which I'd never consulted. One evening, Naomi, Carla, and I decided to try it. On an Ouija board, participants put their hands on a flat disc called a planchette, which is moved around to spell out words, answering questions posed by the participants. Presumably, the spirits the participants are consulting move the planchette. We thought it was a joke. None of us believed in spirits. We asked a few random questions and got indecisive answers.

Then, either Naomi or Carla asked the Ouija board, "Ouija, oh Ouija, will Terri ever get rich?" The planchette, with all of our fingers on it, shot to "Yes." We gulped. "How will Terri get rich?" one of my friends asked. Unerringly, the planchette, still with all of our fingers on it, sped quickly, letter after letter, to F U C K I N G J E W S. We never touched the Ouija board again.

It was wrong. I never got rich.

The End of Our Marriage

By early 1968, Dave and I recognized that our marriage was falling apart. I traveled some on behalf of my clients; he traveled to perform. When one or both of us was on the road, we had long, lovely phone conversations. But when we were together in our apartment, we turned each other into nervous wrecks. That had never happened before, but we didn't know how to stop it.

That spring, I went to California to book him and the Holy Modal Rounders into clubs and concert halls. When I got home, Dave made some Italian sausage and eggs—something we always enjoyed. But instead of thanking him, I became angry, saying that he hadn't bought enough sausage. Of course it was stupid—it had nothing to do with the sausage; it had something to do with Dave and me.

I would say things like "I'm trying to get the guts to leave you." When he traveled, he said at least once that maybe he wouldn't return home. We would lie in bed at night and I would be so horny I would have fucked anyone—but I didn't want the man with whom I'd had years and years of great sex.

We tried to keep our marriage together. We loved and respected each other, but that wasn't enough.

I didn't know for sure that he was screwing around until a few months before we separated; I was doing the same, although I had started a while later than him.

When we talked about it, Dave said that within the previous year he had trundled some nutty women around with him when he was on tour. But, he said, he always told them that he was married to me, loved me, that whatever brought him to them didn't detract from his feelings about me, and that I was his home. I had no reason to doubt that. I had told my sex partners that I loved Dave, planned to stay with him, wasn't sure whether he was screwing around, didn't know whether he would be angry or hurt or would shrug if he learned that I was, but that if he was to find out, the information had to come from me.

Dave initiated the conversation. A woman he'd had an affair with in California thought she was pregnant, and had contacted him through the record company with which I had negotiated his contract. I was pissed that the record company official knew, and jealous that Dave had started playing around about six months before I had.

Was this a grown-up reaction? Guess not. Maybe a way to not feel hurt and betrayed; even though I, too, was having sex with others, I was bothered that he was.

I agreed that if the woman had his child, he should acknowledge it and help support it. Luckily, he soon learned that the woman wasn't pregnant. So, caring for a kid never became an issue.

We talked about why we both were having affairs—or one-night stands. Dave thought he was because he was traveling and lonely. That sounded reasonable. We'd been together for eleven years, including the two years before we lived together. He had been traveling alone for about six years, since I stopped going with him, and although we usually arranged his schedule so that he never was away for more than three consecutive weeks, being away could be lonely. I thought I was doing it because our relationship was strained and I needed the ego boosts.

We tried to stay together. We talked about taking a vacation in places that had no folk music presence. But that meant small towns or the country, and Dave hated both. Still, we decided that I should learn to drive so we could travel. That venture was a disaster. I took driving lessons from my father and from a driving school. When my father said I was ready, I took a driving test. The tester said I went past a STOP sign, and he failed me. *Note:* I got a license easily after we broke up; my marriage didn't depend on it, so I wasn't stressed out about it.

Then I suggested that we separate our personal and professional relationships. We talked that over a lot before we decided that it might help. I turned his management over to a small company that he chose. He wasn't happy with them. I tried to stay out of it.

Finally, it happened. We had been out wandering around the Village one summer evening, holding hands and being kind of romantic as we walked through Sheridan Square. Did we make love that night? I don't remember. The next day, we agreed that it was a good day to break up. We talked a bit about how to handle things like his getting stuff from the apartment. I asked him for his key and he objected, saying that he'd have to pick up clean clothes and other stuff. I said OK, but that he had to call before he came by. When he left, we walked around each other three times and formally shook hands. We thought it was a friendly Jewish parting ritual; recently, I googled it and learned that at some Ashkenazi weddings, the bride circles around her groom either three or seven times under the chuppah.

Ending a marriage is difficult. Dave and I weren't angry with one another; we just couldn't stop our relationship from being uncomfortable. After he left, I waited for him to come home, knowing that wasn't going to happen. The next evening, I had Maggie and Terre Roche booked into the Gaslight, so I went to the club and spent the evening with the girls and their parents. My god, I was so cool. I never cried in front of anyone. Two days later, Dave came in, using his key to the apartment. "You can't do that," I said. "You don't live here anymore." "I don't have a home other than this one," he said. "And everything I own is here." We negotiated how he could come to the apartment.

We also worked out a way in which we both could continue to go to the bars and clubs we hung out in. If person A walked into a place and person B was already there, A would leave. But if A had a business appointment in that place, they would explain that to B, who would leave. If both of us had business appointments there, we'd both stay. Remarkably, that didn't happen until we'd been separated for several months, and by then, we simply said hello to one another.

A few weeks later, we agreed on how to divide our possessions—and when we did so, we were generous to one another. He asked me to choose either the pewter or White Horse Tavern mugs. I said the best

New Guinea statue was his. We divided the African art. We agreed that he could have the bulk of the Donald Duck and Captain Marvel comic books and I would keep the duplicates—but that he would leave them to me in his will, which didn't happen. We agreed on how to handle money, and I stupidly didn't say that he owed me a percentage of future earnings because I was giving up the part of my income that came from being his manager. We postponed making any decisions about the books and records, knowing that would be difficult.

Months later, Dave suggested that he take a few samples of each kind of record—blues, folk, classical, jazz, 'other'—and that I keep the rest, but he would have borrowing privileges for the records and books. It was an incredibly kind offer from a musician. The arrangement worked well.

About eight months after we separated, Dave gave me the biggest compliment I've ever received from anyone.

He came to the apartment to tell me that he was going to Philadelphia to break up with a woman he'd been seeing. There was a long history behind that. He and she had been friends when I met him; they often played chess at the Figaro. Back then, I once had asked him whether they'd ever had a romantic or sexual relationship. He had seemed surprised at the question and said, "No, of course not. We're just friends." "Well," I had said, "she has a thing about you." He had said I was wrong. Years later, after we separated, when he told me that he was dating her, I insisted that he ask her if she used to "have a thing" about him. He asked her and she said yes. "Naah, naah," I was able to say. "I told you so."

"Why on earth are you breaking up with her?" I asked. "She's smart, attractive, and rich." She had inherited money. Dave looked at me quizzically. "I used to want to marry Madame Curie," he said. "And I did. But I don't want to live with that kind of competition in my house anymore."

Thank you, my first love; I've often hugged that comment.

Of course, when Dave remarried, it was to a smart, funny, talented woman.

It was an odd year. I made new friends. I drank a lot and, after deciding that I would not have sex with people in the socialist or folk music worlds, I screwed more men in the music world than I should have. People told me Dave was drinking a lot. I didn't want to hear that Dave was drunk on stage. He didn't want to hear that I was drinking too much. I learned that once, someone said something uncomplimentary about me to Dave, who became so angry that he almost punched the person. We didn't understand people's urge to dump crap on others and to justify it by thinking they are doing a good thing.

One nice surprise: my family's reaction to our breakup. Given my parents' unhappiness about my relationship with my non-Jewish folk singer, I thought they would tell me that obviously, he was to blame for whatever had happened. They didn't. I asked them to come to the apartment, telling them I wanted to talk with them. When I told them we had separated, they said they weren't surprised; they had sensed that something out-of-the-ordinary had been going on and had wondered whether Dave and I were having a difficult time. They didn't criticize; they didn't dump on him, as I expected them to. That was a relief.

Meanwhile, I was managing the Holy Modal Rounders, Maggie and Terre Roche, and Mark Ross, and doing some work with Paul Geremia. The Roches were still in high school, Mark was still becoming a musician, and both needed a lot of boosting. The Holy Modal Rounders were difficult to book. Although they were an underground legend, a group had to earn a lot more money than a solo act, but they couldn't draw well enough or work in large enough places to get paid decently. So I was earning very little.

And the Village and the music world had changed. As I note elsewhere, I didn't believe in magic, and my neighborhood was full of spaced-out people. Even the clubs and record companies were full of them. I felt that I didn't belong there anymore.

Chapter 7
GREENWICH VILLAGE FOLK MUSIC IN THE '60S

Homes away from home: the Gaslight Cafe, where I heard wonderful folk music throughout the 1960s, and where Dave became a skilled, honored musician; and the Kettle of Fish, the bar next door to the Gaslight, where performers drank, schmoozed, told each other stories about other gigs, introduced new songs and arrangements—but generally, didn't sing or play an instrument.

In late 1959, Village coffee houses started to book folk singers, and I spent the next decade moving through several worlds: graduate school for a year-plus, folk music, and left-wing politics. The coffee house world was the most fun, both exciting and welcoming. I'm still gratified by the acceptance I got from musicians, club owners and managers, photographers, and media even before I started managing folk singers. I never felt that I was being treated simply as a 'performer's wife.'

Some thoughts about that folk music world: it was fun. It was musically exciting. It was full of people who admired one another, taught one another music and songs, helped each other get gigs and recording contracts. Because the music itself derived from many diverse but sometimes-related enclaves, the musicians and the people around them tended to look at the way groups were linked rather than the ways in which they were separate. I treasure the years I spent in it, and I'm honored and delighted that many people remember me, apparently think well of me, and believe that I contributed something to it.

Some readers may have seen the Coen Brothers movie, *Inside Llewyn Davis*. The lead character presumably was based on Dave. But, as I wrote

Carolyn Hester and me

in an article in *The Village Voice,* the film had little to do with the folk music world that Dave and I knew. Aside from presenting Dave as a somewhat incompetent schmuck, which is far from what he was, it presents the folk music scene as a not pleasant, somewhat cutthroat one … which doesn't at all resemble the one where I and dozens of others lived and hung out. Both before and while there were places to work in New York, the folk music world was professionally and personally supportive, and nothing like the bleak one shown in that movie.

In the documentary, *Greenwich Village: Music That Defined a Generation,* Tom Paxton speaks about this. "We were rivals, of course. But we were more than rivals. We were colleagues, friends, and supporters."

Also, although there always were fewer female folk singers than male ones, it was not a sexist scene. Again, I'm thinking of *Inside Llewyn Davis,* in which a club owner tells someone that to be hired, a female musician "fucked" him, saying that was standard procedure for women who wanted to perform. That's nonsense. It didn't happen anywhere. Club owners didn't hit on women performers; nor did they hit on women managers. That's just an invention.

That doesn't mean that women weren't propositioned. Carolyn Hester tells wonderful stories about that. She said that while club owners didn't hit on her, other performers did. Working with one particular all-male group meant that she had to be dexterous to prevent "hands all over my front and hands all over my back." Two noted musicians from another country never directly suggested sex, she said. They simply kept talking about how lonely it was to be far away from loved ones, and how people in that situation could alleviate the isolation by comforting one another.

(A note on the movie: for me, the most infuriating element in the movie is not about folk music, but a different part of the story. Llewyn Davis impregnates someone and goes to a doctor he knows to make sure she gets an abortion. He learns that because someone whose abortion he once paid for didn't have it, he has a credit in that office. He and the doctor have a conversation about both the abortion that didn't happen and the forthcoming one. Abortion was illegal then in New York State, and that section of the movie is an insult to all women. I understand that filmmakers aren't necessarily showing reality, but I don't understand what the Coen brothers were trying to do when they showed abortion in such a cavalier way.)

Hiring folk singers was an experiment that worked for the Commons, a large room on MacDougal Street. Within a few weeks of starting to perform there, Dave was asked to book the performers. They played a set for no remuneration—playing only to be heard. That wasn't difficult. The Commons was the only place around that featured folk singers, so everyone who came to New York wanted to play there. Dave writes in his memoir, *The Mayor of MacDougal Street,* that he "once counted thirteen performers on a single night." I think he was wrong; I remember only twelve.

Great music? Seldom. Reverend Gary Davis appeared there occasionally, and he was great. If you haven't heard him, go online and buy any of his records (I still think of them as 'records'). I'm not a musician and if I wanted to describe his guitar style, I'd have to quote something written by someone who understood what he was doing, like Dave, who worshiped Gary as much as my atheist, unspiritual ex-husband worshiped anyone. Most of the other musicians who appeared there still were learning both their musical art and their performing skills.

Watching folk singers become performers was striking. For musicians like Dave and Tom Paxton, it was a place where you could learn what to do and what to avoid onstage. People who had always looked down at their fingers, or at a few people in a living room when they played music, now had to learn how to simultaneously play, sing, and look at an audience—in fact, look at the audience from different angles so people all over the room felt that they personally were being invited to partake of the music.

They had to learn to talk to or with an audience, which meant not mumbling, deciding whether to explain the derivation of a song, whether to tell stories about why they were performing that song, or whether to talk about something else … or not to talk at all. What could they say that an audience would want to hear? Or did they prefer to be silent between songs?

They had to learn how to handle a microphone—I repeatedly told Dave and later, Bob Dylan, "Don't pop your 'p's." One of the skills needed was knowing how far from the microphone the performer had to be … but there generally was only one microphone for both voice and instrument, mics differed, and being a performer meant adapting to whichever one was in the club or concert hall.

Folk singers had to learn how to develop a set. How many songs could they sing in the time allotted to their performance? Which songs did the audiences like? Which elicited no reaction? Did they want to start with a soft song and end with a strong one? Was it safe to play an instrumental, or would the audience get bored? Each of them was developing a style, and started to build a roster of fans … and got paid for it.

I was good at critiquing. My major criticism of Dave, then and later, was that he wore creased chinos and short socks, so his pants always looked sloppy and often, because he sat when he performed, you could see bare leg between his pants and his socks. Also, of course, that he popped his 'p's.' Other than that, he took to the stage comfortably. Dave was a storyteller; back then, I said he had the "Irish gift of blarney," which probably is considered politically incorrect these days. His last name is Dutch, but he grew up in his mother's Irish family and inherited their storytelling ability.

Financially, the Commons was a boon for Dave and me. It was a basket house, meaning that performers weren't paid a salary. Waitresses passed a basket to attendees, who contributed as they wished, and the proceeds were divided among the performers. Even though occasionally there were as many as twelve performers an evening and the basket

Dave presented the Hootenanny at the Gaslight (note the spelling of Hootennany in the poster above!). *Photo, Don Paulsen*

collection was divided equally among them, Dave sometimes took in about $200 a week, which was a decent income in 1961. There was no health insurance, no social security paid to his account, and no vacation days—if he didn't work, he didn't get paid—but he was 25 and I was 22 and we didn't think of those benefits, especially since he was paid in cash. Dick Weissman says that he once was paid only $3 for the evening, and although I don't remember any such disasters, I'm sure they happened.

After a while, Dave moved across the street, from the Commons to the Gaslight. The Commons was cavernous; the Gaslight was small. It was downstairs, dark, dingy, and dirty. It served execrable food and lousy, weak coffee. None of that bothered me; I never ate the food and I had started drinking coffee at Brooklyn College and had not yet advanced to grinding my own beans, as I learned to do years later; back then, I drank anything that pretended to be coffee.

The Gaslight was a basement room. Two sets of stairs, about 15 feet (5 m) apart but parallel to one another, went down there from the street, into a small entranceway where someone collected your admission fee.

When you walked into the club, you saw three rows of tables running from front to rear; one along each wall and one in the center. The row along the left wall were on a slightly raised platform. The stage was along the wall at the back of the room; the kitchen was to the right, and about 10 feet (3 m) beyond that and upstairs, you were in the green room.

Nice reproduction Tiffany lamps hung from the ceiling—they were attractive enough so that when the club closed, we were tempted to go there and take a few of the lamps. (Of course, we didn't.) Dave once smashed one. He always performed seated on a stool. One evening, Clarence Hood, then the owner, talked him into performing standing up. Dave did, and was so pleased with himself that at the end of his set, he jumped off the stage, somehow hitting and breaking a light fixture.

People have written about the rats and roaches. I don't remember the rats. I'm sure they existed—this was downtown Manhattan, these were old buildings, and rodents ran rampant. We fought roaches in our apartment and certainly, they were even more likely to be prevalent in a basement coffee house that served food. Luckily, we didn't have rats in the apartment, but again, a basement food entity was bound to have them.

The Gaslight became Dave's working home and, for both of us, an important component of our social lives. It wasn't so much that we saw many of the people there outside of work—for the most part, we didn't—but that it and the Kettle of Fish, the bar next door to it, became gathering places for folk singers who worked there and for many who just visited. So I wandered over to the coffee house and the bar when Dave worked there, not necessarily to hear the music but because I knew there would be people to hang out with. And sometimes when he wasn't working there, we both wandered over there to hear the music or just to hang out. And when he started working out of NYC, it was a comfortable place for me to go. I always found congenial people there.

That went on for years.

Poets and Comedians

In its early years, the Gaslight featured an eclectic group of performers. Before it started to book folk singers, it was a venue for poetry readings. I've never been able to appreciate much poetry. I haven't the patience, although from time to time I've tried. Of course, I still have some of the classic poetry collections college students owned in the late 1950s: Emily

Dickinson, William Blake, Robert Frost, Charles Olson, Dylan Thomas, T. S. Eliot, W.H. Auden; and some of friends: Joel Oppenheim and Shel Silverstein—but I don't read them. I've tried to like poetry, but I just can't do it. (I like some of Charles Bukowski's poetry, despite his male chauvinism and his admiration for strong, male leaders.)

At the Gaslight, you could hear Bob Kaufman, a Beat poet who seldom wrote his poems but orated them on the street, in bookstores, and in coffee houses. Bob wrote 'Green Green Rocky Road,' conceived from words in a children's ring game, with Len Chandler, a classically trained musician who also sang folk songs and was one of the stalwarts at the Gaslight. Len was also one of the few Black folk singers to appear in the Village.

You could hear John Brent, who we knew as a Beat poet, but who was actually a comedian later involved with Second City, the comedy club in Chicago that produced an improvisational theater troupe which became a training ground for actors such as Bill Murray, Alan Alda, and Tina Fey. I liked to listen to John declaim *Bibleland*, a sarcastic fantasy dream about a place that sounds like an adult Disneyworld. I've read that John wrote it when he saw an article about plans to build a Bible Storyland theme park, which never came to being. The poem featured such figures as Shadrach, Meshach, and Abednego. It wasn't great poetry, but we were young and thought it was brilliant. I still have a printed copy somewhere; I remember the yellow cover.

Or, you could hear LeRoi Jones, who later changed his name to Amiri Baraka. When I knew him, he considered himself a Beat poet. One evening, LeRoi challenged me to listen to poetry readings every night for a week. I was in graduate school and couldn't take the time to do that, but I gave him a weekend and spent Friday, Saturday, and Sunday evenings immersed in readings. I wasn't converted. A year later, no longer a Gaslight poet-reader, LeRoi traveled to Cuba and decided that he should link his art with his emerging politics, based somewhat on an appreciation of Malcolm X. He eventually called himself a Marxist–Leninist. Many people, including me, found some of his later poetry anti-Semitic, and after he read a poem suggesting that Israel knew in advance about the attacks of September 11, 2001, he was asked to step down from his position as New Jersey poet laureate. He refused, claiming that he couldn't be fired, whereupon New Jersey abolished the position. He sued but lost in court.

My favorite of the poets who read there was Hugh Romney, who later became known as Wavy Gravy and had his legal name changed. In the late '60s, he turned a hog farm north of Los Angeles into a commune for artists, and it became an entertainment collective. Wavy Gravy was the MC at all three Woodstock festivals, a job he's politely described as "exhilarating and exhausting."

The Folk Music Clubs

I was more interested in the folk singers—people like Noel Stookey, who became Paul in Peter, Paul and Mary (a job Dave turned down) and who told hilarious stories. Tom Paxton, a smart, funny, excellent songwriter and performer who was Dave's best man when we got married. Don Crawford, also an actor who appeared in the television drama, *The Cube*. Len Chandler, a classically-trained musician. Jose Feliciano, born without sight in Puerto Rico, a brilliant guitarist who brought a jazz inflection to his music and skyrocketed to fame. The truly great Reverend Gary Davis. The superb musician and charming Mississippi John Hurt. And John Winn, who often has been called a "minstrel-troubadour" because of his lovely tenor voice.

The coffee houses really were a community.

Shortly after Dave started to work at the Gaslight, while I was studying for end-of-term graduate school exams, I started to receive obscene phone calls. The phone, like everything Dave and I owned or rented, was in my name; Dave hated lawyers, banks, and documents, and preferred that I sign them alone. So, my (female) name was listed in the phone directory; phone companies published printed directories back then. The apartment had one window that faced a courtyard, people across from our building could see into it. So, perhaps the caller had seen me. Or, perhaps he knew who I was from elsewhere, or perhaps he picked my name from the phone directory at random.

The caller had a male voice. "Hello, Terri, how are you?" I wouldn't answer. "Do you know what I want to do to you?" I wouldn't answer. "Would you like that?" I would hang up. If Dave answered the phone, which he seldom did, the caller would hang up without speaking.

We called the police, who, as we expected, said they couldn't do anything. The caller never directly threatened me, and the police wouldn't tap my phone (which was almost funny, because, we learned later, the FBI was tapping it); they said the caller wasn't doing anything criminal, and for them to intervene, I'd have to stay on the line with the caller for several minutes while he specified how he'd harm me, and they couldn't spend the time needed to be available when he called.

I was scared. Dave was concerned. The week I had to prepare for graduate school exams, Dave worked at the Gaslight, and I stayed home, alone, to study. Dave told the Gaslight performers what was happening, and they worked out a "Terri sitting" brigade—a grown-up babysitting committee. Performers would come and just sit quietly in the apartment, so I could study. The roster included Tom Paxton, Noel Stookey, Hugh Romney, and Bill Cosby. Non-performer friends Jimmy Herman and Jack Arnold hung around for full evenings.

A lot of coffee houses and even some liquor clubs found homes in the Village of the '60s. This isn't a history, so I won't describe all of them. But to me, a few were key.

The Gaslight was my home less than a mile from home. I could go there any evening and find friends and good music.

During the first few years that the Gaslight booked folk singers, musicians spent most of their non-performing time in the coffee house, often in the so-called dressing room. It was a small, not-very-clean room behind the coffee house. It wasn't a dressing room, since no one ever changed their clothes to go onstage, it was a place to hang out. At some point, folk singers started to play poker between sets. I seldom sat in on those games; the room was small and dirty, and when I went upstairs, it was to hang out briefly. Over the years, the games went from a nickel or dime ante to one of several dollars, and Dave, who had occasionally participated, decided the game was too rich for his blood.

I was welcome to listen to performers or to wander into the kitchen or the dressing room. I took that for granted. Sometimes, at folk music events, I was the only nonperformer who took part in the conversation; no one ever objected, and I was always welcomed, so it never occurred to me that my participation was unusual. Much later, I realized that something about me drew respect from the musicians, and that Dave's tacit assumption that I should be included anywhere I wanted to be ensured that when he and I were together, no one would object out loud.

Someone objected once. In 1961, the performers who worked at the Gaslight fairly steadily, and who were paid salaries, decided that the basket houses which collected donations from audiences to pay the performers should be forced to pay salaries. Dave led the group, and I assumed that

I would be part of the organizing group; the action had been partly my idea, I was an active socialist who believed in working-class organizing, and I was a good strategist. At the first meeting of the organizing group, Len Chandler objected to my participation because I wasn't a performer. Dave was outraged; he wanted me there, I wanted to be there, and he was used to having his way. There was an argument; there was a vote; and I was part of the organizing group. Objection overruled. It never happened again.

Recently, I came across a receipt for $1 for 'dues' signed by Noel (Paul) Stookey. It took a few minutes to figure out that the dues payment was for membership in the coffee house union we tried to organize more than forty-one years ago. Noel must have been treasurer.

We took the organizing effort one step further. Two of our organizers, both members of the American Federation of Musicians, met with Local 802, the New York City chapter, and were told that the union didn't think folk singers were musicians and it wasn't interested in organizing them. We thought that was outrageous, since folk singers who played in liquor clubs had to join the union. Mostly, we thought that union chapter sucked.

Ultimately, the whole effort dissolved. The basket houses remained basket houses for as long as I can remember.

By 1962, the New York folk music scene comprised several coffee houses that paid performers salaries, and at least one liquor club.

The Gaslight booked both new and older performers such as Dave, Mississippi John Hurt, Gary Davis, Doc Watson, Skip James, Tom Paxton, Patrick Sky, and Richie Havens. The Bitter End featured more 'commercial' acts: Taj Mahal, Peter, Paul and Mary, the Chambers Brothers, Odetta, Chad Mitchell.

I wrote earlier that the Gaslight was my home. It was that before I started to manage musicians, and continued to be afterward. I had unfettered access to musical greats such as Mississippi John Hurt, Reverend Gary Davis, Sonny Terry and Brownie McGhee, Lightnin' Hopkins, Doc Watson, and mandolin virtuoso David Grisman.

Hearing and meeting these musicians was a privilege. A few years earlier, many of them wouldn't have been performing in Greenwich Village. Part of the musical excitement of the '60s was the growing interest in blues and blues musicians. Young aficionados were going south to try

Dave and me on the roof of 190 Waverly Place, NY. *Photo, Ann Charters*

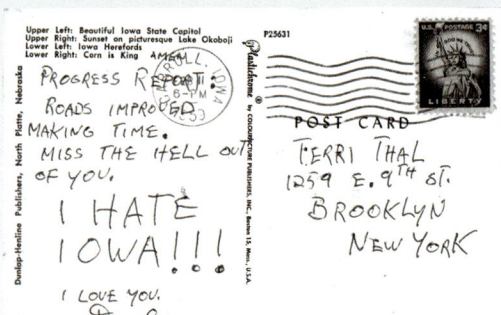

In February 1959, a socialist colleague drove Dave to California, where David expected to find work as a folksinger. Dave sent postcards home

I HATE IOWA!!!

NEBRASKA. DAMN.

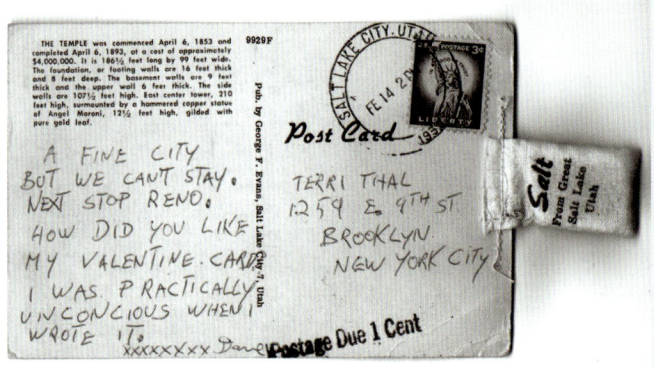

NEXT STOP RENO.

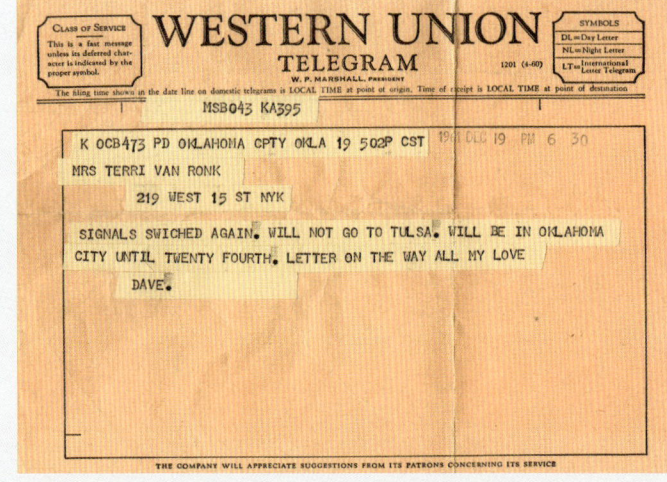

Dave sending a personal message via Western Union was unusual, 1961

Dave Van Ronk, when I met him in 1957. He was 21

Dave in Central Park in spring 1958, with a banjo, which he had played years before

A list of the members of the Folksingers Guild, 1958

Roy Berkeley and Dave, c.1958

Receipt for membership in group organizing the basket coffee houses, 1961

August 1, 1961, to celebrate booking our wedding Dave and me bought coloring books. Bob Dylan decorated and dedicated a picture in my coloring book

September 6, 1961, I recorded Bob Dylan playing a set at the Gaslight. I took the tape to club owners and concert producers to introduce his sound to them, trying to get him gigs. This has become known as the First Gaslight Tape!

Dylan Tape

Some thoughts from Bob Dylan on his 1st album – dedicated to Dave and me, 1962

Bob Dylan album cover

To Dave & Terree Walrus
If this ain't the bestest godest
wholest, suziest, dylanist, ronkish
egotisticish, columbyaist,
greatest record I ever made that you Listened to
I give you my all permission to put in the middle of
your
spear and shit on it — Lots of Love Listening and —

Try to do it while Listening to
this here record — "Highway 51" — it's the
greatest way — better than any of that
rag time and classical crap —
Your Friend,
Bob

To Dave & Terree Walrus

These were giveaways from the Kettle of Fish, the bar next to the Gaslight Cafe

White Horse Tavern mug — a wedding gift from the bartenders at the White Horse Tavern. I kept this when Dave and me split up

Promotional poster for Dave Van Ronk performing at the Cafe Au Go-Go, mid-1960s. *Courtesy of Barry Ollman, Photo by Dara Ollman*

Anthea Joseph, manager of London's The Troubadour, and me, London, 1967

Dave Van Ronk and the Ragtime Jug Stompers: l-r Barry Kornfeld, Sam Charters, Danny Kalb, Dave, Artie Rose. *Photo, Ann Charters*

DAVE VAN RONK AND THE HUDSON DUSTERS

TERRI THAL MANAGEMENT
190 WAVERLY PLACE NEW YORK, N.Y. 10014
(212) 255-2856

The Hudson Dusters. I'm pushing the cart, which carries (standing) Dave, Ed Gregory (bass), Rick Henderson (drums), Dave Woods (guitar); and seated, Phil Namanworth (Pot) (keyboards)

Suze Rotolo book art, 1993. This is one of several that Suze gave me and that I still have. *Photo, Norman Savitt*

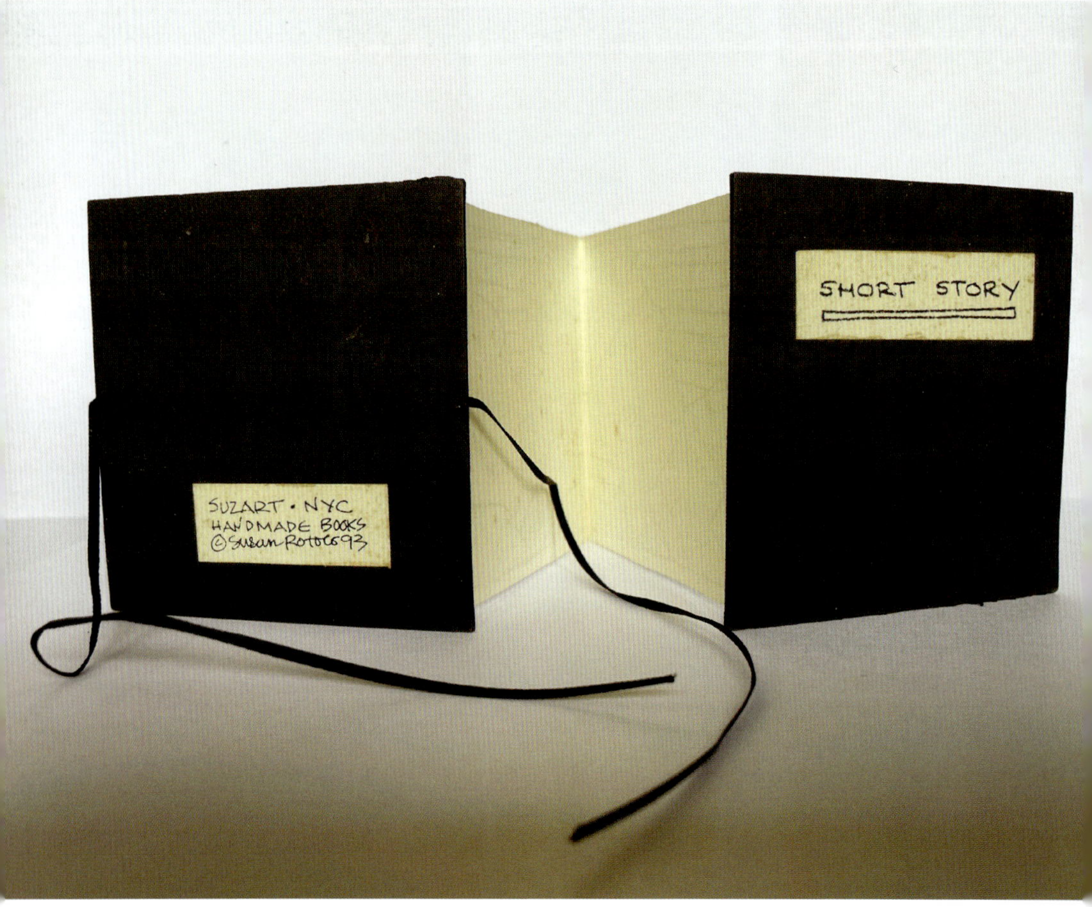

Suze Rotolo, 1993

My brother Leon and me, Anza-Borrego Desert

My sister Joyce, my brother Leon and me at my 60th birthday party

Paul in Tin Can Alley Antiques. *Photo, Bill Mitchell*

Me with my uncle, Jack Beller, my cousin Robin Swados and my aunt Bette Swados

Martus and me

Peter Stampfel and me at Gerde's Folk City reunion, 2010. *Photo, Jeannie Myers*

With Suze Rotolo at Washington Square Bluegrass and Folk Music reunion, 2009. *Photo, Frank Beacham*

With John Hammond Jr at the Museum of the City of New York, 2015. *Photo, Frank Beacham*

to find the bluesmen they worshiped—and for me, the result was meeting the people I just listed, and suddenly finding 'Son' House or 'Skip' James or Robert Wilkins walking down the street or showing up at the Gaslight, the New York City home for the blues. I'd sit in the Gaslight and one of those men would get up on stage and tell a few stories, then would produce tense or light, but always incredible, blues. Or I'd be in the Kettle of Fish and they would walk in and knock back drinks with us. It was mind-blowing.

I have more of an overall memory of being in the Gaslight than memories of specific performances. If I was alone, I usually sat at a table along the northern wall, leaving the more desirable (if they were that) center tables for paying customers. My favorite seat was toward the front, so I could watch musicians' hands. Mostly, I was quiet during performances. I've always been annoyed with people who talk or rattle dishes when someone's singing or playing music or presenting an oral performance onstage. It's rude. And back then, there weren't any cell phones, and audience members didn't disrupt shows by taking photographs or recording shows, although that was happening by some time in the early 1970s. And with few exceptions, there wasn't banter between performers and their colleagues in the audience. There was some, of course, since many were friends, but mostly, folk singers listened to their peers with respect and admiration.

When Dave and I were together in the audience at the coffee house, the same self-imposed rules held, although he and whoever was on stage occasionally would make comments to one another, either about the music or the culture it came from. But that happened only if the performer was someone of his own age. It just about never happened if the performer was someone he had admired from afar, such as Gary Davis or John Hurt or Doc Watson or Jean Ritchie.

The Gaslight had several owners over the years. The most noted was John Mitchell, a temperamental man whose bursts of anger terrified people working there. It was then sold, and was managed by Clarence Hood, a southerner who, we were told by members of his family, had been part of the Truman administration, and had made and lost fortunes. I wondered how comfortable Clarence felt in his role as the caretaker of a coffee house that featured folk music, which at that time was not regarded as "real music" even by the musician's union. If he felt that it was a lesser form of business than those of his southern friends, he never hinted at it.

I saw a non-businesslike Clarence Hood one afternoon when I went to his apartment to pick up Dave's pay after an appearance in the Gaslight. Clarence was very, very drunk. He muttered some phrases about conducting business that wasn't "worth his time," (not the words he used), and invited me to have a sexual interlude with him. I recoiled, but he repeated several times what he was asking me to do. I fled in horror and disgust, and ran home, yelling to Dave, "That mother fucker tried to get me to go down on him." I stayed away from the club for a few weeks. However, I realized that Clarence hadn't hit on me to make any kind of professional exchange; he did so because he was drunk and I happened to be there and was sexually appealing. So I went back to hanging out at the Gaslight and doing business with Clarence Hood, and neither of us ever mentioned that occurrence.

After a few years, Clarence turned management of the Gaslight over to his son, Sam, who was torn between being a businessman and a friend of the folk singers he hired. Sam was able to take back part of the money he paid them by being a consistently big winner in the poker games that went on in the 'dressing room.' Later, he married folk singer Alix Dobkin, and they opened a club that featured folk singers in Coconut Grove, Florida, and after that folded, opened one in Woodstock, New York. That also folded. Very few people made money owning folk music clubs.

The Blues Musicians

John Hurt may have been the most loved musician who performed at the Gaslight. A Black man in his seventies, he had been brought to New York by one of the blues fans who sought out musicians in the south. It was especially interesting to see him develop a good relationship with Clarence Hood, a white man who came from the same part of Mississippi as John. It was disconcerting to learn that once, many years before, they had attended the same lynching; John never talked about that, but I've always wondered what he really thought.

John wasn't a hard drinker. But when we hung out and drank in the Kettle of Fish, next door to the Gaslight, one of the bartender-waiters would bring him a drink. Mark Ross reminds me that John occasionally would ask the waiter, "Why do you bring me a drink before I order?" The waiter would reply, "Because I know what you drink. You always drink bourbon and branch." "What if I want something different?" John would ask. So the waiter would take the drink back to the bar and ask, "What would you like?" "Bourbon and branch," John predictably would reply. Yes, it sounds like a bad joke, but it was funny when it happened.

I learned a hard lesson about racism when John died in 1966. Dave and I wanted to tell his family in Avalon, Mississippi, how much we honored him. We decided to send flowers, something neither of us ever had done. I went to the florist shop on West 8th Street and told the man there what we wanted to do. He refused. "I don't ship the actual flowers," he explained. "I send money to a local florist down there, and that store delivers the flowers. If I tell them to deliver flowers to a Black family, your friend's family will receive weeds, not flowers. You want to pay tribute to your friend, but his family will be humiliated. I can't take your money to do that." He told me to honor John in another way. Again—this was in 1966. So, instead of trying to send flowers, we wrote a letter to John's family.

My other musical god was Reverend Gary Davis. Gary was born blind in South Carolina, where he learned to play guitar using only his thumb and index finger. When he moved to North Carolina, he joined a musical scene in which he played gospel, ragtime, and blues. He became a minister in the 1940s, moving to New York with his wife, Annie. Gary became prominent among folk music fans in the 1960s, but even before that, his home was a school for would-be blues musicians, many of whom became his 'lead boys,' helping him get around New York City.

Barry Kornfeld, an excellent musician who subsequently was our downstairs neighbor, drove Gary to a major initial gig in Boston where they both performed, and later, to the 1959 Newport Folk Festival, where Gary was featured at one of the Sunday afternoon concerts. Barry recalls that they drove from New York City to Newport and back in one day because of a problem getting a Black man a hotel room in Newport—and consider, that was in a New England state.

Dave wasn't one of Gary's 'lead boys,' but he virtually worshiped Gary; the Reverend's guitar style and ability were superb, and his singing, which resembled—and actually was—southern preaching, was an intrinsic part of who he was. Gary was not a blues musician or a jazz musician; he was a preacher and, I think, a musical genius. I recently saw a 12-minute tape of Dave introducing his version of 'Spike Driver Blues' in 1997, saying that the first time he saw Mississippi John Hurt, he thought, "There's God. He's alive." But although that was close to true, it was a bit off—Dave was forgetting that always, his first God was the Reverend Gary Davis.

I still play Gary Davis's and John Hurt's records more often than any others of that era. If you want to know what moves my soul, find them on YouTube.

In the early years of the Gaslight, its two most popular performers other than Dave were Len Chandler and Tom Paxton. Tom showed up in 1960, and even then, he wrote songs that were so good that I never thought of him as a singer-songwriter, but as a folk musician. Some of his songs, such as 'Ramblin' Boy' and 'The Last Thing On My Mind,' have entered the folk tradition. Tom was—and still is—funny, often devastatingly so, and smart, and still wants his songs to move people.

The Folklore Center

Before we leave MacDougal Street, I have to introduce you to Izzy (Israel) Young, proprietor of the Folklore Center, which was almost next door to the Gaslight. There's no place like that around anymore, which is a pity. It was a tiny store owned and managed by a man who was constitutionally incapable of running a business or making money. Izzy sold stuff needed by folk singers: records, capos, guitar strings, finger picks. His prices were ridiculously low, even for then, and he probably gave away as much as he sold. Folk singers could hang out there, have mail sent there, get phone messages there, meet friends there … but mostly, you could find out who was in town, what was happening, what new publications had been started, who edited them. You could find out who was or no longer was managing whom. Or who had just cut a record. You also could find out, if you asked nicely, who was going with whom and who had just broken up. Lots of news.

Izzy let folk singers hang out in the tiny back room of the Folklore Center, including Bob (Dylan) newly arrived in the Village, although Izzy was later somewhat turned off by what he saw as a condescending attitude on Bob's part. And, occasionally, you could see Izzy dressed for Morris dancing, bells and all, on the landing in front of the store.

In 1973, Izzy moved his store to Stockholm, where, I've been told, he made as small an income as he had in the United States. I saw him once, when he came back to visit several years before he died. He asked me to meet him and a few other people from our folk music scene in Manhattan. We spent some time schmoozing in Matt Umanov's instrument store on

Bleecker Street (now gone), and in the evening, heard the incredible mandolinist David Grisman at City Winery.

Gerde's Folk City

Gerde's Folk City, a few blocks east, was a liquor club, and booked a cross-section of musicians. It featured many of the same performers as the Gaslight and paid them a bit less, but it became the most prestigious folk music room in New York, perhaps because it brought in both non-commercial and commercial musicians. To work there, performers had to be members of the American Federation of Musicians and have a cabaret card, and attendees had to be old enough to drink legally.

I heard everyone there: the Greenbriar Boys, Brother John Sellers, the Clancy Brothers, Ramblin' Jack Elliott, Judy Collins, Lonnie Johnson, Andy Statman, Buffy Sainte-Marie, Cisco Houston, Bonnie Dobson. And I heard my good friends: Dave, of course, Dylan's Pat Sky, Tom Paxton, Happy Traum, Caroline Hester, John Winn and Paul Clayton.

New York folk singers developed a routine to close evenings in clubs and, occasionally, concerts. It was introduced by John Winn. He or the closing act would start to sing 'Lloyd George Knew My Father,' and they would be joined on stage by the other folk singers in the room, all bellowing, "Lloyd George knew my father, My father knew Lloyd George," to the tune of 'Onward Christian Soldiers.' It would be repeated over and over, more and more loudly, until everyone who was expected to be on stage was there and the room sounded, as John Winn put it, "like a huge Carnegie Hall symphonic crescendo," and then with one more round it would end. I always went on stage or was called on stage and joined in—one of the only times I ever sang. I couldn't and can't carry a tune and don't ever sing when another person is nearby. But I would sing 'Lloyd George.'

The ditty was an English song from the early twentieth century. It worked well for a crowd of Greenwich Village folk singers who wanted to end a night of music on an upbeat, raucous note. And at the volume used, no one heard me butchering the music.

One evening, Jean Redpath, a wonderful Scottish folk singer who knew and sometimes explained the derivations of all the songs she presented, was ending her performance at Gerde's. As the final notes of her voice faded, Patrick Sky wandered onstage to tell Jean how much he loved her singing and to start to intone 'Lloyd George knew …'

Jean looked annoyed, and turning to Patrick, seemed to be about to say something, when Pat, never a male chauvinist, loudly said, "You're discriminating against me because I'm a man. I'm not a sexist. Terri, come up here so Jean knows I'm not a sexist." So I went. Jean shrugged, put an arm around me, and we joined Patrick and the other male folk singers who found their way onto the stage in a bellowing rendition of the song.

I wrote above that singing 'Lloyd George' was one of the only times I sang in public. The other was with Dave. He sang a song called 'Mr. Noah,' with a chorus that included the line "Doodely doo, doodely doo, doodeley doodeley doodeley doodely doodeley doo!" Dave developed a habit of calling me up on stage to sing that chorus, often with him, sometimes alone. Mostly, I'd half-sing, half-recite it alone the first three times and the fourth, we'd do it together. Was I embarrassed? Of course. But it was fun.

Although, over the years, folk singers moved from drinking lots of coffee to drinking lots of booze, Gerde's Folk City wasn't a place to get drunk. People went there to listen to the music, and that was the predominant focus. Liquor was very secondary. Most of the heaviest drinkers in the folk music world, including Dave and me, tended not to get smashed at Folk City.

The club was owned by Mike Porco, an immigrant from Italy whom I never would have imagined enjoying American folk music. In 1960, Mike had allowed two people, including Izzy Young, owner of the Folklore Center, to turn his bar into a folk club. It was successful, and after a few months, Mike took it over himself.

I liked Mike; I was the person, or one of the people, who talked him into hiring Bob Dylan, and in the first year of running the club, he occasionally asked my opinion of someone he thought of bringing in. It didn't occur to me then, but in retrospect, I wonder whether I offered him a woman's perspective on potential acts. Although he was open to booking in anyone whom he thought would pull in an audience, Mike wanted assurances that the musician wouldn't attract unsavory characters, wasn't a lush, had decent manners, and wouldn't hit on customers. Mike had good business acumen; he didn't have to love someone's music to feature the performer in his club.

Mike's grandson, Bob Porco, has spent years keeping the spirit of the club alive. In the 1990s, he interviewed many people who had been associated with it for a film he hoped to make. I've always regretted putting him off—I did so not because I didn't want to be in the film, but at that time I was trying to organize stuff in the house that's 30 miles (48 km) from Manhattan where Paul and I had moved. If Bob ever makes the film and I'm not in it, I'll be angry with myself.

Women Folk Singers

Most folk singers were male. Recently, I listed everyone I could think of who was either a folk singer or something related—manager, club owner, photographer, producer, waitress (there were no waiters), record company owner or producer—in New York in the late '50s and through most of the '60s who lived in New York, performed there often, or spent a lot of time there. The vast majority of the people on the list were musicians.

Of the three hundred thirty-eight names on the list, only fifty-eight are female. While there was no discrimination against women, and no one I knew tried to coerce them into sexual activity, there was sort of an assumption that there were factors distinguishing the female folk singers from one another in ways that were never considered for the men. Why were there so many discussions about whether Joan Baez or Judy Collins was a better singer? Both were superb, and their musical approaches differed. Why did I occasionally hear people wonder whether there was room in the folk music pantheon for both Joan Baez, who was not a New York-based musician, and Caroline Hester, who lived in New York? The women didn't think they were competing against one another; why did some male folk singers think there wasn't room for more than one woman?

Carolyn and I have talked about that. "No one ever said there can be only one guy folk singer," she said. "There were hundreds of them. I was working in the clubs, and when other women started to play, it was fabulous. The idea that there should be only one or two women drove me nuts. No one compared women jazz performers to one another; why did they do it to folk singers?"

The editor of one of the folk music magazines wrote something about 'The battle of the folk queens,' which ruined Caroline's enjoyment of one of the folk festivals. "We needed one another," she emphasized. "It was a case of the more, the merrier."

Some people have asked whether there was an accepted way for women to dress in the Village or in the folk music world at that time. That's happened partly because of a well-known photograph of Dave,

Bob Dylan, Suze Rotolo, and me on our way to breakfast one day. A part of this photograph is featured on the cover of this book. In it, I'm wearing slacks that end above my ankles; I've been asked whether women wore pants like that in the 1960s. No, it wasn't a style. My slacks were short because I was 5'11" and too slim to buy clothes in Lane Bryant, a store that sold clothes for tall women. To wear them, the woman had to be large; I remember the term 'broad-boned.' I wasn't broad-boned. I was slim and large-breasted. Finding clothes that fit, including pants that were long enough, was a torturous adventure.

Later, I became friends with Trina Robbins, who was associated with the science fiction and comics fans on the East Side, and who also made clothes. She made several wonderful pairs of slacks for me, with waistlines around my hips, below my navel. The best outfit she created was a striped, heavy silk pants suit with a high-necked top that ended just below my breasts, low-cut pants, and a mandarin-style jacket that went below my hips so I could wear the garment to business meetings. I still have this outfit, and I'm delighted that I'm still able to get into it.

A few years ago, when my house was renovated and I had to empty it temporarily, I came across at least six pairs of black slacks and four pants suits. I owned that many because it was so difficult to find slacks that were long enough and could be taken in to fit me, so whenever I found them, I bought them. I know a wonderful seamstress who could make anything fit me; Anna Palaia has remade suits that were several sizes too large for me.

My own preferred outfit was very large sweaters and slim slacks. I dressed like that until several years ago, when I switched to slim—but not tight—sweaters. During those early years of hanging around the Village, several women in the folk music world and some in the Trotskyist movement envied me my huge, oversized sweaters. How did I get them? My father worked in the textile industry, and while the company my uncle owned and Dad worked for didn't manufacture clothing, my father sometimes brought me samples that had been worn in a fashion show or photo shoot. Most of them were men's sweaters. I loved them.

No one I knew wore a costume. Carolyn Hester wore casual dresses. I think Carolyn came closest to having a country look. Suze Rotolo, Dylan's girlfriend, generally looked as she does in the photograph in this book. Alix Dobkin preferred skirts. Most women performers wore skirts or dresses, but there wasn't any uniform.

There was one item of clothing we all wanted: custom-made sandals. There were two sandal makers in the Village. Both custom-fit. Both used only brown or tan leather. Fred Braun's sandals were a bit less rough-looking. He used thin straps, sometimes wrapped around a woman's ankle. Allan Block's had arch supports, were more obviously handmade, and every woman I knew wanted Allan Block sandals. I did, very much. I remember how excited I was when we finally could afford a pair. And yes, they lasted more than twenty years.

Allan Block also was a folk musician. He played fiddle, and the shop was a gathering place for old-time musicians such as Doc Watson and 'Son' House, people the younger folk singers admired and emulated. Dave and I knew of it, but didn't hang out there; we hosted a different scene in our apartment.

His daughter, Rory Block, has become a good and successful blues musician.

The Café Au Go Go

For a while in the mid '60s, one of the most exciting clubs in the Village was the Café Au Go Go. It started as a jazz club, but soon booked a lot of rock and South Side, Chicago blues groups. I never heard the Grateful Dead there, but I devoured such performers as Muddy Waters, the Paul Butterfield Blues Band, James Cotton, the Chambers Brothers, and 'Big Joe' Williams. And my friends in The Blues Project, who included its originator, Danny Kalb, and Steve Katz, both of whom had been guitar students of Dave's; I briefly managed Danny as a solo act before The Blues Project and again many years later.

I remember hearing and meeting Muddy Waters at the Café Au Go Go more clearly than I remember anyone else there—except the Paul Butterfield Blues Band and the Blues Project. Muddy grew up in Mississippi, where the Delta Blues was developed, and started playing electric guitar in Chicago during the 1940s. By the late '50s, he was an influence on some English bands, and many of the American blues musicians who played acoustic guitar were impressed by him. Dave and I were knocked out by his recordings. Dave recorded Muddy's signature song, which boasts of the singer's sexual prowess, on *Van Ronk Sings*, his second album for Folkways in 1961, spelling it 'Hootchy Kootchy Man' in the album notes, while someone spelled it differently on the cover. (Eric Von Schmidt designed the jacket cover, but I don't know who set the type for the names of the songs.)

When I heard Muddy Waters at the Café Au Go Go, I found him a personable man and as musically exciting on stage as on records. Fifty years later, in 2016, I heard and met his son, Larry 'Mud' Morganfield, also a wonderful blues musician.

The Café Au Go Go hosted comedian Lenny Bruce, who, with the club's owner Howard Solomon, was arrested and convicted on obscenity charges. Howard's conviction later was overturned, and Lenny Bruce was eventually granted a posthumous pardon by New York State Governor George Pataki.

The Village Gate and the Blacklist

The Village Gate featured mostly jazz, not folk music. It was the one place where I didn't have free entrée; although I knew Art D'Lugoff, the owner, I didn't know the people at the door, and they had no reason to comp me; they didn't comp folk singers, either. The space now is a club called (Le) Poisson Rouge.

Art D'Lugoff was a jazz impresario who had booked musicians such as Billie Holiday, Duke Ellington, Dizzy Gillespie, Aretha Franklin, Miles Davis, Chico Hamilton, and Charles Mingus.

Art was either left of liberal or a socialist. After ABC-TV started the *Hootenanny* TV show in 1962, folk singers learned that Pete Seeger would not be invited to appear in it. He had been convicted of contempt of Congress for refusing to discuss his political affiliations with HUAC in 1955, but the conviction had been overturned on appeal in May 1962. Art loaned us the Village Gate for meetings of musicians who were furious and declared that they would boycott the show. Among those who said they wouldn't appear were Joan Baez, Carolyn Hester, Barbara Dane, Alix Dobkin, Ramblin' Jack Elliott, Tom Paxton, Happy Traum, Phil Ochs, and Dave. The Greenbriar Boys also attended but later performed on the show, though without John Herald. Joan Baez, Barbara Dane, and Tom Paxton were asked to perform and declined.

Carolyn Hester, who facilitated the initial meeting, has an especially interesting story. She had appeared on the show before she knew that Pete Seeger was being blacklisted. As soon as she learned about the decision to ban Seeger, she told her manager that she wouldn't participate as long as the ban existed. Although both people from ABC-TV and her booking agent pressured her to reconsider, she kept her commitment to fight for Seeger's right to take an unpopular political position.

Pete Seeger was later invited to perform, but only if he signed a statement stating whether he ever had been affiliated with the Communist Party. Of course, he refused, and the show remained contentious for folk singers until it folded.

The Other Clubs

There was another group of coffee houses: the basket houses. I didn't go to them often, but some excellent music was being played there. The Four Winds, the Basement, the Why Not, The Cafe Wha?, and others enabled musicians such as Fred Neil, Tim Hardin, Lisa Kindred and Vince Martin to showcase their altered, updated folk songs. They didn't totally rewrite the songs, but they didn't feel that the music came from a tradition that should be preserved; they were content to maintain the spirit, if not the notes, of the traditional material. Tim Hardin wrote original songs, some of which became classics. The basket houses also featured more traditional performers such as Susan Martin Robbins, who later played at the Gaslight, and still can be heard, mostly in Houston, Texas; and Jay Ungar, who wrote 'Ashokan Farewell,' the theme song for the TV series *The Civil War*. Karen Dalton, who has become something of a legend, performed in the Cafe Wha?, sometimes accompanied by Bob Dylan on harmonica. Several of those folk singers later played at the Night Owl, which was not a basket house, but wasn't licensed to feature live music.

The Four Winds, in particular, introduced some musicians who became very well-known: Janis Ian, Emmylou Harris, Steve Goodman, and Peter Tork of the Monkees.

Later, these clubs also hosted some of the early folk-rock and rock groups. The Velvet Underground members began their careers in Café Bizarre. When Jimi Hendrix still was Jimmy James, he performed at the Cafe Wha?; Bruce Springsteen's band played there weekend afternoons in the late '60s. The Lovin' Spoonful worked at the Night Owl Café.

Performers and managers could go to any of the clubs without paying an admission fee. That meant that I was able to hear some of the best folk and early folk-rock music being played. All of the clubs and coffee houses were exciting places to be. If you walked into any of them, there was an air of expectation—and more often than not, that expectation was met. There was also a feeling of fun, with good conversation and good will backstage. *Swinging* is an old-fashioned word to use for a place, but that's what all of those rooms did.

The Music Was Changing

Musical changes were occurring, too. In the early to mid '60s, folk singers started to write their own songs. Tom Paxton was writing songs when he first came to New York, although his first record became a secret because the record company crashed. Bob Dylan and Phil Ochs were writing songs by 1962. Patrick Sky was writing satiric, funny, ribald songs. Others started to do so, too.

Joni Mitchell showed up in New York in 1966, and knocked everyone out. Dave had heard her in Winnipeg and had raved about her. When her album *Song to a Seagull* was released, I played it repeatedly. Dave and I both thought her songs were amazing. As I write elsewhere, he recorded 'Clouds' with his band, Dave Van Ronk and the Hudson Dusters, and Joni successfully pushed him to include the original title, 'Both Sides Now.'

Pop groups such as the Kingston Trio and the Chad Mitchell Trio had been around since the late 1950s, and while the folk singers I knew were revolted by some of their recordings and commercial presentations, they had to admit that these groups helped generate interest in the old field recordings we listened to and the young musicians who were trying to make a living by emulating—and changing—them. Tom Paxton says he was entranced by the Kingston Trio's recording of 'Tom Dooley' in 1958, a song about the murder of a woman in 1866.

The Paul Butterfield Band, with Michael Bloomfield, an astounding guitarist who became a friend, appeared in New York and galvanized the folk world, as did the Beatles in 1964. Even before that, folk groups had started to appear. The Even Dozen Jug Band and the Jim Kweskin Jug Band both came into being in 1963; Dave created Dave Van Ronk and the Ragtime Jug Stompers in 1964—which I call The Year of the Jug Bands because they were so visible; there weren't many of them, but they seemed to be ubiquitous. Danny Kalb started the Blues Project in '64—not a folk band, although it had many folk elements and a folk flavor. A lot of other folk singers now wanted to augment their instrumentals with drums or flute or tambourines.

Those were heady days in the folk music world. Lots and lots of exciting events; a lot of exciting new and old music; and much experimentation, which often worked.

Years later, after Dave and I separated, I swore I would not go out or have sex with anyone in the music or socialist worlds. It was an absurd oath. I was turned off by the idea of going out or having sex with any of the socialists I knew, but the music scene was my professional and social one, and that's where I continued to work and hang out. So that's where I wound up having affairs—or one-night stands. One night, I tumbled into bed with the owner of a club; the sex was boring, but I was amused and annoyed afterward when he earnestly told me that I could go to his establishment without paying an admission. Amused, because I'd been going to his club gratis for years, courtesy of the people at the door. Annoyed, because he sounded like he thought he should gift me for the (lousy) sex. I choked and thanked him. He meant well.

The Village Neighborhood

Art D'Lugoff and Joe Marra, owner of the Night Owl, were said to have the distinction of being the only club owners in the Village who got away with not paying off the police. I don't know whether that's true or, if it is, how they managed it. The Gaslight's owners always had a line in their books labeled "grease." Other coffee houses and clubs also earmarked funds for the 6th precinct. What would have happened if they didn't pay? Noise complaints. Dirt complaints. Department of Health violations. Time spent in court. Fines. They all paid.

We got along with the policemen who regularly patrolled MacDougal Street. Generally, they were pleasant. Recently, I saw posts on Facebook by people who extolled their thoughtfulness to people who lived in the neighborhood. But, they were the same guys who took payoffs from the coffee house owners and sometimes beat up guys they thought weren't polite enough to them.

One spring night in 1962, my friend Lenny Glazer was in the Gaslight, apparently in a lousy mood. Later, I was told he had been loudly insulting folk singer Alix Dobkin and had been asked to leave the coffee house. As he walked up the stairs outside the Gaslight, one of the neighborhood policemen came by; perhaps the police had been called. I don't know what their conversation was like, but clearly, Lenny annoyed the cop, who beat him with his nightstick until he was bloody.

There was another aspect to the interaction between the clubs and coffee houses and the Village. We destroyed a neighborhood. The Village had been a residential Italian neighborhood. Sure, it had stores and restaurants, but people lived there. They raised families and socialized on the streets as well as in their homes. It was their community. Over a period of a few years, as entertainment places opened, MacDougal and Bleecker and West 4th and West 3rd Streets and the surrounding area were filled with a zillion young tourists noisily going from club to club, from subway to club. Loud, rude, walking on the sidewalks and in the streets, dumping cigarettes all over—this was before people smoked grass in public. Then, there were the cars. The performers recognized that they needed the tourists who came to hang out in the neighborhood and occupy seats in the coffee houses and clubs, but they—and I—despised the New Jersey drivers who cruised the streets, blew their horns, dropped beer cans in the gutters, tried to get laid, and occasionally were so drunk they drove up onto the sidewalk. We were convinced that none of them knew how to drive.

One weekend night, I was walking on MacDougal Street when a car jerked to the right, came up over the curb, knocked down a young woman who was only a few feet away from me, and screeched to a stop. Someone ran to the nearest open store and called an ambulance. It took more than an hour for the police to arrest the drunk driver and impound the car. Meanwhile, they closed the street to traffic. I never found out what injuries the woman suffered. This wasn't a very unusual event.

The Italians who lived in that section of the Village didn't like us. Occasionally, a performer would be taunted by one or more neighborhood kids and would wind up being pummeled by their fists. The young men hated the guys with beards; they hated the folk singers' success with the swarms of young women who were sexually available to the people they considered 'beatniks,' and they hated that their neighborhood was under siege.

We were respectful to the Italians who lived there, partly, I suspect, because we understood that some of the clubhouses where the elderly men gathered were Mafia-affiliated. And, I think that like many Americans then, we had a little bit of secret admiration for the people who sold liquor during prohibition and murdered one another over 'territorial' rights. (Consider the extraordinary success of the movie *The Godfather*.)

We knew some of the younger Italian men dealt in marijuana. It didn't occur to us that they also sold heroin, which we avoided.

When I hung out in the Kettle of Fish, the bar next door to the Gaslight, both Guido Gampieri, the owner, and Babe, the manager, treated me with respect. They should have: Dave and I drank prodigiously, bought drinks for friends, and tipped well. Years after Dave and

I separated, I found some old checkbooks from the mid '60s, and was shocked to see how much money we spent on booze.

Meeting Paul

About a year after Dave and I broke up, I was sitting in the Kettle of Fish with Mark Ross, a young folk singer I managed for a while and who is still a good friend. A man walked up to the table and said, "Mark, introduce me to your friend." Within a few months, Paul Solomon Orentlich and I were living together.

I was surprised to learn that Paul had been a bartender at the Kettle; we'd never before met. He had worked there days and I hung out there nights, but occasionally our paths must have crossed. We didn't think so—but, then, we wouldn't have paid any attention to one another. I was married and would have had no reason to meet Paul, and he would have had no reason to meet me.

We inadvertently put Babe in an uncomfortable position one evening, soon after we started to go out. I was meeting Paul at the Kettle of Fish. He arrived there before I did, and Dave was seated at the bar. Paul later told me that as he walked in, Babe moved forward to near where Dave was sitting and put his hands behind the bar; Paul knew there were items back there that could be used as weapons. He said he walked up to Dave, and as they said "Hello," a palpable deep breath was felt throughout the room. When I heard about it, I was baffled. Everyone in the Kettle knew that Dave and I still were good friends and everyone there knew Paul and I were together. Why, I wondered, would they think there would be any problems if they met?

Paul was well-regarded by all of the Kettle staff. When he stopped working there, he was regularly invited to Guido's famous private lunches. After Paul and I became a couple, Guido invited me to lunch. I was flattered, and wanted to go, but I was working uptown and a midday jaunt to MacDougal Street would have been very inconvenient. I've always regretted that I didn't take the time to do it. I understand that Guido was a fabulous cook and a gracious host.

When did that music scene start to deteriorate? I can't be specific about it, nor do I like to say that when it changed it was deteriorating. But, sometime in the late '60s, the music world I knew there did change. Folk singers such as Dave and Tom Paxton worked in the Village clubs only occasionally; their careers now took them on the road more frequently than before. Tom recalls that other clubs such as the Bitter End and the newer Bottom Line paid so much more than the Gaslight that he performed in them rather than the Gaslight or Gerde's. "I owed it to myself and Midge to make a decent living," he commented recently.

New Yorkers felt that the city was changing. More young people who took drugs other than pot were on the streets. Beads and candles abounded. In the music scene, the singer-songwriters had replaced the folk singers. The music I heard comprised too many songs that I found soppy—I was not interested in hearing a young man sing, "My candle burns for you, my love, Will you love me tomorrow," nor was I interested in whatever else was going on in his head. Emotions had replaced stories, and I thought most of the songs about them were badly written. I didn't believe in magic.

One night at about 2 a.m., I left the Bitter End on Bleecker Street to go home, and the streets were fairly deserted. For the first time since I had started to go to the Village, I felt a bit unsettled. It was uncanny. I had been walking those streets at any hour of the day or night for more than thirteen years, and I'd never been uncomfortable or felt unsafe. But, suddenly, I was both. Uncomfortable enough that I went to the Kettle of Fish to find someone to help me get a taxi. John Hammond, Jr., was there, and offered to walk me home. I was grateful and embarrassed. It was disconcerting. This was my city; these were my streets; what was happening?

Within a year, I stopped managing folk singers.

Chapter 8
THE BUSINESS OF FOLK MUSIC

No one became a folk music manager or music publisher or started a record company to make money in the early 1960s. There wasn't much money to be earned in that world. Most of the people who entered the business did so because they loved the music and were happy to be around it. There were some commercially minded managers; I wasn't one of them.

I became a manager because Dave's manager gave him good advice that Dave didn't like. Dave and I had been delighted when Paul Endicott, a manager from the Midwest, wanted to handle his business. Contract? I'm sure there wasn't one.

Endicott booked Dave into a new club in Pennsylvania, near Philadelphia. It wasn't well known and had a small advertising budget. When Dave appeared there, blues greats 'Brownie' McGhee and Sonny Terry were playing at the older, well-known Second Fret in Philadelphia, and many people who might have gone to hear Dave went there instead. It was clear to us that the new club wouldn't be able to pay Dave, so we called Paul Endicott. "Fulfill your contract," Paul advised. "If you walk out, you'll never be able to collect your money." It was sound legal advice.

Dave completed the engagement, got stiffed, couldn't sue, and asked me to take over handling his business. I did. I dropped out of graduate school; I thought it was a temporary hiatus, but I didn't go back for more than twenty years, and when I did, I was in another career.

Initially, I didn't consider myself a 'grown-up' manager—whatever that was. I knew that a manager was someone who planned and guided the careers of her/his artists, but Dave was unguidable. Not by me, not by any subsequent manager. He did his own thing, and no one was going to change him. Not tell him how to stand or sit; not tell him not to drink on stage; not suggest that he wear longer pants. But, in folk music, very few managers did try to change performers. You managed them as you found them.

Albert Grossman was superb at developing and guiding folk singers. When Albert conceived of and organized the trio Peter, Paul and Mary, he asked Dave to become Paul. Dave and I talked about it, but we decided that Dave's musical abilities would be drowned in that group. And, since Mary Travers refused to speak to me (although I still don't know why), we thought it would be a difficult personal relationship. Dave turned down the offer and Noel Stookey became Paul. The group became the smash hit folk group of the era. Dave and I were sure that if he'd become part of it, that wouldn't have happened. Dave lacked a smoothness that lent itself to commercially oriented music. He was craggy and rough and sometimes growly, and in those years, that made him commercially unviable.

Also, for some reason, Albert freaked me out. I've been in a few situations in which I and someone else look at each other and just don't like one another. I don't understand what's behind that, but it's real. I also don't understand why I froze as much as I did in Albert's presence. If I was at a table of people in a bar, enjoying my friends and the booze, and Albert joined us, I shut up. I stopped speaking. I stopped laughing. Dave called Albert "The Great Stone Face," because he never showed any expression. As a fairly gregarious person, I usually wasn't put off by people. I was put off by Albert.

We made this business card for Dave, but he never carried it with him

Becoming a Manager

I became a good manager, although it took me a long time to realize it. I didn't send the performers I worked with to voice coaches or carefully advise the (few) women I worked with on makeup or hair. I was able to suggest how to stand or sit on stage, how to approach a microphone, and I could help move them up from small clubs to larger ones, and to concert performances. I could approach record companies and negotiate record contracts. I was able to expand their careers.

There was a geographic pattern to booking, which still exists. You'd know how long ago the performers had appeared in, for example, the Midwest (by which we meant Oklahoma). If it had been more than six months, it might be time for a return engagement. Very often, the major club in the region would call me at about that time; sometimes, I would make the call. To make the engagement pay, the performer usually needed one or more other gigs in the area. In Oklahoma City, the club was The Buddha. I'd book Dave there for a week or a long weekend, and if there was a club in, for example, Denver, I'd try to get work there for him just before or after The Buddha. Even if it paid less, it usually would be worth doing it, as long as it wasn't too far from the major engagement.

Many club bookings came about for Dave because the club owner called. Others, I solicited, but I was able to ask for good pay with confidence.

As I gained confidence, and as Dave became better known, booking was sometimes fun. I still can hear a conversation I had with Manny Rubin, who owned the Second Fret Club in Philadelphia. Manny had called me, and I had asked for a higher fee for Dave than he'd ever received from a club. As I waited for Manny's reply, I heard him say to someone, "Don't bother me; this is a very important call." I chortled privately and quietly, knowing that he'd pay the money I wanted. He did, and I felt good, and Dave got paid.

Concerts were another matter. Colleges and the few concert producers who put folk singers on stage determined who they wanted. I learned how to find the people who handled college bookings, which generally paid as much for one night as coffee houses did for a week. Usually, campus concerts were arranged by a student group. I still encounter people who are or were in the folk music world, or who were in CORE or SNCC or later, SDS chapters who tell me that they brought one or more of the performers I managed to their campus back in the '60s. They've mentioned engaging Dave, Danny Kalb, Alex Lukeman, Mark Ross, and the Holy Modal Rounders. I'm always surprised if I don't remember the event ... but it was a long time ago.

Recording contracts were crucial, but not very lucrative. Folk music artists seldom received record royalties, and manager and performers tried to get a large advance payment at a time when a good one was in the hundreds, not thousands, of dollars. Musicians—certainly, folk singers, who didn't sell a lot of records—had no control over their albums. They couldn't approve album jackets, although they usually decided who wrote liner notes; they sometimes couldn't approve which songs or versions to release. I've written a story elsewhere in this book noting that when Dave made his first Folkways record, he hated the cover, which, it turned out, was made by the man I later lived with. No one at Folkways cared whether or not Dave liked it; Moe Asch had decided to use it and neither Dave nor I had any input.

We made one mistake. In 1964, I negotiated a recording contract with Mercury Records for Dave. He recorded one solo album and one jug band album for the company. The jug band album was good but sold poorly. The solo album was OK, but not as good as it could have been. The person who was supposed to be supervising the recording had no idea of what Dave's music was about, so I took over. Dave and I were drinking fairly heavily at that time; he had a bottle of Irish whiskey with him and swigged it all throughout the session; I drank less only because I preferred Scotch and didn't have any with me, so I had to drink his Irish whiskey. The music sounded good to us.

We listened to the tapes the next day; they still sounded good and we approved their release. Later, when we heard the record, we were

My business card, stylishly adapted after we moved to 190 Waverly Place

horrified; the music was sloppy. We never should have allowed it to be released. Lessons learned. First, a performer shouldn't get drunk while recording. Second, the A&R person shouldn't drink while supervising a recording session. Third, let some time elapse between when you record and when you listen to the product. *Note:* I wrote the liner notes for that album, which were about Dave, not the music, and they were pretty good.

Managing Dave presented some special problems:

- I was already friendly with some club owners who knew me as Dave's wife; now I had to ask them to do business with me as his manager.
- Everyone in the folk music world knew Dave and I were married. Was I going to say, "This is Terri Van Ronk and I want you to book Dave Van Ronk?"
- If Dave and I disagreed about something, how would we handle it? If the disagreement was a bitter one, how would the loser cope?
- If someone I approached for a gig said she or he thought Dave was not a good musician, would I be able to keep my cool?

My solution to one of those: when Dave and I got married, I started to use his last name. Now I stopped, and tried being Terri Thal professionally and Terri Van Ronk socially. But even I couldn't handle that; it was too complicated. I went back to being Terri Thal, not Terri Van Ronk, in all aspects of my life. I found that I preferred using my own name both professionally and personally. As Terri Van Ronk, I was Dave Van Ronk's wife. As Terri Thal, I was myself, not an appendage of 'the famous man.' People could like or dislike me for myself; Dave's persona wasn't involved.

We were able to work out disagreements between us. Most of them weren't major. Once, I forgot to book Dave a hotel room when he went to a club gig in Cambridge. He wound up staying with a friend, something he didn't like to do. It was my goof. He was furious with me. But, he got over it.

A worse gaffe: Prestige Records (the company he recorded for then) was approached by an afternoon television show that wanted Dave to appear on it in a swinging cage, singing 'Samson and Delilah,' a song he had learned from Reverend Gary Davis. Dave said "no" clearly and flatly. I hoped it would get him some publicity, and talked him into doing it.

I can't explain how excruciatingly awful it was. There was Dave, a large, ungainly man, dressed in tan chinos that had lost their crease, and a heavy sport shirt, hanging in what looked like a huge birdcage, swinging back and forth, singing "Samson and the lion …" while an underdressed girl chorus below the cage danced—presumably provocatively. If Dave had fired me, I'd have understood. Our only consolation was that no one we knew saw it—if anyone had, Dave would have been the laughing stock of the folk world and would have been even angrier with me than he was.

I learned that not all publicity is good publicity—and that you have to create and control it rather than allow the shmucks to do so.

The Year of the Jug Band

1964 was the year of the jug band. Six years before, Dave and Sam Charters—blues collector, ethnic musicologist, record producer, and writer all about the blues—had played together in a jug band that Dave and Sam organized just to make one record. The group, which included Dave on guitar, Sam on cornet and guitar, ragtime pianist Ann Danberg (who became Ann Charters) on washboard, a jazz enthusiast named Russell Glynn on jug, and jazz writer and musician Len Kunstadt on kazoo, was called The Orange Blossom Jug Five; they issued one record called *Skiffle in Stereo*. The record was fun to make and, I still think, is fun to listen to. The group wasn't supposed to last; it made the record and dissolved.

But, in 1963, Jim Kweskin started a good, enjoyable jug band. Stefan Grossman organized the Even Dozen Jug Band. Dave, who had incorporated some of the ragtime he loved into his repertoire, said, "I want a jug band."

With my reluctant blessing—I was not nuts about jug bands—he organized a jug band. He had good musicians in it: Sam Charters again, this time playing on jug; Danny Kalb on guitar; Artie Rose joined to play dobro and mandolin; and Barry Kornfeld on banjo. Dave? He played guitar, washboard, kazoo—whatever was needed.

The group was musically solid. Its album for Mercury Records included three rags, two traditional jug band tunes, some folk tunes, and some jazz. And a superb rendition of 'Mack the Knife,' Dave's first attempt to incorporate Kurt Weill and Bertolt Brecht into his repertoire (which he did more of brilliantly years later).

Having a jug band rehearsing in your living room isn't fun. I wasn't in love with the music of the jug, or the washboard, or the kazoo. I wasn't in love with listening to five guys repeating their songs over and over again. But, the group was good ... for a jug band.

Booking a group is very different from booking a solo performer. Five people (if that's the number of musicians in the group) have to earn enough money to make the group pay. Five people have to travel together. Five people have to sleep someplace. The economics is staggeringly different. But for a new group, the places to perform are the same ones as for an established performer. And a club owner is not going to pay a new group five times as much as they paid the solo performer. So, it was difficult.

One night, I answered the phone and a male voice said, "Hello, this is Max Gordon." I gasped. Max Gordon was the owner of the most prestigious jazz club in New York. I thought the call was from a joker. "I'm Mickey Mouse," I responded, and put the receiver down. The phone rang again. "This is Max Gordon. Do you have anything to do with Dave Van Ronk's jug band?" I gulped, and said I was the band's manager.

Apparently, Gordon had heard that there was a jug band revival and had asked Robert Shelton, music reviewer for the *New York Times*, to recommend one. Bob had told him about the Ragtime Jug Stompers, Dave's new group, and Gordon was calling to book it into the Village Vanguard.

Dave and I were thrilled, as were the other members of the Ragtime Jug Stompers. Danny Kalb had to join the American Federation of Musicians because the Vanguard sold liquor, but Max Gordon was able to book him in even before Danny joined.

Dave and I were embarrassed when the jug band was given top billing for the engagement, superseding the truly superb jazz trumpeter, composer, and educator Clark Terry. This man was mentor to Miles Davis, Quincy Jones, Herbie Hancock, and other truly great jazz musicians. And here was Dave, a jazz fan, being billed above him with a jug band in a jazz club. Ouch.

Ouch indeed. The jug band bombed. Jazz audiences thought it was a joke. Folk music audiences didn't even know the jug band was at the Vanguard; jazz publicity didn't reach Dave's audience. And Dave's audience didn't yet go to liquor clubs; folk music mostly still was heard in coffee houses.

Strike one.

Then came the Newport Folk Festival. Danny Kalb was ill, so our friend Bob Brill, an excellent guitarist, replaced him for that concert. The set was going well ... until Jack Elliott decided to retrieve the hat he had left on stage a while before. He furtively went onstage behind the band, picked up his hat, and waved it at the audience. The performance was interrupted as the crowd giggled, but the band had no idea what was happening, and I was enraged. As Jack came off the stage, I punched him as hard as I could. It was the first and last punch I've thrown in my life. I hope I hurt him.

The Ragtime Jug Stompers broke up, but the record is good.

Then, an Electric Band

In 1966, Dave decided that he wanted to be part of an electric band. I thought it was a lousy idea. I couldn't see him being absorbed into a group rather than making his own music. But he pushed, hoping to make some money and good music simultaneously, and we decided to finance the band with the money he had earned from Peter, Paul and Mary's recording of 'Bamboo,' a song he and Dick Weissman had written.

I still think it was a lousy idea.

Dave recruited superb musicians to the group, starting with Dave Woods, a blues and jazz guitarist he had known for many years. We rented a large room that had been used for storage in the basement of our apartment building as a rehearsal room. The musical arrangements were primarily the work of the two Daves: Van Ronk and Woods, but the bass player, drummer, and keyboard player helped create them, and the guys rehearsed until they could play each song meticulously and interestingly. They named themselves Dave Van Ronk and the Hudson Dusters, which had been a street gang on Manhattan's West Side in the 1890s, and had developed political connections with Tammany Hall, the Democratic Party's political machine.

For me, aside from—correctly—foreseeing a financial fiasco, managing the group was not fun. Dave Woods was married to a musician named Doris Stone; they had a history of fights that sometime resulted in items thrown at one another. Ed Gregory, the bass player, was married, and the other two musicians either were married or had girlfriends. The band decided that they did not want visitors when they rehearsed, and the women were furious. The wives and girlfriends yelled that my being able to be around during rehearsals was wrong, and although I was both manager and one of the financial backers of the group, and the musicians came up to our apartment during rehearsals, they made my life hell. "Why can she be there?" they whined. Because I had a professional relationship with the group—and a sizeable financial investment in it! Actually, I spent very little time at the rehearsals; I had a business to run, which included trying to help group members earn money.

Dave was signed to Verve/Forecast, and the Hudson Dusters became part of that contract. They recorded a phenomenal arrangement of Joni Mitchell's song, 'Both Sides Now,' which Dave renamed 'Clouds (from Both Sides Now).' It was so good that we thought we'd actually have a hit record, and it gained a growing listenership, until Judy Collins recorded it ... and, of course, she had the hit record. While I admire Judy tremendously, I still think the Hudson Dusters' version of that song is a better presentation of its mood.

I figure we put about $18,000 and a lot of my blood into that venture, in addition to Dave's dream.

Managing More Folk Singers

After I started to manage Dave, other performers asked me to represent them. Bob Dylan was one of the first.

In 1964, I heard a trio of two women and one man play at the Tuesday night Gaslight hoot. I thought they were terrific; they had interesting arrangements of the few songs they played, and Sue Manchester, the lead singer, had a clear voice with the kind of relaxed but enthusiastic phrasing I didn't often hear in a young, not very experienced singer. I offered to manage them. I had a disc made of a tape recording and booked them into the Gaslight and the Second Fret in Philadelphia. Jerry Schoenbaum, who supervised the production of Dave's album *No Dirty Names* for Verve Folkways, was interested in them, but the group's members decided they should go back to school rather than keep trying to succeed in the music business. I've always regretted that; I still think they could have had a successful career.

I did some booking for Paul Geremia, one of the best white acoustic blues musicians anywhere, and one of the most egoless on the scene. Paul has an amazing repertoire, is a superb guitarist, and is comfortable with music from any region of the United States. Several years ago, I came across Dave's John the Conqueror root in the same desk drawer as our old pot pipe, and was trying to find a way to publicly give it to Paul. I hoped I could do it at a concert or when he performed at the Turning Point, a wonderful club in Rockland County, New York, where I live. Unfortunately, before I was able to arrange that, Paul had a stroke and had to stop playing professionally.

John the Conqueror is a legendary African-American folk hero who played tricks on people. He's represented by a tubular root called *Ipomoea jalapa*, said to give the user the ability to create sexual spells, an association that probably came about because when dried, it resembles the testicles of a dark-skinned man. It's carried in a mojo bag, which contains several magical items. It's known in the folk world through the reference to it in Muddy Waters' song, 'Hoochie Coochie Man.' Mississippi John Hurt gave Dave a chunk of the root, which Dave considered an honor. I regret not being able to pass that honor on to Paul.

Before the band the Blues Project started, I also worked with Danny Kalb. Danny had been one of Dave's guitar students the first year Dave and I lived together, and was a wonderful musician as well as a marvelous guitarist. He not only had great chops, but he became part of whatever music he played. Danny didn't consider himself a blues singer, but when he played blues, he didn't try to sound like an elderly Black man from the south, as so many young white folk singers did. As I write elsewhere, he was the guitarist in Dave's jug band, the Ragtime Jug Stompers.

Some years later, he took what apparently was an overdose of acid, and had mental health problems for the rest of his life. He never lost his musicianship, though, and during the last ten years of his life, he amalgamated blues and jazz guitar in a musically exciting and touching way. I wish he had been able to record that work.

Alex Lukeman was another talented folk singer who I worked with for a while. When he stopped performing he later became a well-received author.

Holy and Modal

The strangest management experience I had was with the Holy Modal Rounders. I've never been able to describe the group to my own satisfaction. *Took country music and stood it on its head*, is one of my old descriptions. *Psychedelic country music before psychedelic music was invented*, is another.

The Holy Modal Rounders, Steve Weber and Peter Stampfel.

The group was a duo, comprising Peter Stampfel and Steve Weber. Both were tall and slim; both loved music of the 1920s and '30s, but they partially rewrote the songs, incorporating current images and slang into them, and retaining sexual innuendos that had been in the originals but had often been removed from later recordings.

I met Peter in fall 1959, before any substantive folk music scene began for the younger musicians like him, Dave, and others. Peter knew Tom Condit, a good friend of ours from the socialist movement, whom I considered a walking encyclopedia of useful and useless information. Peter remembers the day he introduced us: "Condit took me to meet Dave and you. You were a teacher, but you were playing hooky that day. I was hugely impressed with Dave; he was one of the two white guys I met who could play blues and sound legitimate."

Peter became part of a bunch of guys Dave got together with at McSorley's Old Ale House once a week, and came to "poker games you and Dave hosted, where a big winner would make about a dollar." Later, when he met Antonia Duren, whom he lived with, they visited us regularly. Peter reminds me that, "You turned me onto Philip Dick and Frank Herbert's *Dune*. I'd given up rock and roll because there were all these girls screaming at all these Italian singers, like Frankie Valli, but in 1963, Antonia and I were immersed in it." Peter and Antonia brought us records like 'Be My Baby,' sung by the Ronettes, featuring Ronnie Spector; I still think it's one of the best pop songs ever.

The Holy Modal Rounders made two records for Prestige Records, produced by Sam Charters, who told me they were incredible musicians who never would earn a living because they and their music were weird. Maybe I thought that was a challenge, and I decided to manage them. The group disbanded almost immediately, and I continued to work with Peter, but then he and Antonia started to take speed.

One of my memories of those days is that Peter sometimes would call and ask me to go to their apartment, explaining that the music that left a radio station's studio would become changed and distorted in transit to their place, so it entered their radio differently from the way it sounded when it was broadcast. I would wend my way there late at night, and behold the strange musical distortions wouldn't be there for me! Recently, Peter explained that when I went there, Antonia would do something to "make the music normal." I don't know why taking lots of speed made them keep their apartment incredibly hot, except that it decreases body temperature and apparently, they were compensating, but the apartment felt like the air in it was well over 100 degrees; maybe it affected the soundwaves.

Antonia, who grew up in Brooklyn, was a superb songwriter; she wrote 'Bird Song,' which was featured in the movie, *Easy Rider*. She was paid a pittance for that—only several hundred dollars, with no royalties; that was standard procedure for films then, and was a disgraceful practice by Hollywood.

Musician Norman Savitt, a friend, reminds me that the Rounders had a large, loyal following, comprising many people who also were fans of the Fugs, a rock group known for its scatological and anti-Vietnam War lyrics. Peter and Steve played with the Fugs for a while, and Peter suggested that I manage that group, but Dave and I thought that some of them used heroin, and we had agreed that we wouldn't allow users it into our apartment. (They didn't use it, we learned later, but Steve did.)

Meanwhile, Peter experimented with playing with other musicians, trying to get a new group together. When he met Sam Shepard, a young drummer, Peter reunited with Steve and signed a contract with ESP Records without consulting me. Neither Peter nor I has ever understood why he did that. The contract said that the musicians were supposed to get a miniscule fee but no royalties. That was surprising. Most recording contracts have a clause stipulating that the performer gets royalties after the record company has earned enough to cover its production costs. Although most folk and surreal records didn't sell well enough to earn royalties for the performers, it was unusual for a contract to not include them at all. Also, ESP owned the publishing rights to any of the songs on the album the musicians had written, and although songwriters collect royalties starting with the first record sold, the contract stipulated that they didn't receive any.

All of the Holy Modal Rounders, except Sam Shepard, were taking excessive amounts of dope. The record for ESP, *The Holy Modal Rounders: Indian War Whoop*, is so strange I can't try to describe it. When it was released, I brought a copy home and played it for Dave's rock group, the Hudson Dusters. They were baffled, including Ed Gregory, the bass player, who had worked with Jimi Hendrix; and Rick Henderson, the drummer, found it so unsettling that he went into my shower while it was playing.

After making the ESP record, Peter asked if it was OK if the Rounders performed in a play Sam had written. I said, "Sure," and they appeared briefly in Shepard's play *Forensic*. Later, they performed in another of his plays, *Operation Sidewinder*, at the Repertory Theater of Lincoln Center (now the Vivian Beaumont Theater). Opening night was amazing: every theater critic on the East Coast was there. I hadn't known who Sam Shepard was, and I was incredibly impressed.

Sam was an actor, playwright, author, screenwriter, and director, who won ten Obie Awards for writing and directing. Many of the people he wrote about didn't fit into American society, and his surrealistic approach was a good match for the Holy Modal Rounders' blend of country music and psychedelia.

Peter then put together another group, which included Sam and two other musicians. Frazier Mohawk, a producer for Elektra Records, one of the better folk music record companies, flew the group out to Los Angeles to record. It was a typically odd experience with the Holy Modal Rounders.

I went to the airport with the musicians when they left for California; I planned to join them a few days later, when they went into the studio to record. Everything went well, except that the flight attendants wouldn't allow Antonia onto the plane. Their reluctance was understandable; her face was almost totally white, drained of any color; her mouth was black; her eyes had no expression. I knew she was stoned, and I was terrified that the group would have to go without her and I would have to take her home and explain to Dave what was happening. And then, what would I do with her?

In those days, there were people to talk to in most businesses, even in airports. I asked for an airline supervisor and completed the most difficult sales job of my life. "She's never flown and she's terrified," I told the man. "She's pale and shaking from fear. But she wants to go with her husband and I'm sure she'll be OK once she's on the plane. She'll be very quiet on the plane. She won't be sick," I assured him. "She looks like she is just because she's afraid the plane will crash. Once she gets up there, she'll be fine."

The airline staffer apparently didn't know much about dope. He finally said OK, and I watched Antonia board the plane with the band. Then I fled home.

Two days later, I flew out to Los Angeles, planning to go directly to the studio where the band was just starting to record. Flying then meant either an expensive taxi ride to Idlewild Airport (now Kennedy Airport) or a long subway and bus ride. I opted for the latter, and when I got to the Los Angeles airport, I looked for a bus to take me to the studio. A man who was obviously trying to pick me up introduced himself as a cinematographer and offered me a ride. Of course I took him up on it.

I walked into the recording studio, and Frazier ran to me, almost yelling, "You have to get Steve. He's still in the motel." "Why?" I stupidly asked. "Just get him," Frazier said. So the nice guy who had driven me there took me to the motel, where Steve had just finished shooting something into his arm. I bundled him into my new friend's car and got him to the studio.

It was that kind of trip.

I booked the band into a few places in California. But everywhere we went, people in the music world in crazy, dope-ridden California told me, "They take too much dope—take them back to New York."

Elektra Records loaned me a car while I was there. I didn't have a driver's license, just a New York State learner's permit. A marketing official at Elektra told me to take the car anyway, adding that if I got busted, they'd say they didn't know me. So, we were able to get around.

I didn't take drugs; I had stopped smoking pot several years before then, and happily swigged Armagnac or Scotch … but because I was driving, I temporarily stopped drinking. Yet, the scene I was immersed in affected me. One day, I drove the band someplace and we stopped at a diner to eat. We seated ourselves and waited for service. And waited. And waited. The waitress ignored us. "We'd like to order," I called to her. No reply. "Would you please take our order?" Silence. Twenty minutes later, we understood that our business wasn't wanted. Finally, I said, "Let's go," and as we walked out, I swept all the condiments and tableware off the table, yelling: "We just wanted food, you stupid fucks." The Rounders saluted me. I was embarrassed, but also a bit proud of myself; I had defended my people. (The Elektra record is called *The Moray Eels Eat the Holy Modal Rounders*.)

As Good as Paul McCartney

Managing Maggie and Terre Roche was musically and personally exciting. Dave discovered them. He came home from MacDougal Street one night and said, "I've got you a new act." That afternoon, Maggie and Terre had walked into Izzy Young's Folklore Center asking to appear on a show Izzy hosted on WBAI, a small alternative radio station (which still exists) in New York. Izzy asked them to play a few songs, and Dave, who was visiting Izzy, was so impressed that he talked with them about my becoming their manager.

I was knocked out, too, when I heard them. The girls wrote their own songs, and their lyrics were witty, observant, thoughtful, and had wonderful harmonies. Terre later said, "Maggie wrote the lyrics, and I fit the music around them." Of course, the girls were so young: Terre was 15 and Maggie was 16. I had them perform at hootenanny nights at the Gaslight, then got them booked into the club. In fact, the evening after Dave and I broke up, the girls were to appear there, and I went there, acted like a businessperson, smiled, and didn't talk about my personal life. No one knew what was happening.

During the next year, Maggie and Terre still were too young to be booked into week-long engagements. Their parents trusted me enough to offer to go to court and execute a management contract, but I was finding that the folk music world had turned from an intelligent, interesting, exciting one into one permeated by drugs, magic, and many singer-songwriters whose self-indulgence bored me to tears. I felt that I wouldn't be able to help the girls professionally in the new music scene, and I didn't want to tie them down legally. I did work with them for a fairly long time.

One personal memory is of an event that occurred about a year-and-a half after Dave and I broke up. Paul Orentlich was living with me by then. He clearly wasn't at ease with young people. One night, Maggie and Terre had appeared somewhere in the Village and were sleeping in our apartment. Late at night, the phone rang, and I went into the living room to find Maggie in tears. She had picked up the phone receiver and heard an obscene rant—obviously meant either for me or for any female who might have answered the phone. Paul was remarkably unsympathetic, and I realized that it was a good thing that neither of us wanted to have kids.

By then, I had decided to stop managing and to do something else, although I didn't have any idea of what I might be able to do.

I was able to help the duo leave my professional nest in two ways. I knew that a concert-booking outfit would be auditioning performers at the Bitter End, and took the girls there. Of course, the bookers wanted them, and the Roche sisters went on an extensive college concert circuit.

Around the same time, I wanted to introduce them to Paul Simon. Paul was teaching a songwriting class at the New School for Social Research, and I suggested that Maggie and Terre enroll. They very tentatively approached Paul as he went to teach his class. According to Terre, Paul asked them, "Do you think you're as good a songwriter as Paul McCartney?" and Maggie said "Yes." He wound up mentoring them.

Music Publishing Pays for Songwriters

Sometime around then, Peter Stampfel put together a new version of the Holy Modal Rounders, and after a while, the other group members said they felt that I represented Peter, not them, and that they wanted to work with someone else. Peter was not happy, but, as he told me, "My bands are democratic and I was outvoted."

I was still handling Dave's music publishing. Over the years, he developed as a songwriter, but when we separated, he had written only nine or ten songs that he considered good enough to record. I had started a music publishing company called Obscure Music, and had the rights to his songs and to several written by Peter Stampfel and Antonia Duren.

When Dave signed with another manager, that person wanted to handle Dave's music publishing. Dave and I knew why: songwriting and song publishing could be much more lucrative than performing. If a musician cut an album, they would get a small royalty for every album sold—after the record company reimbursed itself from the royalties for whatever cash advance it had paid the performer and for production costs of making a record, including studio rental, use of side musicians, pressing the actual recording, and album covers.

Songwriting, though, generated two royalties from the sale of records. The songwriting royalty of two cents was divided equally between the songwriter and the songwriter's publishing company. That meant that if a musician recorded an album with eleven songs on it and had written all of them, that musician would collect a penny per song per album sold as the songwriter. If the publisher was a different person or company, that entity would collect the publisher's royalty of a penny per song per album sold. But, if the musician handled their own music publishing, they would collect both the songwriter's and the publisher's royalty.

If a song is used in television or a film, the songwriter, music publisher, record company, and recording artist all are paid a flat fee. No royalty. As I've said, Antonia Duren's song 'Bird Song' was used in the movie *Easy Rider* in 1969. She was paid only $600 for that. I understand that the average fee now is about $15,000 (much more generous, even allowing for inflation), but that was 50-plus years ago, and it was not a negotiable offer.

If a song is used in a commercial, only the songwriter and music publisher are paid, and the payment is a royalty.

This, I am convinced, is partly why many people who might have become folk singers instead became singer-songwriters. Writing all of the songs you record pays a hell of a lot more than just collecting a royalty of a penny or two for every album sold.

One example: Dave and Dick Weissman filed a copyright as writers of 'Bamboo,' a song Peter, Paul and Mary recorded on their first album. Since they co-wrote it, they shared the songwriters' royalty of a penny per song per album sold. Each of them received between $12,000 and $16,000 for that (which would be between $115,000 and $154,000 now). Later, the song was used as a European shoe commercial and brought the writers another $5,000, and royalties from sale of the sheet music added about another $5,000 to their bank accounts.

Most songwriters don't earn anywhere close to that amount of money. It represents a huge number of albums sold, and a majority of records or CDs sell fewer than 10,000 copies. Still, the writer's royalty is larger than that of the performer.

When he started to work with a new manager, Dave asked me to continue to handle his music publishing, and I did so for a while. Later, record companies never sent any publisher's royalties to me, and I didn't try to collect them. I don't know whether they were paid to anyone. It's too late to do anything about it. I simply regret making a bad business decision. It was based on two odd, personal concepts. One was that when Dave and I separated, our business relationship ended. That was an absurd way of thinking. I had helped develop his career and had a signed contract (which Dave had requested) that entitled Obscure Music to certain payments. The other was that I was independent and shouldn't take anything from him. That, too, was absurd; on a business basis, because of work I had done, Obscure Music was entitled to ongoing payments. Many people think that if they work with their spouse, they are entitled to a fair share of money; I'm the only person I know who didn't get mine because of some strange idea of independence.

I have no idea of what amount of music publisher's royalties I should have received over the years. I just know that legally, I was or am entitled to payments I never got, and I should have done something about it a long time ago. I certainly am not trying to collect now.

I wasn't that careless with the music publishing of members of the Holy Modal Rounders. With Peter and Antonia's consent, I sold Obscure Music's rights to their music publishing to a larger company. Later, though, Obscure Music occasionally received small royalty checks from a record company for one or more of the songs whose rights I had sold, which I always sent back with a note reminding them that I no longer had the publishing rights to the songs. Peter has told me that he never received royalties for the songs he wrote. The music business is rife with inefficiency and corruption.

Now, royalties, whether for recording or songwriting, are miniscule. I follow many of the complaints musicians and songwriters have with the music industry; people who make and write music are getting ripped off.

One important managerial note: for a performer or manager, it's crucial to have a good lawyer. I've seen dozens of cartoons and notes all over media poking fun at lawyers and saying they virtually steal from their clients. In my experience, they've protected both my performers and me; and the same holds in my personal life.

I retained a lawyer when I first negotiated a recording contract for Dave. That person subsequently became attorney for the record company. Representing both it and a performer signed to it would constitute a conflict of interest, so he notified me that he no longer could work with Dave. I had frequently turned to Bill Krasilovsky, a noted attorney specializing in music publishing, for legal advice, so I asked if he would represent Dave. He agreed. When I asked him questions or when he reviewed contracts, he would say, "Grab a pencil," before he streamed masses of information at me.

Bill was co-author of *This Business of Music*, considered the definitive reference book for musicians. I met him when Dave first recorded for Prestige Records, and found him available, kind, and comprehensible—and the last was very important. His information was lucid and sensible.

The first time I consulted him, I waited for a bill. And waited. And waited. Next time I consulted him, I waited again. No bill. Finally, I asked when I'd receive one. "I'll start billing you when Dave becomes rich and famous," Bill said. Never happened.

Bill would not be lawyer for my other clients. Just for Dave. And for me.

Divorce Time

About a year after Dave and I separated, he suggested that we not get a divorce. Soon after we broke up, he had met a woman—who was engaged—and they had quickly become very involved with one another. "I thought I was in love," he told me later. "It was a classic rebound reaction. If you and I hadn't still been married, I would have married her. It would have been the biggest mistake of my life." The affair had lasted about two months, then, he said, he had come to his senses, "and she went back to her fiancé."

"Let's hold off on divorce until neither of us is in danger of doing something stupid," he said. It was OK with me; I already knew about Dave's quixotic adventure, and while I didn't think he'd ever become that blinded to reality again, I didn't feel that I needed a legal divorce. I had no intention of remarrying.

Several years later, when I was living with Paul and Dave was living with another woman, I decided that although we still were good friends, we should make sure we had no legal obligations incurred by marriage hanging over us. It was divorce time.

When I told Bill Krasilovsky that we wanted to divorce, Bill said he would represent me, not Dave, and that although he wasn't a divorce lawyer, he would prepare the separation agreement. He sent it, but no bill. I called to ask why he wasn't charging me for the agreement. He said, "Terri, I'm not a divorce lawyer. I copied that out of a book. I can't charge you any more than the cost of a secretary's time putting it together and sending it to you."

Bill also sent the separation agreement to Dave's new manager, who retained lawyers who represented both the business and its clients. A few days later, Bill called to tell me that one of Dave's new lawyers had called him to suggest that they bill both Dave and me at high rates. Bill said he had asked the lawyer why he should charge a lot. He told me that they had said that they thought Dave would become successful and should be billed accordingly. "I told them that you're still friends, that neither of you is contesting the divorce, and that you could go to a Caribbean island, get a quick divorce, and have a vacation for very little money," he explained. He wanted me to know what was happening; and he obviously wanted me to tell Dave.

I called Dave, but no one answered the phone, so I left a message urging him to get back to me as soon as he got my message. I then quickly called Dave's new manager. "I haven't said I'm speaking for Dave since I stopped managing him," I said. "But I'm speaking for Dave now. If you don't fire those lawyers from representing Dave by three o'clock this afternoon, you will not have Dave Van Ronk as a client." They pulled the lawyers off Dave's divorce case that day. When I told Dave what had happened, he approved of my handling of the situation. He fired that manager a short time later.

Eventually, when Bill prepared the divorce papers for me, he charged me $110; he said that again, he had copied them from a book.

My advice: if you're in the music business, get a lawyer you trust.

In Closing: Everyone Goofs Once

One last word: everyone who ever has been in the entertainment business has a tale to tell about their big gaffe. Mine involved a singer-songwriter. A tall, slim, pleasant young man approached me one day, asking if I'd be interested in managing him. I invited him to the apartment, which also was my office, to play for me and to talk. His music was OK, but very soft, and his songs were about his internal thoughts.

I politely told him he was talented and probably could become successful, but that my abilities were in managing people who didn't perform only their own material. "My own predilection is for a different kind of music. I wouldn't be able to promote you properly," I said, and it was true.

James Taylor and I parted company that day with good will.

Chapter 9
DYLAN, FRIEND AND CLIENT

One night in 1960, when Dave was out without me, he came home and said, "I just heard this kid who's a fucking genius. You've got to hear him." Within a few days, I made a point of going to a basket house, where I was sure Bob Dylan would play a few songs (for no pay, just to be heard). He played, and I agreed with Dave.

Bob was neither a great guitarist nor a great singer. His voice was rough and he had a distinctive, disconcerting way of emphasizing odd syllables. He stumbled about on stage and one leg twitched. Dave and I thought he had brilliantly absorbed the way Charlie Chaplin had moved, and that his music was effective. This was before Bob started to write songs; at that early time, he mostly emulated Woody Guthrie.

Bob started to come to our apartment, and he became a friend. For the first few months after he came to New York, he slept in people's houses: Eve and Mack McKenzie's, Sid and Bob Gleason's, Camila Adams', and ours. He was an easy guest to have around. Slept on the couch. Ate whatever I produced. And ravished our bookcases and record cabinets.

I am only two years older than Bob and Dave was only five. But, I had graduated from college and was in graduate school. Dave had been on his own since he was 16, had been a merchant seaman and a jazz musician, and had been part of the New York City folk music world for several years. We had lived together for only two years, but we had books and records, accumulated more records whenever we had any money, were involved with socialist organizations; and to Bob, I think we were sort of grown-up.

I've been told that when he stayed at Eve and Mack McKenzie's, Bob acted like a young man in need of a home and a mother. When he visited or stayed with us, it was as a friend—a younger one who wanted some guidance, especially professionally and intellectually, but still as a friend, not a son. Dave and I weren't surrogate parents and didn't regard ourselves as Bob's mentors. Yes, he slept on our couch, and we lectured him on the class struggle, and introduced him to music he'd never heard, and Dave taught him about blues and folk history, and showed him new guitar techniques. But, we all giggled a lot and got stoned and listened to different types of music and Bob colored in my coloring book.

When Bob met Suze Rotolo, she became a friend, too. My relationship with her lasted long after she and Bob broke up; we were friends until she died of lung cancer in 2011.

Before we met, Dave had become interested in the goliard poets, clergymen in Europe who wrote comical Latin poetry in the twelfth and thirteenth centuries. It often has been portrayed as satire meant to mock and lampoon the church. That was probably Dave's interpretation too; he was raised in a religious Catholic home and rejected all religion, especially his family's, quite fervently. I'm sure the ribald elements of the poetry were attractive to Bob, whose many invented stories about his upbringing belied a mind still searching for ways to evaluate the world. Bob would become immersed in the books about those poets, and Dave would lecture him about them as happily as he would lecture about Trotskyism. Later, when we visited Bob and Suze's apartment, we noticed a well-thumbed book on those clerics.

We probably bored him with our interminable rants on socialist politics; we had socialist friends, who visited often, and Bob and Suze heard our discussions. But, Bob was less interested in theories about capitalism and why it was important to mobilize the working class to change society, and paid more attention to specific events, like the death of 51-year-old Black woman named Hattie Carroll, whose white killer was sentenced to six months in jail for manslaughter and assault.

Bob didn't argue politics or political theory with us; I think he absorbed as much as he wanted to and ignored the rest. Certainly, a song like 'Masters of War' recognizes that one group of people consciously wields the massive power they have on their own behalf, and 'The Times They Are a-Changin'' doesn't just recognize that social protest was occurring but touts it. Interestingly, those songs, which I think are among his best, are neither stories about events nor theories about society and change, but are commentaries on society as a whole. I think they represent the way Bob saw the world more than his songs about current events do. I see them more as a parallel to Bertolt Brecht's 'The Legend of a Dead Soldier' or Patrick Gilmore's 'When Johnny Comes Marching Home,' which, although written about certain wars, are commentaries about war in general.

"I don't want to lecture anybody," he told me once. "I'm not like you. I don't want to tell anybody what to do. I want to tell my truth." Sounded a little like Reverend Gary Davis saying he didn't write a song: "It was revealed to me."

I thought that was fine for his music. I wasn't trying to convince him to write or sing political songs. I was trying to bring him, not his music, into left-wing politics. That was not going to happen. Bob was not about to join anything or to become enmeshed with any group. He was neither interested in nor capable of doing so.

It might have been more possible to recruit Suze. Her parents had been members of the American Communist Party, and although she didn't respond to our tirades about the class struggle, she certainly had more of an understanding of what we were talking about than Bob did. After they broke up, she became active in politics and art; I thought she went overboard in her enthusiasm for Cuba, which never abated, regardless of how the revolutionary government changed over the years.

I didn't even like most political songs. They were usually badly written and trite, and the tunes tended to be bombastic or repetitive. Dave didn't sing overtly political songs; he didn't try to separate his politics from his music—they just intersected when they intersected, and didn't when they didn't. To the extent that Bob wrote songs with a political slant, they tended to be good songs.

Bob and Phil: Fame and Money?

I've read and heard a lot about the so-called competition between Phil Ochs and Bob about who was a better songwriter. If there was a competition, and I think there was, it was one-sided. When Bob started to write songs, he wasn't competing with anyone. "I'm not trying to be better than anybody," he once said to me. "I write what I see." But that was the only time he ever specifically referred to the putative feud.

I saw hints of it in my living room. Soon after Bob had started to write songs, he and Phil were in our apartment with their guitars. Phil played 'The Ballad of John Henry Faulk,' about a radio show host who successfully sued a corporation that had told radio stations he was a Communist in the 1950s, resulting in his being blacklisted. Bob then played 'The Ballad of Emmett Till,' about a 14-year-old Black boy in Mississippi who had been lynched for whistling at a white woman in 1955. Phil played another topical song. Bob then played 'Talking Bear Mountain Picnic Massacre Blues.' That back and forth went on for a while. Did either of them "win?" Not that evening. Ultimately, their paths diverged.

Phil was a prolific songwriter. Several evenings in 1962, he sat in our living room and played newly written songs for an hour. At some point, my eyes glazed over, but many of those songs were substantial.

Years later, although they went in different directions as songwriters, their relationship deteriorated. Phil combined description with a left-of-center analysis. Bob wrote songs that reached beneath political action to sense how people felt. And the two men sometimes exchanged harsh words that went beyond mutual digs.

Dave, who was very perceptive about people, thought the competition was less about who was a better songwriter than about who was going to become rich and famous. It was clear that Phil wanted as much. I found it less clear that Bob wanted it. But, I think Dave was right. Phil and Bob and David Blue (whose real name was David Cohen) all wanted to be famous; I think they equated fame with money; if they were famous, of course they would have a lot of money. I doubt that any of them ever thought of what they would do with the money. Of the three, I suspect Bob had the least conception of what a lot of money would mean; I'm sure he equated fame with his music being well known, but money was an ephemeral entity. Eventually, when he became famous, he found himself less enthralled by it than he expected to be, although he certainly sought it out.

As Bob continued to write, my impression was that his songs were even more important to him than performing. He considered them songs, not poetry. In interviews, although he's been elliptical about his personal life, he has consistently emphasized that to him songs are straightforward and to be taken to mean what they say. He once told a magazine writer that his songs were influenced by poetry recited by poets who were backed by jazz bands.

He said several times that he perceived himself more as a lyricist or poet than as a songwriter. He started with a poem or proposed song. "I'm not in the old music any more," Bob commented once, after he had started to write songs. "I have to write what I see, and it's not back there. It's what I know now."

Hundreds of books have been written about Bob, and some of his songs have become anthems. For me, the most memorable is 'Mr. Tambourine Man,' perhaps more because of its haunting tune than its lyrics. On Bob's recording of it on *Bringing It All Back Home,* Bruce Langhorne's electric guitar is gentle, speaks softly, and is the voice of a top-notch jazz improvisator.

Blues, Wine, and Poker

People ask what Dave and I and Bob and Suze did when we were together. We talked. Dave and I talked politics a lot. Bob and Suze listened. They asked questions. They were probably sometimes bored. We smoked pot. We listened to a lot of music. Dave and I shared a predilection for acoustic blues; we listened interminably to Folkways and Library of Congress albums; to albums of songs collected or produced by Sam Charters. They included John Hurt, 'Blind Lemon' Jefferson, Blind Willie Johnson, Arthur Cruddup, Robert Pete Williams, Peg Leg Howell, Reverend Gary Davis, 'Bukka' White, 'Pink' Anderson, Blind Boy Fuller, Sonny Terry, Lightnin' Hopkins, 'Skip' James, 'Son' House, Charlie Patton, Blind Willie McTell, 'Kokomo' Arnold, Blind Blake, Leroy Carr, 'Furry' Lewis, Willie Dixon, Manse Lipscomb, 'Brownie' McGhee, Sonny Terry, Big Bill Broonzy, Lead Belly, Snooks Eaglin, and Bessie Smith.

Dave had introduced me to jazz, and we tried to introduce Bob and Suze to Louis Armstrong, Jelly Roll Morton, Scott Joplin, King Oliver, Fletcher Henderson, Duke Ellington, Lester Young, Bix Beiderbecke, Frankie Trumbauer, Eddie Lang, Johnny Dodds, Art Tatum, Charlie Christian, 'Johnny' Hodges, Benny Goodman, Billie Holiday, Chick Webb, Cab Calloway, Bessie Smith, Victoria Spivey, and all the other greats and not-greats. It's fabulous music—and I still have a record player and a CD player and wallow in it. Bob never seemed to become emotionally affected. Perhaps he found it more interesting later, but in the early 1960s, most of it didn't appeal to him. Neither did classical and East Indian music.

The blues singers did. He met and recorded with Victoria Spivey and 'Big Joe' Williams in September 1961, backing each of them on harmonica.

We spent a lot of time playing penny poker in our kitchen. Bob couldn't afford or couldn't stand to bet more than a nickel per game, and that's all he would allow Suze to lose before he cut her off. Dave and I couldn't afford to play for much money, but we were appalled by Bob's attitude toward Suze, and I didn't understand her acceptance of his 'allowing' her to play or not play. They hadn't been together long and she was finding her way with him, so I never said anything about it to her. "If you're broke," we said to Bob, "we can play for matches." But he insisted that he wanted to at least do it for pennies.

Bob developed a reputation for being cheap. I don't know whether his reluctance to spend money even after he was doing well financially was because he was intrinsically frugal or because he had lived for two years earning very little and counting dollars. I find stories about him and his minions holding court in the Kettle of Fish in the late '60s amusing. People write that he played music there and the bar locked its doors so he could do so. Maybe. If so, that was a change from earlier years, when he played in the basket houses and then, infrequently, at the Gaslight, and hung out with other folk singers at the Kettle of Fish. Back then, the bartenders at the Kettle didn't like him; he didn't spend much on booze and he didn't tip. I can't imagine Babe, who managed the Kettle when Guido Giampieri, the owner, wasn't there, being very patient with Bob and Bob's followers when they virtually took over the Kettle. Babe came from Italian Greenwich Village stock, and had no use for people who put on airs—especially for people who didn't tip well.

However, when Bob started to earn money and to hang out with Albert Grossman's crowd, he developed a taste for wine—especially for Beaujolais —and he frequently showed up at our place with a bottle, something no one else ever did. Everyone else, including close friends, smoked our grass, ate our food, and drank our liquor, but never thought of contributing anything.

One notable characteristic of his was a dry sense of humor. I had an answering service. Not a machine, not an electronic device. Real people—all women—answered the phone when I didn't, took and relayed messages to me. Often they would tell me that Albert Einstein had called. Sometimes they would tell me that Nikola Tesla had called. At first, I was baffled. Then, I realized that Albert Einstein and Nikola Tesla were Bob Dylan … or vice versa. I don't know what my answering service ladies thought of those messages. I thought they were funny.

Managing Bob

One day in spring 1961, Bob asked, "Would you get me gigs?" Of course I said, "I'll try." I didn't think of asking him to sign a management contract. Dave and I never had signed one; I wanted to work only with people whose music I thought was great, and it never occurred to me that if I helped build someone's career they might switch to another manager. Bob and I agreed that I would be his manager and would get fifteen percent of any job I got for him, but that I wouldn't take a commission until he was earning enough to pay me. That became my standard way of working with new performers. It was an investment. I learned later that other managers kept track of their initial expenses, and that when the performers started to make money, they reimbursed the manager—but I didn't even think of that when I started to work with Bob. I simply wanted him to be heard. I never took a penny from him.

Getting Bob Dylan work was difficult. Folk singers in New York started to agree with Dave and me that Bob was distinctive and remarkable, and that he had great promise. But he didn't yet have any other audience. Other folk singers went to hear him, but musicians couldn't constitute enough of an audience to support the cost to a club owner of bringing in a performer. In fact, musicians didn't pay admission fees; they were comped, so a club earned very little from having them in the audience.

Bob didn't need anyone to book him into basket houses or the Gaslight—although he seldom worked at the Gaslight. But, of course, I wanted other appearances for him. I approached Manny Rubin, the owner of the Second Fret, the major coffee house in Philadelphia, who asked, "Why should I hire a Jack Elliott imitation?"

I called the owner of the Café Yana, a coffee house in Boston. "He won't draw," the man said. "I'd lose money. When he can pull in an audience, I'll hire him." Bob did work at the Yana eventually—according to its website, in 1963, but that website is incomplete. It says Dave also appeared there in 1963. He did, but he first performed there earlier.

In an attempt to get Bob work, I joined Carolyn Hester and Richard Farina, then her husband, on a trip in summer 1961 to Springfield and

Cambridge, Massachusetts, where they were performing. In Springfield, the manager wasn't interested in a new, unknown performer. He wanted Dave, which was fine, but I had gone there primarily to try to get a booking for Bob. I could have booked Dave just by calling, but I had known that I'd have to generate interest in Bob, and had brought a tape to play.

The Club 47 in Cambridge, where there was a flourishing folk music scene, wouldn't hire Bob. "He's too freaky for a folk music audience," the manager told me. Later that year, Bob wound up playing there for no pay just to perform with Carolyn Hester, whom he considered one of the best singers around.

I asked Manny Greenhill, who managed folk singers and who produced concerts in Boston, to feature Dave and Bob in one in Jordan Hall; he said Bob wouldn't draw anyone and Dave wouldn't fill a hall by himself.

Years later, Manny told me that he found a note he'd made about meeting with me and refusing to produce the concert. "Boy, did I kick myself," he laughed ruefully. But he shouldn't have—when he turned me down, his reasoning was correct. I doubt that Dave would have filled Jordan Hall alone at that time, and Bob wouldn't have drawn many people.

The audition tape Bob made before I went to Massachusetts was recorded in the Gaslight. It's a quarter-track, reel-to-reel tape made on the Ampex I had bought for Dave. I had a studio make a vinyl recording of the tape, and insisted that the studio promise not to make any others, as I always did to protect my clients. Was I nuts? Did I really expect them not to make copies? They didn't make copies because he was the 'famous' Bob Dylan—he still was unknown. They probably did it routinely.

Years later, a pirated copy was used to produce a bootlegged album. The bootleg includes a rendition of 'Pretty Polly,' 'This Old Man,' 'He Was a Friend of Mine,' 'Talking Bear Mountain Picnic Massacre Blues,' Bob and Dave singing 'Car, Car,' and Bob's tribute to Woody Guthrie. There's also a version of 'Mr. Tambourine Man' on it that wasn't recorded during the set at the Gaslight. It's played at a slower tempo than any other recording of the song that I've ever heard … and I like this one better.

I had not played the original tape since 1961, when it was made, and didn't know whether there still was any sound on it. In early 2023, writer

Richard Barone introduced me to Steve Addabbo, owner of Shelter Island Sound, a studio that has worked on Bob Dylan recordings. Steve played the tape in his studio. Not only was there still sound on it, the sound is clear and stunning. It's a wonderful sample of Bob's early music. By the time this book is published, there may be a resolution to what will happen to the tape. I hope there's a way for you to hear it.

I got Bob one important out-of-town appearance. Bill and Lena Spencer had opened the Caffè Lena in Saratoga Springs in May 1960, and featured folk singers on Friday and Saturday evenings. They paid a negotiated fee. Dave played there often; he was there four times that first year. Lena adored him, and he drew large crowds. I went to the club with him the first few times that he performed there. On one occasion, the Spencers didn't have a waitress. I offered to help, and wound up being waitress all evening. I didn't drop or spill anything, and people left tips for me, which I gave to the kitchen staff.

Whenever Bill and Lena Spencer found themselves without a performer, they called me, and I would find someone to quickly go there. When I asked Lena to book Bob, she objected that he was too new and unknown. "Every time you need an act at the last minute, I find one for you," I said. "You owe me a favor, and this is what I want."

Bob played at the Caffè Lena in July 1961—and bombed. The audience talked throughout his performance. Finally, Bill Spencer went on stage to say, "You may not know what this kid is singing about and you may not care, but if you don't stop and listen to him, you will be stupid all the rest of your lives. Listen to him, damn it." At the end of the weekend, Lena called and told me never again to ask her to book Bob Dylan into her club. Of course, after he became famous, she was proud to have had him in her coffee house, and for years, one of Caffè Lena's boasts has been that Bob Dylan performed there at the start of his career.

I booked him into some other places in New Jersey, Long Island, and Connecticut. I thought it was important that he play in Gerde's Folk City, then a fairly new folk music club in the Village. It served liquor, which meant that performers had to have a New York City cabaret card, issued by the police department. Performers there also had to join Local 802 of the American Federation of Musicians. The AFM was pleased to take their dues, but otherwise, it didn't regard folk singers as musicians and did nothing for them.

There's been controversy about who convinced Mike Porco, the owner of Gerde's Folk City, to book Bob. It doesn't matter; everyone in folk music wants to have helped Bob get started, to own a piece of his fame. I spent a lot of time nagging Mike to hire Bob. If others were doing the same, so be it. Mike finally told me that he would hire Bob—and when he did, he came through like a mensch. He accompanied Bob to the AFM and declared himself Bob's guardian so Dylan, who was not yet 21, could get his union book. He also paid for photos so Bob could get his cabaret card.

In April 1961, Bob opened at Gerde's as second act to John Lee Hooker, the legendary blues musician. Although he had desperately wanted to work in coffee houses and clubs, Bob found performing in a club a restricting experience—he had to play on schedule several times each evening for most of a week, and he hated it; he wanted to play at will. As soon as he was more successful, he appeared only in concerts. They involved less routine, less time, less being on call than did clubs. A performer usually played a longer set at a concert than at a club, and got paid as much as or more for that one performance than for the two sets per evening over four or five or six evenings required for a club gig. Concerts also gave a performer more stature than clubs.

I was able to get him a slot early in the day at an all-day folk music concert at Riverside Church in July 1961, before his appearance at Caffè Lena. Other performers liked him so much that he wound up also closing the show with Jack Elliott, a well-known devotee of Woody Guthrie's. After that, I couldn't get any more work for him until Mike Porco booked him into Gerde's Folk City again in September. Then the *New York Times* published a rave review. That was followed by a concert produced by Izzy Young, owner of the Folklore Center. It was a flop; only a few people came, and most of them were musicians who didn't pay the admission fee.

The next day, Bob accompanied Carolyn Hester on one of the songs she was recording for a Columbia Records album. Carolyn says his participation was a last-minute decision.

Although I hadn't been able to interest the manager of Club 47 in Cambridge into booking Bob, he was determined to play there, and he admired Carolyn Hester so much that he hitch-hiked from New York to Cambridge, and was allowed to open for her—that is, to perform a short set before she did hers—without getting paid. The next day, he asked whether he could open for her in any concert or club gigs she was doing over the next few months. She wasn't going to perform for a while because she was about to record an album for Columbia Records. But, she said, Bruce Langhorne would be backing her on guitar and Bill Lee would be backing her on bass, and perhaps Bob could back her on harmonica. Bob immediately accepted her offer.

The producer of her album was John Hammond, who is best known for his work with jazz musicians such as Benny Goodman, Art Tatum, Fletcher Henderson, Charlie Christian, and Billie Holiday; and who later recorded Aretha Franklin and Bruce Springsteen. He suggested that she and the musicians rehearse before they recorded together, and at the end of the rehearsal, asked her whether Bob had a recording contract. She said that as far as she knew, he didn't.

The rest is history; John Hammond recorded Bob, and although Bob's initial album did not sell very well, Hammond stuck with him.

The Riverside Church concert resulted in another interesting relationship for Bob. Victoria Spivey was a blues singer and songwriter who had performed with 'Blind Lemon' Jefferson, Louis Armstrong, Lonnie Johnson, and a host of other greats. She was the mother-in-law of Vince Hickey, a traditional jazz drummer Dave became friendly with when they both were in an anarchist organization. Victoria married Len Kunstadt, a blues and jazz historian who also was a friend of Dave's. Victoria and Len met Bob at the Riverside Church concert, and they were impressed by his ability on the harmonica. There were very few harmonica players in that world in the early '60s, and they asked Dave about whether he thought Bob could make it playing with them. Dave said he thought so, and Bob was thrilled to appear on a record 'Big Joe' Williams and Victoria made for the new label, Spivey Records. Len Kunstadt, who had been very leery of bringing Bob into the studio with Victoria and 'Big Joe,' was surprised at how smoothly the recording session went and how well Bob's playing meshed with that of the lead musicians.

According to Bob, he already knew 'Big Joe' Williams. When he came to New York, Bob told a lot of "Bob adventure stories" about his childhood and teenaged years, which many of his new folk friends doubted were based in reality. In one, he had traveled with 'Big Joe' Williams, a Mississippi Delta blues guitarist who started performing in the 1920s and wound up playing in blues and folk clubs and concerts in the 1950s and '60s. It sounded spurious to us. But, one day in 1961, well before the Riverside Church concert, 'Big Joe' Williams was to perform in Gerde's Folk City—and several of us were at the bar when Bob approached Joe, who greeted him warmly and reminisced about their traveling together. Vindication for Dylan!

A Former Client

Soon after playing harmonica on Caroline's record, Bob came to our apartment and said, "Albert Grossman wants to manage me." Even I think my reaction was odd. "Oh," I said quickly, "how wonderful. He can do so much more for you than I can." Of course I was a bit hurt, but I knew that Albert would be able to foster Bob's career in a way that I couldn't. Bob didn't tell me then that John Hammond, one of the most noted producers in the recording industry, had approached him about a recording contract with Columbia Records. Bob went on to fame and glory, and other musicians asked me to manage them.

I continued to represent only people whose music I loved, but I asked them to sign a management contract. Bob and Suze and Dave and I continued to be friends—until Bob moved into the world of fame.

Dave and I watched Bob and Suze go through thrilling and confusing times. I sympathized with both of them. He needed someone to lean on and to support him; and she needed to function as herself, not just as Bob's appendage. I was especially attuned to Suze's situation. I was married to a man who knew he had to be a musician, who attracted followers and supporters, who was probably never going to be famous but who had a strong personality, was brilliant, witty, and engaging. Sometimes, we'd walk around the Village and strangers would walk up to us and say, "Hi, Dave," and try to engage him in conversation. I'd stand there, annoyed but polite. Dave, remarkably, usually would say, "Do you know my wife, Terri?"

I had a life and interests other than Dave. I had been in the socialist movement before I met him and stayed in it when we lived together and when we were married. I had academic interests. Still, much of my world revolved around folk music—and that meant around Dave.

Suze was interested in art and theater and politics, and like me, didn't want to live as a muse to a musician.

Suze's mother was possibly as unhappy about Suze's affiliation with Bob as my parents had been when I started to go out with Dave. She enticed Suze to take a break from Bob with an offer to go to Europe with her and her new husband, and then to a school in Perugia to study Italian. Suze was torn. She wanted to go to Italy and she wanted to stay with Bob. I wasn't about to get involved in helping either of them make decisions about their personal lives, and when Suze asked me what I thought she should do I pointed out that her mother was offering her a chance to do something she might love, but the separation might prove disastrous for her relationship with Bob. "If it's a really strong love, it might withstand the separation," I speculated.

Suze went to Italy, and Bob was pissed with me for not trying to stop her from going. "You should have told her not to go," he said. "That," I pointed out, "wasn't for me to do. She had to make her own decision." I was shocked to learn later that my not telling her to stay with Bob became legendary among people in the folk music world. Apparently, she was expected to stay with Bob and to be his adjunct. In reality, when she returned, they lived together again … until they didn't.

Many people have said that Bob was ungrateful to us—especially to Dave, who had been something of a mentor—by not continuing to see us as his career careened upward. I disagree. Every time I've left a job, or every time someone I worked with took a job elsewhere, we've said, "I'll miss you and we'll stay in touch." We never stayed in touch. The person who took a new job moved on to a different professional and, possibly, a different social place. That's just one of the realities of modern life.

We were all still friends when Bob made his first album. One day, he asked Dave if he could record Dave's new arrangement of 'House of the Rising Sun.' Dave had worked hard on that and was, I think, justifiably pleased with it. "I'd rather you didn't record it yet," he said to Bob. "I'll be going into the studio soon and I want to be the first person to record that." Bob looked away and said, "Well, I recorded it yesterday." Dave went into a righteous rage. He yelled a bit and told Bob he didn't want to have anything more to do with him. Bob had done a stupid, inconsiderate thing. At that time, no one talked about covering a song; if someone had written or arranged a song you liked and you wanted to record it, that was fine. But there were some unspoken rules, and one of them was that if a friend wrote a new song or arranged an old song, while you could record it, you checked to see whether the originator wanted to record it first. Bob had broken that rule … and had screwed a good friend and supporter.

Dave stopped speaking to Bob. I understood why; I was angry, too, and agreed that Bob had been a shit. But Suze and I wanted to remain friends, and it would have been very difficult to see one another if she was with Bob and Dave wasn't speaking to him. Also, Bob besieged me with requests to get Dave to forgive him. It took months, but I finally got Dave to back down, and the four of us hung out together again.

The Famous Walk

I'm often asked about the apparently famous walk Jim Marshall photographed of Bob, Suze and Dave and me going to breakfast one morning. Breakfast together wasn't unusual; Dave and I often went out for breakfast, sometimes with Bob and Suze, but Jim, an excellent photographer who went on to shoot many of the best-known rock groups, was taking photos of Bob that day. We all went for a walk in the West Village, to Hudson Street, to Seventh Avenue South, and to wherever we had breakfast—I don't remember where.

Who was the woman in the photographs who joined us? None of us knew. No, she wasn't Karen Dalton, as people have suggested. Whoever she was, she was out by herself, she walked alongside us, but we didn't know her. Why didn't we ask her to leave? Because we were young, friendly, polite people.

'Don't Think Twice'

There was another contretemps around then, about Bob's recording of 'Don't Think Twice, It's All Right.' The story behind it: Paul Clayton was a wonderful folk singer who sang many Appalachian songs, New England sea shanties, and ballads. Paul had studied folklore, had written about the dulcimer, and had been recording since the mid '50s. When I met him, he and Dave were friends, and Paul and I became friends. Dave was one of the few people in New York who knew that Paul was gay. I didn't know until Paul had been a friend for a year or so.

When Bob came around, he and Paul became friendly. Then, in 1962, Bob used Paul's recorded, copyrighted arrangement of 'Who's Gonna Buy Your Ribbons (When I'm Gone),' for his own new song, 'Don't Think Twice, It's All Right.' All the folk singers we knew were angry—they all felt that Bob should have credited Paul with the arrangement. Ultimately, it turned out that Paul had used a traditional tune for his own song, and had copyrighted it.

Meanwhile, Paul had become very taken with Bob. And Carla, Suze Rotolo's sister, had become very taken with Paul. It got complicated. Carla, who said she and Paul planned to get married, had a history of being infatuated with unavailable men: married men, men who were friends but who didn't want to be lovers. Now, a gay man. We wondered how realistic that was. One night, Paul came into my kitchen, closed the door, and kissed me—a deep soul kiss. I never regarded it as a sexual act. My sense was that Paul trusted me enough to try to find out whether he could enjoy kissing a woman. We never spoke about it, and I knew Dave would agree with me about why Paul had done it. Of course, when I told Dave about it, he did.

In 1964, Paul went on a tour of the U.S. with Bob and several other people in what then was Bob's entourage. Paul's role was supposed to be one of Bob's 'mind-guards,' whatever that was. I understand the tour was rife with drugs, booze, and incoherence. Paul left it early, but he continued to use drugs.

Paul came to the apartment one evening in 1967. He was ranting, especially about women. I listened to Paul for about 16 hours. Later, a therapist told me I should have found a way to call the police, who probably would have had him institutionalized ... but I never thought of that and I don't know whether I could have done it, if it had occurred to me.

A week later, Dave was working in a club in Oklahoma City when I learned that Paul had gotten into his bathtub, filled it with water, and pulled a plugged-in radio into the water. My first instinct: to call the club and ask the people who worked there to try to keep news of Paul's death from Dave, which they did. Dave didn't find out about it until he got home and I gave him the bad news. I've always been sad about Paul's demise; he was a sweet, kind, interesting man and a good musician and scholar, and I liked him a lot.

Other friends often came over, however the four of us, Bob, Suze, Dave and I regularly hung out together. New Year's Eve 1963, we all decided not to go anywhere. Dave and I thought New Year's celebrations were kitsch and noisy and stupid, an opinion I generally still hold, although I've been going to a lovely one for more than ten years. We hung out at our apartment, but at about 11 p.m. we said, "OK, let's go to a party," and left to go to one we'd been invited to uptown. We walked a short block to Seventh Avenue to hail a taxi. There weren't any empty cabs; it was New Year's Eve and they all were taken ... except for two that simply passed us by. We figured we weren't dressed well enough for the cabdrivers, who would assume that we wouldn't tip well.

Bob ran out into the middle of the street, waving his arms. "Hey, stop. I'm Bob Dylan. I'm Bob Dylan. You want to stop for us," he yelled. "If you don't stop, you'll be sorry some day." Big ego? I didn't think so then. He was just a 22-year-old. Maybe a 22-year-old who had large plans for his future.

If his ego needed a boost, it certainly got one later. When Bob gave his first major concert at Carnegie Hall, Albert Grossman, his manager, anticipated large crowds accosting him after the performance. Suze and I were asked to play decoy so Bob could leave unhindered. I've never been in that kind of scene at any other time. After the concert, Suze and I went to a car with someone from the Grossman office, and a horde of young people, mostly girls, followed us, screaming. We got into the car and the kids literally threw themselves on it. They thought Bob was inside, as they were supposed to. The car actually rocked because they were pounding it so hard. It was like something out of a movie, or like TV newsreels of rock stars and their fans. Meanwhile, Bob was able to leave Carnegie Hall quietly, in reasonable peace. I had hated mob scenes before that, and I hated them more afterward.

Gone Electric

Folk music was characterized in part by people playing acoustic instruments. Guitar, banjo, mandolin, fiddle. Never electric instruments. Electric instruments were for rock musicians, not folk singers. Even when people like Dylan and Tom Paxton and Phil Ochs started to write songs rather than perform only old, traditional music, their accompaniment was an acoustic instrument.

When Bob startled the folk world by 'going electric' at the Newport Folk Festival of 1965, performing three songs backed by musicians playing electric instruments, a lot of folk singers and folk fans were appalled and horrified. They yelled, "He's betraying his origins. He's betraying us." That was absurd. Bob had been heavily influenced by rock when he was young. His musical background was rock 'n' roll; his hero when he was in high school was Little Richard, so his going in that direction wasn't shocking. Rock already was affecting the folk music world. We listened to blues bands and loved them. We didn't think anyone had to stay locked into a certain kind of music. Bob was moving in an inevitable direction, and the musicians he played with who used electric instruments were great; he was not going into a world of bad music.

Dave and I were at Newport when the infamous performance happened. Some of the rumors that flew around afterward simply weren't true. The audience didn't hiss; part of it did, but I think it was more unhappy because the sound system was dreadful than because of what was being played into it. The sound of the band blasted toward the seated audience in front of the stage, and Bob's voice carried through speakers on the side of the field. They didn't blend. The story of Pete Seeger yelling for an axe didn't mean that Pete wanted to destroy the sound system. It probably was just a call for an acoustic guitar for Bob after Bob's songs with the band ended (folk singers often referred to their guitar as their 'axe'; the word was used by jazz musicians for their saxophones in the 1950s; I don't know when it was picked up by guitarists). Pete was not happy about what Bob was doing, but he certainly was not going to attack Bob or the group on stage or off it.

Later

About a year after Dave and I separated, Bob rang the bell to my apartment and visited for a while. Before he left, he handed me his corduroy cap, saying: "I want you to have this." It floated around the apartment for years; hanging on to a lot of stuff in a three-room Greenwich Village apartment is hard. I once found it behind the radiator in the bedroom and put it in 'a safe place.' (I guess it didn't stay there, because by the time that I moved from the apartment to Rockland County, NY, it had disappeared.)

A few years after Bob gave it to me, I was home one day when he rang the bell and came up to the apartment. We talked—mostly, he talked. He had been living in Woodstock for several years, hadn't been performing, and wasn't sure whether he wanted to return to the life of a traveling musician. He said he didn't need money, but didn't know what he could do other than perform. I wasn't surprised to hear that he thought his songs were more important to him personally than his performances, and were what he wanted audiences to take away from hearing him, although, like me, he detested the term 'singer-songwriter.'

"It's a fake dichotomy," he said. "It's another way of tagging people. You don't have to be a singer and a songwriter, whatever that is, to write songs. You don't have to do either to do both."

We talked some about hanging out in my living room years before. Bob spoke of my old habit of walking around in panties and a bra. "You always wore droopy drawers. You looked great, but I always wondered why you didn't get some that fit you," he said. It reminded me that he had commented on my 'droopy drawers' in the past. Bob liked giving us nicknames and often referred to Dave as Walrus due to his large moustache!

He asked to see the corduroy cap he had given to me on his previous visit, so I showed it to him and, of course, I offered to return it. "No," Bob said. "I want you to have it. I don't want it." He looked at some other items I had in the apartment, and asked for a poster Eric Von Schmidt had designed, but I liked it and kept it, although since then, it's disappeared. He seemed to be looking at old times … and in retrospect, this was at least six and probably more years after he had moved out of our orbit. Several other people who knew him when he hung out in the Village have said that he got in touch with them, too, and seemed to be trying to work out what kind of future he wanted … and could have.

Last time I saw Bob's cap, I was moving out of the Waverly Place apartment. I should have taken better care of it—for Bob and me—as it was a thoughtful gift.

Chapter 10
SOCIALISM, HERE I COME

To me, my politics seem almost preordained. The philosophy that's always guided me came from my family: treat everyone well. My parents said it repeatedly, not because they were socialists—they weren't, but because they were ethical people.

As I became a committed socialist, I don't know what they thought of my constantly bombarding people with my concerns and my criticisms of the social order; I know they believed I was going overboard, and my constant ranting (a practice I've thankfully stopped) must have driven them crazy. They probably also worried about my getting in trouble with the government, but they never talked about that.

One of my earliest memories is of when Roosevelt died. I was six, and my first-grade class was on an outing in Brooklyn's Prospect Park. My teacher must have had a portable radio with her, or perhaps she heard the news from a bystander; it was the only time I ever saw a teacher in tears. She sent us home early. When I got there, my mother and aunt were in tears, too.

Outside of family discussions, one of my earliest encounters with political thought was in 1954, when I was still in high school and visited my sister at Brandeis University. Brandeis was an innovative college, its students tended to come from liberal Jewish homes, and, as I wrote earlier, I was entranced by the intense discussions about whether *The Birth of a Nation*, a blatantly racist film, should be shown on campus. My sister hated the movie but insisted on the right of a student group to bring it to campus. This was seen as a civil liberties issue, and I agreed with Joyce.

Soon afterward, I found photographs taken in German concentration camps in my parents' desk. They made me nauseous for days. I also discovered the main branch of the Brooklyn Public Library, where I found fiction such as *The Jungle*, Upton Sinclair's classic book about the meatpacking industry in the U.S. I drowned myself in a host of his other books, including all eleven of the Lanny Budd series; George Orwell's *1984*; Maxim Gorky's *Mother*; John Dos Passos' trilogy, *The 42nd Parallel, 1919*, and *The Big Money*; and probably a dozen or more other 'socially conscious' novels. *The Threepenny Opera*, which I saw with my sister at the Theatre de Lys in Greenwich Village, introduced me to the writing of Bertolt Brecht.

In the school year that started in September 1953, I was a junior in high school. In our American History class in spring 1954, one of the topics we studied was the difference between socialism and communism. At the close of the session, my history teacher asked me to see her after school. It wasn't a disciplinary meeting; she wanted to make sure I was clear about the distinctions.

The Cuban Missile Crisis and the Kennedy Assassination

I thought my socialist analyses were confirmed the night of the Cuban Missile Crisis in October 1962. The United States was concerned about Soviet nuclear-armed missiles that were installed in Cuba as the result of an agreement between Soviet First Secretary Nikita Khrushchev and Cuban Prime Minister Fidel Castro. Since both Khrushchev and Castro believed that a U.S. invasion of Cuba was imminent, they planned to move the missiles into Cuba secretly. On October 22, 1962, Americans braced for what many thought would be a nuclear war; I don't know anyone who was an adult then who wasn't terrified. Complicated negotiations led to President John F. Kennedy assuring us on Sunday, October 28, that the crisis had been averted.

That evening, Dave was scheduled to play at the Gaslight. My Marxist analysis had predicted exactly what was going to happen; negotiations between the United States and the Soviet Union were already going on and the crisis would be averted ... and I was correct. That said, I did call my parents in case my Marxist analysis was wrong, to talk to them and tell them I loved them and to know that I had said goodbye. I went to the club with Dave so we could be together when whatever was going to happen happened. The Gaslight was almost empty; I guess most people were home or on the phone with their families. Around midnight, when the sparse audience was gone, Dave and I gathered up everyone who still was in the club and treated them to a meal at Sam Wo, then our favorite restaurant in Chinatown. Then, about eight people went home with us to smoke grass and listen to records and breathe sighs of relief that what I predicted wouldn't happen hadn't happened. Our social-democratic friend Jimmy Herman and the Trotskyist Jack Arnold were there; Tom Paxton and a lady friend spent the night on our couch; Barry Kornfeld and Danny Kalb were there.

The day President John F. Kennedy was killed, I again found myself accurately predicting what would happen. Dave was booked into the Club 47 in Cambridge, MA. By 1963, I usually sent Dave off to out-of-town gigs without me. This time, though, I accompanied him because my sister and her family lived in a suburb of Boston and it would be a good time to visit them. Dave developed a bad cold even before we got there. We spent Thursday night at the home of David Wilson, then the editor of *Broadside* magazine and still a friend. The next day, folk singers arrived at David Wilson's house, wanting to socialize. I turned into a concerned wife: Dave was sick, he didn't want to see anyone, and I kept visitors out of the bedroom where he was resting and insisted that they be quiet so he could sleep.

That afternoon, Kennedy was shot. That evening, we took a taxi to the club; Dave was going to work. It was closed. Oh yes, we realized, this was Cambridge, next to Boston—John F. Kennedy's land. Of course the club would close.

A friend who has read the manuscript of this book asked me whether my predictive talents were purely rational analysis or something vaguely ethereal. I've never been able to figure that out.

I Become a Trotskyist

Somewhere in my left-wing travels after Dave and I started to live together in the summer of 1959, I became friendly with a Trotskyist whose political name was Jack Arnold. Jack adopted Dave and me, telling us repeatedly that we would wind up in the Trotskyist movement. He became one of the people who were likely to be in our apartment any evening, and we argued politics incessantly.

Trotskyists said that the Soviet Union could have become a socialist force, but instead, turned into a repressive force as it developed, one that actually betrayed socialism.

To my surprise, within a few years I decided the Trotskyist movement was more relevant than the Socialist Party, and Jack and I then convinced Dave. A while later, Dave joined the Trotskyist Socialist Workers Party (SWP), but despite my leanings toward Trotskyism, I felt that joining something that called itself a political party was a commitment that I wasn't ready to make. But, when he and some other members left the SWP and started a small group called the American Committee for the Fourth International, later renamed the Workers League, I joined it.

Marxists distinguish between people who own the facilities that make things, the capitalists, and those who don't own the facilities that produce goods, the workers. It posits that when there are surpluses of resources, they should be shared among everyone, not just among a limited group. There were very few workers in jobs deemed working-class in the Workers League. It had a fairly static view of what a worker was. Theoretically, it recognized that anyone who traded work for remuneration is a worker, whether the person is a teacher, a factory worker, a delivery person, a musician, a lawyer, a writer, etc. But in real life, there was an unstated attitude that factory workers or others in jobs that generally aren't considered middle-class jobs are purer workers. This bias wasn't limited to the Workers League, it permeated the organized left.

Members of the Workers League included me—then a manager of folk singers; Dave—a folk singer; several social workers; a printer; some others; and when one factory worker joined, I was amused at the adulation he got from my comrades.

If I sound flippant about my experiences in the socialist movement, please understand that my personal style sometimes seems to conflict with my beliefs—I think sometimes I sound caustic, but I believe strongly. I am passionately committed to social justice, but in the 1960s, even as I participated in socialist organizations, I was skeptical of their ability to make any substantive movement toward achieving it. I used to tell people that there was "a little green man sitting on my shoulder, saying 'Dig yourself,'" as I struggled to make a better world through the radical movement.

What could I contribute to the Workers League? Like almost all other members, I sold the weekly newspaper we published on street corners, although there were very few buyers. (The first thing any socialist group in the U.S. at that time did, regardless of size, was publish a newspaper.) I was a good soapbox speaker; I had a Brooklyn accent, which was not a negative in downtown Manhattan in the 1960s; I wasn't afraid to yell, and I could keep my sentences short—important for any public speaking, I knew. Years later, I learned that Tim Wohlforth, the leader of our small group, couldn't stand listening to my Brooklyn accent and avoided me because of it. I wonder even now how he thought he'd deal with other people from ethnic backgrounds if our organization grew. Would other accents not have been as distasteful to his purist ears as mine?

As for Dave, who was politically much more self-assured than I was—once he decided he was a Trotskyist, he always was sure that he was correct about both theory and strategy. When the Cultural Revolution was launched in China in May 1966, ostensibly intended to purge whatever capitalist elements had resurfaced there, Dave jumped up and announced, "I'm going to the Workers League office. I have to make sure Tim understands what our line is on China." I'd barely had a chance to think through what was happening in China, and certainly was not ready to make any declarations about the implications of the new policy.

None of the socialist organizations Dave joined knew what to do with him. He was a good theoretician. And, of course, he was a musician. Musically, Dave considered himself a craftsman, not a reporter or a lyricist or a political preacher. He didn't sing political or protest songs; most of the old political songs, even those whose messages we liked, were hackneyed. When people like Phil Ochs and Bob Dylan started to write songs about social issues, they were commenting on the day's events. Many of those songs didn't survive the test of time. Of course, some did, especially Bob's, many of which moved beyond immediate commentary to vision.

Dave was willing to publicly say he was a member of whichever organization he was a member of, and was open about being a Trotskyist, but that wasn't what the leadership of the organization wanted. They wanted him to sell the group's newsletter on street corners. And, although the man was an extrovert, he was a lousy newspaper peddler.

I was asked to speak at a SNCC (Student Nonviolent Coordinating Committee) rally in Baltimore in 1964. The group of 500 was the largest I had appeared before. I presented the Workers League perspective that racial unity was needed to bring about substantive social change, and was applauded soundly. I was a bit surprised; I hadn't thought that perspective would generate such a positive reaction.

After the rally, several SNCC organizers asked me to go to Mississippi to help register Black people as voters. I said I'd think about it, but that since I was a one-person management business, I probably wouldn't be able to leave my performers with no one to handle their career decisions. That may have sounded like a thoughtful reply, but the reality was that I was scared to go south to organize. I've always been embarrassed by that.

Marching on Washington

Some of my political activity was separate from my membership in the Worker's League. I helped chapters of CORE in New York City by finding folk singers to appear at benefit concerts gratis. Dave, Tom Paxton, Alix Dobkin, the Greenbriar Boys, Carolyn Hester, Danny Kalb, and others, I recruited them relentlessly. I participated in sit-ins at Woolworths. I went to every march on Washington that took place, starting with the 1958 Youth March for Integrated Schools when I still was in college. There, I joined 10,000 high school and college-aged people who marched to the Lincoln Memorial to promote desegregating American public schools. A smaller group of students went to the White House to try to meet with President Dwight D. Eisenhower, but neither the president nor any of his assistants made themselves available. After staging a half-hour picket, the students left a list of demands to be forwarded to him.

In April 1959, I was part of a larger group of 26,000 who repeated the march. This time, the delegation to the White House met with President Eisenhower's deputy assistant, who told them that "the president is just as anxious as they are to see an America where discrimination does not exist, where equality of opportunity is available to all." We wanted Eisenhower to take action, but no legislation was passed that would have enhanced the 1957 Civil Rights Act and speeded up school integration.

Four years later, in August 1963, I was on the speakers' platform when 250,000 Americans took part in the March on Washington for Jobs and Freedom. As Martin Luther King Jr. talked about his dream, I looked out and saw a tremendous sea of people, all like-minded, all wanting decent civil rights legislation, an end to school segregation, a federal law prohibiting discrimination in hiring, a minimum wage (of only $2/hour, which was not a good income even in 1963), and more. It was exhilarating.

I'd felt part of something huge in earlier marches; it was inevitable when you were walking from the Washington Monument to the Lincoln

Memorial with thousands of people who had a unified goal. But here I felt that the momentum of the civil rights movement finally was having an effect.

I was on the platform because of Dave. He had been asked to perform there, and I had planned to go with him. The morning of the march, he was sick, too sick to go, but he insisted that I shouldn't miss the event. So, I flew to Washington, D.C. with performers I knew: Peter Yarrow, Noel Stookey, and Mary Travers (Peter, Paul, and Mary); and Odetta. I was thrilled to be on the same stage as Mahalia Jackson, a singer I'd admired for years and had heard once in an inspiring concert Dave and I had gone to at Brooklyn College. Marian Anderson should have sang but like Dave, didn't make it. Odetta, who I knew from the Village, did. She was accompanied by Bruce Langhorne, a superb guitarist who had lost most of three fingers on his right hand, but who played better than most musicians could with five.

Many people I knew were there. Both of the men I lived with later, Paul Solomon Orentlich and Martus Granirer, went to Washington that day, although I didn't know them yet.

I wish I could say that I realized then that I was hearing a speech which would become a legend. But, while Reverend King's presentation was riveting—he was a superb speaker with a remarkable sense of timing—I was also intrigued by the visual effect of masses and masses of people silently listening, as I was. That's not unusual, I know. People often don't know that they are living in a historic moment. That's determined later.

In the Socialist Movement

Meanwhile, I was identifying myself as a Trotskyist, and was a member of the Workers League.

In late 1964, even before the anti-Vietnam War movement began on college campuses, the Workers League protested the U.S. bombing of military targets in North Vietnam. I'm sure we never obtained permits for our street corner meetings. We just went out and held protests. We didn't demonstrate outside federal buildings or draft board offices; we weren't looking for media coverage—we were trying to convince people in the neighborhood where our office was located that the U.S. was invading a country whose citizens didn't want us there.

That neighborhood included Tompkins Square Park, east of Greenwich Village (the neighborhood now is called the East Village). I have mixed memories of that park. The good: it's where Dave and I were when he first told me he loved me. The bad: it's where my socialist group was attacked while we were holding a demonstration there.

The attack in Tompkins Square Park was a physical one. They were large men. Most of us weren't used to fighting; I was totally unused to it. I was speaking when they decided we shouldn't be saying what we were saying, and all I could think as they approached was, "Oh my god. No. No." Unfortunately, the reality was "Yes. Yes." No one hit me; I was pulled off the orange crate I was standing on, and fell (or was pushed) to the ground. One of the guys in our little group was punched; two were thrown to the ground (not Dave … he wasn't there). Of course we didn't call the police. Afterward, we thought the police were just as likely to complete the job the attackers had started as they were to go after them.

Demonstrations and marches were a very small—although very important—part of what we did. Mostly, we produced a newspaper, tried to sell it on street corners, and went to meetings.

We were encouraged to read and discuss anything published by the Socialist Labor League (SLL), an English Trotskyist organization with a long history of membership in international coalitions.

One year, there were discussions about a possible merger between the Workers League and the Spartacist League, another small group that had split from the Socialist Worker's Party. They were spearheaded by the head of the English Trotskyist movement. Dave and I were part of the Workers League group that met with others in Montreal to discuss the proposed merger. I remember little of the discussion. I mostly remember that on the ride home, before we crossed the border back into the U.S., we stopped at a diner where one comrade was supposed to get rid of any documents that could identify where we had been and with whom. A while after we left the diner, Tim Wohlforth asked that comrade to reassure us that he had properly disposed of the papers. "Yes, I dumped them in the wastebasket in the men's room," we were told. "Why the hell didn't you flush them down the toilet?" Tim demanded. "They might have clogged the pipes," the comrade said. So much for New York City revolutionaries.

Tom Paxton tells the story of one evening when Dave walked into the Gaslight, loudly talking about an exciting meeting he had just left. As

Tom tells it, Dave boasted of the intense disagreement among Workers League members and the high intellectual level of the debate. Tom says he asked Dave, "Dave, how many people are in this revolutionary organization?" "About seventy-five," he says Dave replied. Tom roars with laughter when he thinks of this miniscule group generating that much interest on Dave's part and his apparent belief that it could change the world. Of course, it couldn't and didn't ... but sometimes I've wished Tom wouldn't tell that story in public.

Trotskyism Abroad

In the summer of 1966, Dave and I went to an international Trotskyist conference held in London. We knew that we'd been elected as delegates, not so much because of our political acumen, but because we were willing to pay our own airfare. My major memory of the event revolves around the delegation from Ceylon. I was awestruck to be at a meeting with people who had spent time in jail because of their political beliefs and were willing to do so again. I had known a few people who went to prison in the United States because of their political activity, but that had been back during the McCarthy era. In the 1960s, while we knew we were under surveillance by the FBI, we were sure that we weren't going to go to jail for our politics. We were careful not to break any U.S. laws, and the government apparently wasn't interested in prosecuting members of what's known as the 'Old Left,' although a few years later, it went after the Black Panthers and some members of SDS with a vengeance.

The following summer, I was a delegate from the Workers League to a summer Trotskyist encampment held in Sussex, England, about 60 miles (96 km) southeast of London. Before we left the United States, we were told that when we got off the plane in London and were asked where we were going, we should give the address of the Socialist Labor League. I thought that was idiotic. I said I could give comrades the addresses of several folk music clubs and record companies, and we could say we were visiting one of them. I was ignored, and when we got to London, we all honestly told the English immigration officials that we were going to a political organization that was not liked by the English government.

On the plane, a tall, middle-aged Englishman engaged me in conversation and bought me drinks. We spoke in Spanish, which was a challenge. I had studied Spanish in high school and in college, but we weren't taught to speak it, just to read *Don Quixote*. The effort to converse in Spanish was fun, though, and I muddled through. Of course the man was trying to pick me up, and when we reached London he gave me his business card, then got off the plane to be greeted by his wife. I was used to pick-up attempts and was amused. But my Trotskyist colleagues were furious because I had talked with a stranger. They said I might have given him information about where we were going. I thought that was irrational, since we all had been instructed to tell English immigration officials where we were going. Of course, I hadn't told him, but what if I had? What would he have been able to do with that information that we weren't about to do ourselves?

They stopped speaking to me. I was isolated. Ignored. And pretty angry. I had paid to go on the trip, was loyal to the organization, was sleeping on a cot in a tent in the outdoors, which was not my idea of a good place to be; and I thought my comrades were not being comradely. I felt like I was in purdah, and I thought they had gone insane.

The trip had turned into a nightmare; I'd never before seen the Workers League act in such a restrictive way. After two days of this, I left the encampment. I got a ride to London, checked into an inexpensive hotel, where I slept in a room only about 2 feet (60 cm) wider than the bed, and called people in the folk music world. I had planned to go to London when I left the encampment and already had a few business appointments there, but I was in the city several days early. Anthea Joseph, who still managed the Troubadour, was home, and I stayed with her.

I tried to interest club managers in London and nearby places in the Holy Modal Rounders, but the group was neither sufficiently strictly folk music nor strictly underground rock for the English folk world, and I couldn't book enough gigs for them to earn enough to go to England.

The flight home was fun. The Air India plane was almost empty; I counted about ten passengers. After we had taken off, I was invited to visit the cockpit, where I stayed for the rest of the flight, although I had to leave it when the pilot prepared for landing. Of course he invited me to his hotel, and of course I went home to Dave.

Dave was outraged at the way I'd been treated at the encampment. We agreed that it was an example of sectarian stupidity, and that the Workers League was acting in ways that reminded us of old stories of American Communist Party narrowmindedness. Shortly before my ill-fated English trip, we had gone to a Workers League meeting at which we were treated to a lecture on why it was bourgeois and counterrevolutionary to go to therapy. The reason: therapy was a frivolous expense—if we had money to spend on therapy we should, instead, give it to the Trotskyist organization. That reminded us of a story we had heard about the American Communist Party banning female members from wearing lipstick in the 1940s, because it was a 'bourgeois' activity.

Dave and I paid dues of about fifteen or twenty percent of our earnings to the Workers League, and we also voluntarily donated the money he earned from one concert a year to the organization, which in 1967 ranged from $400 to $800. We were not interested in hearing that it could dictate how we spent the rest of our modest incomes.

Home again, comrades resumed speaking to me. I don't remember how Dave and I handled our anger at my being mistreated and insulted on the trip. I think we didn't talk about it, but it was part of why we both substantially reduced our political activity. Also, Dave was touring a lot and I was very involved with the Holy Modal Rounders, and later that year, with Maggie and Terre Roche and Paul Geremia.

When Dave and I separated and worked out an agreement on how we would handle being in the same bar or club, I don't remember whether it included political meetings. Probably not. By then, he had stopped going to Workers League meetings. I went to some. But I no longer felt comfortable there.

I never resigned from the Workers League; I just wandered away. I decided that I couldn't stay in a group that limited itself both theoretically and in action by defining itself through its analysis of what had happened to the Soviet Union in 1917. I continue to believe that any viable political movement has to be international, but I also believe that while you should build international relationships, your primary task is to find a way to move forward in your own country.

Tim Wohlforth wrote in a political memoir that Dave resigned from the Workers League toward the end of 1967 because of a political disagreement, but Dave and I still were together then and I don't remember that happening. At any rate, Dave insisted that he was a Trotskyist until he died.

The years in the Workers League helped me understand more clearly than I had before why people who had been members of organizations such as the Communist Party USA, whose policies or philosophies had become untenable, hung on—or tried to hang on—to their old loyalties.

The old group represented home; whatever its belief, it provided a tool that you could use to assess what was going on. I felt that way about the Workers League. Without an organization, even though I still had the Marxist tool, I felt lonely and politically insecure.

Chapter 11
THERE'S LIFE AFTER FOLK MUSIC

When I stopped managing folk singers, I had no idea of what kinds of jobs people had. I knew about traditional women's jobs—nurses, teachers, and secretaries. My temporary teaching license had expired, and I didn't want to go back to school to take the classes I would need to retrieve it. I didn't know anyone I could consult about a possible career.

I took a series of jobs that were absurd. The first was working for an agency that placed people (men) in sales positions. I was supposed to help them get jobs in the textile industry. My father and his brothers were in that industry, which is why I decided to specialize in it, but I knew nothing about it and never consulted my father so I would have a better idea of how to go about helping people in that field. I just tried to get men jobs. The agency didn't train me; it provided me with a script to use when talking to prospective employers, which of course didn't work. I failed miserably. At the end of three months, I hadn't placed anyone. When he fired me, the agency manager told me he'd hired me only because he wanted to "fuck Dave Van Ronk's ex-wife." At least he hadn't tried, and it never happened.

After that failed experiment, I became an 'administrative assistant' to an editor in a commercial publishing company. It became complicated because people I was involved with were involved with one another in ways that affected me. I met and went out with someone who, as it happened, was also dating the director of human resources of that publishing company. Meanwhile, the editor I worked for started to take me to the expensive bar that people in the publishing industry hung out in after work … and, of course, we wound up in bed. And, of course, the director of human resources fired me.

Next try: I idiotically accepted a job in a brokerage firm. Why? It was one of those *It seemed like a good idea* moments.

Finally, I realized that since I could write well and I had been able to manage folk singers, which involved 'selling' their musical and stage abilities and getting them interviews and media coverage, I could adapt those skills to other areas. I don't remember who suggested that I do freelance marketing, or how I came to the attention of Miklos Szabo Pelcoski, who wrote a newsletter on economic trends in Eastern Europe for fairly wealthy investors. He wanted to retain someone to help market the newsletter.

Unlike my job in a brokerage firm, this did not involve working with 'jocks,' men who struck me as interested in nothing but sports. Miklos was smart, interested in music, art, and food, and had a substantial list of contacts who were possible subscribers to his publication. My job was to enroll them as subscribers.

In retrospect, it's amazing that I was able to persuade people to spend $500 a year in 1970 on Miklos' newsletter. I knew virtually nothing about the subjects he wrote about. But somehow, I did.

Working for him was fun. When I'd managed folk singers, I was out at clubs at night and slept late. When I went to work in offices, I had to get up in the morning, along with the rest of the world, which was difficult. Now, I again kept my own hours.

Many of the people on his contact list either took my phone calls or returned them. I was still doing it when I met Paul. Miklos jokingly (I think jokingly) told Paul that he'd been intrigued when he interviewed me and I stood up, "unwinding the longest legs I've ever seen." He added, "Then she started to speak, and she had a brain and charm." And no, he never made a pass at me. We talked about current events, but we mostly talked business.

After about six months, Miklos' full-time job took him to Switzerland. I regretted losing both the work and the intelligent man.

Paul Enters My Life

I met Paul Solomon Orentlich at the Kettle of Fish about a year after Dave and I separated. I was there with Mark Ross, a talented folk singer I managed for a while, when a man walked up to us and said, "Mark, introduce me to your friend." Paul and I went to two more bars that night, and he invited me to Fire Island, a small beach community on Long Island, for the weekend. I'd never been there. When we arrived there Friday night, we went to the beach. I'd never before had sex on a sandy beach; it was interesting, and yes, I wound up having to get sand out of my body and my clothing. The rest of the weekend was a round of being fed wonderful seafood at people's tiny houses and hanging out at the one waterside bar in the small community where Paul rented a room in a house for part of the summer. With lots and lots of booze.

When I returned home at the end of the weekend, I called Dave and said, "We thought we could drink. I just met people who make us look like children." But, after a few years, Paul decided he didn't want to drink that much. It took me a lot longer to slow down. And longer than that to stop.

Deciding to live with someone other than Dave wasn't easy. We were still good friends. We even still acknowledged that we loved one another, although we weren't 'in love,' whatever the difference was. For a while after we separated, a little piece of me thought that after a few years, we'd reunite and grow old together, although neither of us had a clue of what 'getting old' meant. But I realized quickly that our lives would not mesh again.

Paul had an apartment on MacDougal Street, over the Gaslight and the Kettle of Fish, which he shared with a friend. For close to a year, while I figured out what I wanted to do about us, he kept the apartment; you didn't give up a rent-controlled Village apartment without being very certain you wouldn't want it later. In those days, living with someone wasn't something you spent a lot of time considering. Paul spent more and more nights with me, and eventually, it was absurd for him to continue to pay rent, even a low rent, someplace else. So, he gave up his share in the apartment.

As I've noted before, he was twenty years older than me, but at the time, I shrugged off the age difference, which never affected our relationship. I fell in love with him and we spent twenty-seven very happy years together, although I was alone again at a fairly young age; he died at age 77, when I was 57.

Paul was a writer, a sculptor, and an actor—although, to earn a living, he often worked either as a bartender or a public relations practitioner. It was Paul who told me that every time I had gotten a newspaper or magazine story written about a musician, or booked a folk singer onto a radio or television show, I was getting that person publicity—and that professionally this was called public relations. Wow. I hadn't realized that it was a profession I might enter.

Years before, not even knowing what a press release was, I had looked up the proper form to use to notify media of musicians' appearances at Folksingers Guild concerts. Later, when the folk singers I managed performed, I researched the music critics or features editors in the area, sent press releases and announcements, and followed up with phone calls. As a result, the musicians I managed had many radio interviews (television didn't cover folk music then) and received very good newspaper and magazine publicity.

When we met, Paul worked in a financial public relations firm, promoting corporate and business clients through media coverage. The agency he worked for did a large special event each year for the Benrus Watch Company, featuring people who had accomplished time-based successes: they had run the fastest, hit the most tennis balls, pitched the most home runs, etc., and Paul suggested that they hire me to work on that campaign on a temporary basis. I elicited a lot of press coverage for Benrus, and the public relations firm offered me a full-time job. But I didn't want to work for corporations, and I knew Paul and I shouldn't work in the same place. I'd managed Dave, wasn't sure it had been a great idea, and didn't want to risk my relationship with Paul by working alongside him.

Ethical Culture: A Wonderful Job

That experience, and a part-time public relations job I took in an agency that specialized in not-for-profit organizations, gave me confidence to look for a job doing public relations. In 1972, when I was 33, I became public relations director of the New York Society for Ethical Culture. I was thrilled to work there. It wasn't a socialist organization, but it had a left-of-liberal thrust. Technically, Ethical Culture is a religion; it defines itself as "a humanist community dedicated to ethical relationships, social justice, and environmental stewardship." What's important is how people treat one another; whether or not a member believes in a deity is irrelevant. It's pretty much defined by the Golden Rule, and that's how I've identified myself ever since I worked there.

Its focus on social justice led Ethical Culture, more than a century ago, to help found the NAACP, the American Civil Liberties Union, and the first settlement houses in the United States. It helped start programs that eventually became the Visiting Nurse Service and the Legal Aid Society. My job was to help it air issues of social concern and to generate publicity that would attract people who might become members.

At the Ethical Culture Society, I was treated with a degree of professional respect I never again received until I became executive director of a not-for-profit organization. The Leaders (an Ethical Culture Leader is a humanist clergyperson) determined which public events to host, and often I was involved in that process. I then handled the event, sometimes contacting the speakers, and always initiating publicity.

We sponsored one of the first public meetings in this country featuring an Israeli and a Palestinian dialogue; we organized one of the first forums on health care and the aging to be held in New York; we featured as a speaker Leonid Ivanovych Plyushch, a Ukrainian mathematician and Soviet dissident who had been incarcerated in a Soviet mental institution because of his politics.

I hosted a gathering for Plyushch and his wife Titiana in our Waverly Place apartment after he spoke at the large Ethical Culture building on Central Park West, and the next morning, Paul and I found them collapsed on our living room floor, vodka bottles at their sides. We then invited them to Leisure Lodge, our cabins in Ulster County, and again were stunned at their booze capabilities. We now said of ourselves, "We thought we could drink. These people make us look like novices." That's what I had said to Dave after I met Paul; now I found myself echoing myself to Paul.

I left the New York Society for Ethical Culture after five very satisfying years only because it had developed serious financial problems, but I continued to work for not-for-profit organizations until I retired. That enabled me to continue to work for social change professionally as well as in my volunteer activities.

Leisure Lodge: My Place of Relaxation

A few years after we started to live together in the early 1970s, Paul and I bought Leisure Lodge, the cabins in Ulster County that, earlier in this book, I write about Dave and me visiting. They had belonged to my father's sister, but she wanted to part with them, and her son planned to move out of the area. We spent weekends and summer vacations there, and went to them even in winter. I still remember the first Christmas we spent in the cabins, when Paul had bought me 5 lb (2.5 kg) of paté de campagne at Walter's Meat Market in the Village, which closed in 1984.

We'd fill several five-gallon jerry jugs with water at a service station just before we got to the cabins—there was no running water there—turn on the electric stove and some electrically operated gas-filled heaters we'd bought and which cost a fortune to run, go out to dinner, then return to the cabin to crawl into bed under a heavy down comforter. We used paper dishes and carried buckets of water up from the creek that was at the bottom of a small cliff to wash pots.

We visited country auctions and fell in love with early American tools and kitchenware. Paul admired the way the tools were used and we both saw them as striking sculptural objects. I loved to cook, preferred hand tools to electric ones, and enjoyed the feel and overall sensation of older cookware, utensils, and glassware. We found ourselves buying stuff that we couldn't use.

Tin Can Alley Antiques

Paul wasn't happy handling financial public relations for corporations. He had talked about finding another way to earn a living, but by now, he was in his fifties, and finding a new career would be difficult. He couldn't go back to sculpting full-time, which brought in very little income, and he didn't want the lousy hours and physical dangers of being a bartender. He decided that he wanted to start an antiques shop specializing in old American tools and kitchenware.

I loved the idea, and I loved helping him. He found a store on Carmine Street in the Village, and named it Tin Can Alley Antiques. Carmine Street still was home to many older Italian families and didn't have the tourist traffic needed for an antiques store, but Paul thought we could generate enough publicity to attract buyers.

We did that. I was able to get the store written about in *New York Magazine*, the *NY Times*, the *Soho Weekly News* and other weekly community newspapers. People who bought props for theatrical companies found the store. Others were sent by their friends.

We purchased a used Chevrolet Suburban to haul stuff. It's a van on a station wagon base, and Paul kept it until it would no longer start. I was remarkably strong back then, so I was able to load the vehicle with Paul. My body was flexible, possibly because my arms and legs are double-jointed, and I could crawl around the inside of the van, making items fit. I still have large slabs of marble in my backyard that we carried up a hill together; now, I can't even think about picking them up.

Less Folk Music

Paul had been part of People's Songs in the 1940s, founded by Pete Seeger, Woody Guthrie, and others to "create, promote, and distribute songs of labor and the American people." By the time I met him, Paul was no longer involved with or interested in folk music, and he complained that my folk music friends talked mostly about contracts and places to perform, which he found boring. He and Dave liked one another, or, at least, got along, and he was willing to go to hear my ex-husband perform nearby. He listened to other friends of mine, but he wasn't interested in hearing new performers. He listened to jazz and classical music, and liked theater and dance; he introduced me to dance by taking me to the Joffrey Ballet, and I was hooked. We bought subscriptions to the New York Philharmonic, the Joffrey, and the New York City Ballet, and went to jazz clubs. The music wasn't new to me, but ballet and the jazz clubs were. I loved them.

Those years were very happy ones. Great job, then OK ones; great hobbies; a man I loved, who thought of me as much as of himself.

Leaving New York City

We had gotten the *Let's leave New York City* urge, and thought we'd like to move to Ulster County, where the cabins were, but I didn't think I'd be able to earn a living there and we didn't have enough money to buy a house. Instead, my parents, who were talking about selling their summer cottage in Rockland County, which is only 30 miles (48 km) northwest of New York City, offered it to us after consulting my sister and brother to make sure they were OK with not inheriting portions of the house. At my parents' suggestion, we tried it for two years, keeping the Greenwich Village apartment in reserve … and we decided we wanted to stay in Rockland.

The house is in a suburban area, but the surrounding community isn't typically suburban. It's a small house on a small lake that was created in 1928, where two streams converged. In the 1920s, a lot of the land that had been one farm was used to build summer cottages. It's a community of eighty properties. We maintain gravel roads. We have private wells. We are off South Mountain Road, a winding, two-lane, historic road that was the home of many mainstream American artists of the 1930s through the 1950s: actress and singer Lotte Lenya, composer Kurt Weill, playwright Maxwell Anderson, painter and textile designer Ruth Reeves, cartoonists Al Capp and Bill Mauldin, industrial designer Eva Zeisel, and others.

I still live there.

Family Illness

I'd had little experience of illness and death. Dave occasionally had asthma attacks that were severe enough that I'd go to the local emergency room with him; Paul had sporadic bouts of devastatingly painful gout; I'd had an optional tubal ligation to ensure that I didn't become pregnant, but life-threatening illness was new to me.

My parents had given me their summer house because my mother was diagnosed with Parkinson's disease in the mid-late 1970s, and she slowly became bedridden.

I've never felt as helpless as during those years. When my mother became ill, I wanted to spend time with my parents. Although I couldn't help care for my mother, I thought I could at least be present for her, and be a companion for my father. So, every second weekend for sixteen years, I went from work to Brooklyn on Friday, spent the night there, and went home after dinner on Saturday. I felt guilty when I left my parents to go home. I also felt guilty leaving Paul alone so often. He was amazing. When I told him that I felt awful about deserting him so much, he said, "You do what you have to. Someday, you won't have parents to be with. We'll have a lot of time together, and you'll feel that you did the right thing."

We didn't have enough time.

In the late 1980s, my father was attacked by Guillain-Barré Syndrome, an inflammatory disorder of the peripheral nerves outside the brain and spinal cord. He became virtually paralyzed, and lost feeling in his extremities, but my amazing father fought it and exercised his way back to functioning.

My mother died in 1992.

In 1996, my father had a stroke. He was taken to the hospital and after several days, my sister, who had come to Brooklyn from Massachusetts, my brother, who had flown in from California, and I were told that if he recovered, he would have no cognition. He had been very clear about his wishes, but honoring his wish not to live with a damaged brain was difficult.

I went home Friday night or Saturday morning. Late Sunday morning, Paul collapsed with cardiac arrest; he died on the way to the hospital. We'd been together for twenty-seven years. My sister and brother-in-law came from my parents' house in Brooklyn to be with me. When we got back to my house, there was a message from my father's doctor that our father had died.

We buried them both in my family's plot in a cemetery in Queens, NY. After that, my wonderful sister called me every single night for more than a year—even when she was away on vacation.

More Loss

My family tragedy didn't end there. When Donna, my sister-in-law called in February 2007 to tell me that my brother Leon's airplane had crashed and he was dead, I was shell-shocked. He'd been flying from San Diego to the Anza-Borrego Desert, where they spent weekends, and the plane went down in the mountains west of the desert. It was a flight he made frequently. No one ever learned what had happened. I still miss him.

Five years before that, Dave had died. We'd separated more than thirty years earlier, and then settled into good relationships with other people, but we had become adults together and remained good friends who cared about one another. It was an unhappy loss.

Meeting Martus

About three years after losing my father and Paul, Martus Granirer, who I knew slightly, walked past me in a local shopping mall, and he invited himself and a bottle of champagne to my house that evening. Once there, he started to rub my back. "I won't go to bed with you," I said. "You will," he replied. Right, as always, Granirer. For the record, he never again rubbed my back ... it was a good effort, but he didn't do it well. It simply had been a ploy. Within a year of our meeting, he moved into my house.

Martus was a photographer in the 1960s; I write elsewhere in this book about his having designed the cover of Dave's first solo album for Folkways. Commercial record and book photography was partly how

Martus earned a living while creating the photographs that are now in the permanent collection of the Museum of Modern Art and other museums.

When Martus moved to Rockland County in the late 1960s, he lived on South Mountain Road, about a mile from the house I later moved into. He lived next door to Lotte Lenya, and they became close friends.

Martus also went to law school while in his fifties so he could protect land and waterways near South Mountain Road, and led a land trust that protected more than one thousand acres in the smallest county in New York State. Both of us were among the people who successfully defeated an attempt by an international corporation to install a monstrous desalination plant in Rockland.

We had met before we became romantically involved with one another. When my community's little lake became heavily silted, I was one of the civic association members who spearheaded getting it dredged. I had turned to Martus for advice on finding a company to do it and on getting the town government to help us find a low-interest loan. The town took out the loan, and members of the community agreed to be taxed for twenty years to pay off the debt of $1.5 million; most of the cost was for getting rid of the silt that was removed from the lake.

I didn't have to wonder whether I wanted to live with a third man. I welcomed the relationship. I like living with somebody. I like having someone around to talk with, to mumble to—I talk to myself even when I live with someone, but I *have to* talk to myself when I live alone. I like listening to music with someone, and Martus loved and understood music; I've seen him tear up when he heard music that moved him. I prefer going to movies and to the theater with someone, and Martus and I went to Manhattan often to splurge on theater.

I've had great sex with each of the men I've lived with. Of course, living with someone who doesn't help with housework is less than great—and none of the men I've lived with did that. Friends used to say that occasionally I picked Dave up from the couch, vacuumed, and plopped him down again. Paul said he'd help a bit but that he wouldn't do 'stooped labor.' Martus didn't know what the word meant. But he had redeeming characteristics.

He thought I was an excellent editor and writer. He said I was good-looking. He said I was smart. He liked and was interested in my friends and family.

We were together for seventeen years; then he had to have heart valve replacement surgery which, I'm sure, led to the major stroke that killed him. The doctors had told us that people sometimes had strokes after that surgery, but that Martus *almost* certainly wouldn't. Humbug!

That sucked. Martus wanted to live more than anyone I've ever known.

Busted

A few years after I retired, Martus did something that infuriated me. On that same afternoon, he was leaving for California to visit his son's family, and I was supposed to take him to Kennedy Airport. I did, and when we got there I angrily had several drinks, saw him to the airplane, and left for home. I guess I drank the booze to show him that I still was pissed with him. Big mistake. After about an hour of being stuck in traffic, I got off the main road to find a bathroom. If I'd been sober, I would have remembered that all the bathrooms in that area were sealed off. But I wasn't sober.

On a side road, I banged my car on a fence, was busted for drunk driving, and was taken to a jail in Jamaica, Queens. I was a white woman in my early seventies, and the police were reasonably nice to me. They asked me whether I wanted to go into a cell or sit on a bench, handcuffed to a pipe; I chose the bench. They spent twenty minutes trying to fingerprint me using an electronic machine, but couldn't get a clear print and settled for one that, they said, they thought would be acceptable to the 'system.' I've never figured out what happened; I'm able to take my own fingerprints with an old-fashioned ink pad.

Later, they told me that they would keep me in their jail overnight rather than take me to the courthouse, explaining that the jail would be more comfortable. They urged me to go into the cell and try to get some sleep, which I finally did.

In the morning, when I was taken to the courthouse, I was put in a room with about twenty other women; we were seated on benches that lined the walls. All of the other women were young; they obviously were in their teens or early twenties. Some were crying because they were supposed to be home with their children or taking their kids to school.

After a few hours, we were taken to another part of the jail in small groups. When my name was called, I and seven other women were taken to a room that was about twelve feet by eight feet (3.6 × 2.4 m). A waist-high metal barrier ran down the length of the room, dividing it in half. The eight of us were in one half of the room, which contained a small bench large enough to accommodate three people; my young roommates insisted that I take one of the seats. The other half of the room contained an overflowing toilet full of urine and feces. When I called a guard and asked that the toilet be cleaned, he shrugged his shoulders and walked away.

Three hours later, I was taken to talk with someone from the Legal Aid Society. Clearly, the jail's administrators assumed that none of the people held there could afford a private lawyer, but I wondered why we weren't asked whether we wanted to talk with Legal Aid. When I got home, I called Martus—I had not been able to call California from the jail—and he put me in touch with a lawyer he knew who handled drunk driving cases.

I pleaded guilty at my trial, which lasted five minutes. I paid a hefty fine; and I had to relinquish my driver's license for ninety days, although I was allowed to drive for a limited amount of time each week to shop for food or to go to a doctor. I decided that being affected as badly as I was by several drinks (downed very quickly) meant that my body couldn't handle liquor as well as it used to, so I stopped drinking.

I was incensed at the way the women who were arrested were treated. I decided to find a way to improve the way women were treated when arrested or imprisoned. I'll tell you more about this in the Afterword of this book.

Chapter 12
THE REVIVAL OF THE FOLK REVIVAL

I've written that in the late '60s, the Village was changing and its folk music world was deteriorating. But folk music never died, it just became less visible in New York City, and years later, it's very much around, all over the country.

By 1967, the Village folk music scene was waning. A group of clubs still featured folk singers and the new folk-rock groups. The Gaslight and Gerde's continued, although Gerde's moved, and both places closed after a while. The Bitter End always had featured comics as well as musicians. The Bottom Line opened in 1974, and booked a wide variety of musicians ranging from Doc Watson and Dave Bromberg to Billy Joel and Dolly Parton. The basket houses continued to showcase folk and rock musicians.

These performers made good music, but there was a different vibe than that of the cheerful, upbeat Village scene of the '60s. Some sang almost exclusively songs that they had written. Many created bands, which were exciting and innovative, and attracted younger audiences than those of the folk singers. The newer groups used drugs to an extent that would have boggled the minds of most of the folk singers I knew. There were more drug incidents, more fights on the streets, more intervention by the police—and it became a lot less fun.

What's New
Then, in the early 1980s a new group of performers emerged. They gathered at Speakeasy, a club on MacDougal Street newly founded by Angela Page and Vinny Vok. These musicians created a cooperative membership group that came together much as the Folksingers Guild had back in the late 1950s, to help one another find an audience. Dave, who always

had encouraged younger musicians, joined the board of the new club. Over the years, its roster of members included Jack Hardy, Christine Lavin, Rod MacDonald, Roger Deitz, Frank Christian, George Gerdes, Paul Kaplan, Suzanne Vega, Maggie, Terre and Suzzy Roche, David Massengill, Lucy Kaplansky, Tom Intondi and others. A few months later, Jack Hardy and Brian Rose initiated a monthly magazine, with each issue accompanied by an LP (later, a CD) of new songs. The *Fast Folk Musical Magazine* lasted until 1997, when the magazine and records were donated to the Smithsonian Center for Folklife and Cultural Heritage.

Angela Page remembers a thriving scene where musicians knew one another's songs, would join with friends to harmonize, and in which musicians supported one another, "just to get the songs out there."

Speakeasy's members focused on writing and playing their own songs, and they wanted to be considered singer-songwriters. Rod MacDonald, who booked Speakeasy for five years after Angela left Manhattan, calls the era the Second Wave, comprising people who were influenced by the folk singers of the '60s and by the British Invasion, but who "were interested in folk music as songwriters. I'm especially interested in the emphasis Rod MacDonald and Chris Lavin and Terre Roche put on storytelling. "Songs that tell stories," they all say. As someone who loves stories with beginnings, middles, and ends, I'm fascinated by that.

In the '60s, I had an ambivalent attitude toward the singer-songwriter movement. I liked much of what Tom Paxton, Bob Dylan, and Phil Ochs wrote. I thought the songs the Holy Modal Rounders wrote were brilliant. Later, one of the reasons I loved Maggie and Terre Roche was because I liked their songs. I liked the few songs Dave wrote. But, even though Tom, Phil, and the Roches sang only songs they wrote, I never thought of any of them as singer-songwriters. I didn't have a special name for them; they simply were folk singers, or, if I made a distinction, I referred to them as musicians.

That may have been because I disliked most of the early songs of many of the early singer-songwriters; I found them mushy, almost whining, talking interminably about almost nothing but love affairs that happened and love affairs that didn't happen, not even telling what happened but only how they felt about whatever had or hadn't happened.

By the mid '70s, though, I had heard singer-songwriters who were very good. I wasn't managing musicians any more, worked weekdays, went to Leisure Lodge with Paul many weekends, and found it difficult to find time to go to coffee houses and clubs, but I stayed in touch with old friends and tried to keep up with the new folk vibe.

I enjoyed what I was able to do. Club owners occasionally called to ask about New York City musicians, although by the '70s, many were booking electric bands and jazz musicians, not acoustic folk. College booking agencies sometimes sought help locating performers. I remember one call from a young man at a college in Pennsylvania who was looking for Richie Havens. I spent an hour trying to find someone who would know Richie's phone number until finally, I had a brainstorm and looked in the Manhattan telephone directory. Eureka! The man's phone number was listed.

When I was able to, I went to the Gaslight and to Gerde's Folk City. I stayed away from the basket houses, which I now regret; had I gone to them, I might have heard Tim Hardin, Susan Martin Robbins (now a good friend), Fred Neil, Tiny Tim, and the brand-new Lovin' Spoonful.

Pat Sky and me. *Photo, Cathy Sky*

Later, when the new singer-songwriter cohort started, I heard them mostly in the Cornelia Street Café, a small Village restaurant and bar where many of them gathered on Monday nights to swap new songs. Listening to those musicians was a bit like being back in my living room with Dave and Tom Paxton and Bob Dylan and Phil Ochs and Pat Sky.

There was another musical strain at that time—the people who left New York City and moved to Woodstock. Happy Traum, who I think is one of the best folk singers anywhere, and his brother Artie, had a rock band for about two years in the '60s, playing "psychedelic-oriented rock." "I left the band because I moved to Woodstock," Happy told me. "John Herald already lived there, Bill Keith and Jim Rooney came from Boston, Maria Muldaur and Geoff Muldaur moved in, Eric Andersen and Debbie Green came to live there." John Sebastian lives there now.

Happy has pointed out that the Woodstock musicians retained their folk roots, but "wanted the depth more instruments gave the music, so we didn't limit ourselves to an acoustic guitar or banjo, but added fiddles, drums, bass, piano, even cello, although we didn't turn it into folk rock."

Folk music still was happening, he said, "although it wasn't within five blocks of Washington Square." The Village died, he said, but the music just moved.

Happy and others also started to write and publish instructional materials. He and Jane Traum now co-own Homespun Music Instruction, which publishes music lessons by a huge number of artists on CDs, DVDs, and streaming media. It's a good way for would-be instrumentalists to learn one or more musical styles, or to experiment until they find one they want to learn, then to explore it in depth.

It's odd to realize that I'm part of a world seen in retrospect. Good friends and people I hung out with or knew just casually have become historic figures. Dave. Dylan. Noel Stookey. Mary Travers (even though she wouldn't speak to me). John Hurt. Gary Davis. Eric Weissberg. Bruce Langhorne. Pat Sky. Phil Ochs. Danny Kalb. Sam Charters. Izzy Young. So many.

In 2015, the Museum of the City of New York featured an exhibit titled Folk City: New York and the Folk Music revival. It told the story of folk music in Greenwich Village in the 1960s, showing instruments, handwritten lyrics, photographs, and film and video footage. I was in one photograph and recorded a two-minute tape that attendees could listen to. I was also a member of a panel discussion about Bob, featuring me and several people who have written about him: Stephen Petrus, Elijah Wald, and David Hadju.

The Tapes

Listening to the audition tape Bob recorded for me in the Gaslight in 1961, and the tape Maggie and Terre recorded in a studio in 1968, both so I could try to get them gigs, takes me back into the Gaslight in a physical way. I feel it. I smell it. The air is smoky. The Ampex is on a table. We—Bob and Dave and I—are slightly nervous. The audience is small. How will Bob sound? Will the recording be good? I'm in the coffee house, and I'm focused on making a tape that will sell my client. Music can take you back in time. A friend reminds me that one of the strongest memories people have is with the music of their youth. It can be recreated mentally, but sometimes it needs a trigger. Mine was those tapes.

The Dylan tape was made so I would have an example of Bob's work to take to coffee houses and concert producers. Bob did a set at the Gaslight so we could make the tape. As I wrote earlier, I had at least one other tape and at least one cassette made by a commercial studio. I took the cassette to a few clubs out of NYC and to one concert producer in Boston. When Bob signed with Albert, I put the stuff in a closet.

The tape of Maggie and Terre was recorded in the Dick Charles studio. It, too, is amazing. Those young girls had learned to play guitar and write songs by watching someone on a public television show and consulting her guitar book—and they were creating complex, stunning arrangements of songs. Fifty-five years after they made the tape, I'm impressed.

The Music I Still Love

I like a lot of folk music, and in this book you'll find the names of many of the people I listen to. Go back to the chapter on Bob Dylan; there are long lists for you to explore, as well as names that reappear throughout. The ones that are missing are many of the older, traditional musicians I enjoy. Some of them are storytellers, such as Paul Clayton, Ewan MacColl, Jean Ritchie, Clarence Ashley, Ed McCurdy. Of course, I listen to Pete Seeger and Woody Guthrie. But I listen mostly to acoustic blues.

Chris Lavin, one of the best, funniest, wittiest, most prolific singer-songwriters in the United States, still knows every performance site in New York. She mused, "People who love jazz always will love jazz, and

Happy Traum, Terre Roche, Terri Thal, Gerde's Folk City reunion, 2010. *Photo, Jeannie Myers*

people who love the simplicity of a voice telling a story that means something accompanied by a guitar or piano always will love that."

I agree. Martus was happy to go to hear folk singers and singer-songwriters with me, and we often heard old friends of mine as well as musicians I'd never heard before in the Turning Point, a small, friendly club in Rockland County. Since he died, I've been catching old friends and newer performers there and, occasionally, in Manhattan. I also hear a lot of good music on social media, despite my reservations about some platforms.

Recently, I heard Terre Roche keep an audience in a New York City club spellbound, singing songs that she and Maggie recorded years ago or performed as they rode across the United States on their first tour. And during the COVID pandemic, when clubs were closed and we all stayed home, I watched virtual performances by performers such as Dakota Dave Hull, Roy Bookbinder, Deborah Robins and Larry Hanks, John Winn, Tom Paxton, Paul Metsa, Mark Ross, the Piedmont Blūz Acoustic Duo, Richard Limbert, Andrew Cohen, Michael Ubaldini, Howard Levy, Rory Block, and others.

The Revival of the Folk Revival

It is good to see the revival of live music. There are enclaves of folk music people in large and small cities across the United States. There are festivals in places I've never heard of before. I've been to the Newport and Philadelphia Folk festivals, which are many decades old, but there also are festivals in Telluride, Colorado; Wilkesboro, North Carolina; Kerrville, Texas; Butte, Montana; and a zillion others. They blend loud bands with Irish fiddle tunes, contra dancing, acoustic blues, and ballads. Of course, there's the Woody Guthrie Folk Festival, held each year in Okemah, Oklahoma, where Woody Guthrie was born. (I met him once in Washington Square in the mid '50s.) And the annual Greenwich Village Folk Festival, which held annual concerts from 1987 to 1994 and was revived in 2020.

My own favorite musical event for many years has been the annual Washington Square Bluegrass and Folk Music Reunion, a gathering of musicians who played around the fountain in the 1950s and 60s, organized by Jeannie Myers. Some people have turned down paid work so they could be there; some are there every year; some come occasionally. I don't play, of course; I go to listen to the music and talk with old friends.

Washington Square Reunion, 2010

At the reunion, I've been able to catch up with some musician and other friends. They include: John Sebastian of the Lovin' Spoonful. Maria Muldaur. David Bennett Cohen, who was in Country Joe and the Fish. Peter Stampfel of the Holy Modal Rounders. Paul Prestopino, who played with Peter, Paul, and Mary, and was in the Chad Mitchell Trio. Eric Weissberg and Steve Mandell, both of whom were the real musicians who played in the 'duelling banjos' movie *Deliverance*. Terry Mandell. Roger Sprung. Barry Kornfeld. Sylvia Tyson. Happy Traum. John Cohen, who was with the New Lost City Ramblers. Bob Yellin, who was with the Greenbriar Boys. Danny Kalb of the Blues Project. Joshua Rifkin. Suze Rotolo. Matt Umanov, who owned a wonderful instrument store in the Village … and so many more. Many have left us, but all of them are memorable.

A new generation of folk musicians, such as Cole Quest Rotante, Woody Guthrie's grandson, have started to emerge, keeping the music alive. And throughout the United States and abroad, young people are making folk music. It may not sound like the music I remember, but it's their music made in their era, and I'm sure some of it will enter the tradition.

"New York never again will have anything like that moment in the '60s," Chris Lavin says. "But, I think that folk music, like jazz, will always have an audience."

I still listen to folk music. And to some singer-songwriters, and to some bands. You're welcome to join me.

Afterword
MY OTHER PASSION

I'm now in my 80s and most of my life has been driven by two passions: folk music and social justice. I'm still involved in social justice movements, primarily in environmental and climate change as both interact with local policy, and with criminal justice reform, mostly on a state-wide level.

The CIA Illegally Spied on U.S. Organizations

I wrote earlier about working for the New York Society for Ethical Culture. While it had a liberal perspective, not a socialist one, I found it satisfying to create and produce events that explored issues that were alive at that moment. And in the 1970s, Ethical Culture was absurdly regarded as a left-wing organization by the U.S. government.

One day in 1975, a reporter for the *Washington Post* called to tell me that he had just learned that the CIA had been illegally investigating U.S. citizens and organizations, including the Washington D.C. Ethical Culture Society. It was illegal because only the FBI was allowed to investigate U.S. organizations. The CIA was prohibited from having any "police, subpoena, law-enforcement powers, or internal security functions." It was supposed to "collect and analyze foreign intelligence and conduct covert action," but not in the United States. Its oversight of organizations within the country became a huge scandal; many people remembered the persecution of Americans in the McCarthy era, and were horrified to learn that the CIA was spying on Americans.

The Leader of the Washington, D.C. Society during the time it was being investigated by the CIA had been Edward L. Erikson, now the Senior Leader of the New York Society. I hit the phones and called every newspaper, TV station, and radio station in New York, telling them the news and offering them an interview with Ed. I sent telegrams to the ones I couldn't reach on the phone. Only one responded: WCBS News, the local CBS-TV station. We arranged for an interview that evening, but the TV station backed out. Later, this became a big national issue, but when news of it broke, media outlets clearly were afraid to touch the story.

People in Prison are Creative

One project that would be useful to host now as well as in 1974 was an exhibit and sale of art created by men incarcerated in New York State prisons (there were few programs of any kind in women's prisons then). We were trying to show that people in prison could be creative and could produce meaningful works of art. This wasn't changing the nature of society, but we hoped to make it a bit better for some people who needed help. It did create some change. Art programs were started in two more New York State (men's) prisons shortly after the exhibit.

I still like the painting I purchased there. It's a suburban street scene painted by Willie Hamilton, who was serving time in Green Haven Correctional Facility, a maximum security prison in Dutchess County. I wonder where he remembered the street from.

Too Many U.S. Women Are in Prison

That project ties in with the volunteer work I became involved with many years later, after my one-night experience in the jail in New York City. I came out of that jail wanting to do something about lousy treatment of women in prison. But I'm not a social worker or lawyer, I have no credentials in "helping" people, and most of the programs for people in or leaving prison are geared mostly for men.

I wound up in the Rockland Coalition to End the New Jim Crow (RCENJC), named for a book by writer and civil rights activist Michelle Alexander. She showed how the U.S. War on Drugs was a way of using the criminal justice system to incarcerate racial minorities at a higher rate than their white counterparts, although they used drugs at the same rate. Alexander did a good job of substantiating that this practice has evolved a racial 'caste system' that allows legal discrimination measures in all aspects of society.

The United States has four percent of the world's female population, but thirty percent of the world's female incarcerated population. About eighty percent of the incarcerated women are mothers. The children of many single mothers who are in prison are sometimes taken in by people who have registered to be foster parents just to collect the stipend offered by government, and have no interest in caring for the kids. Ouch. That stinks.

What can we do about it? Support the organizations that help women in prison. Join in the efforts to get rid of prison sentences for owning small amounts of drugs, for prostitution, for 'offenses' such as 'talking back' to a police officer. Get rid of rats and roaches and filth in prisons. Get rid of solitary confinement. Get rid of prison guards who rape and maim women prisoners. Follow the lead of places such as Eugene, Oregon, that have mental health professionals rather than police responding to calls involving people known to have mental illness. Improve home care services for the families of women in prison. Put some of the money now spent on police equipment into programs to improve employment opportunities. Make childcare affordable for everyone.

There's been a lot of talk about police reform or prison reform in the past few years. Some reform bills were passed; then came the pushback. And the politicians caved in. In New York State, many bills never got to the floor of the legislature, and some that were passed weren't signed by the governor.

The few bills that were passed have been attacked heavily by the police unions and prison guards, who have a vested interest in putting and keeping people in prison. Other proposed legislation makes common sense, but has become controversial. We continue to work with the many groups advocating for reform.

Pregnant Women and Young Children Need Healthcare

Friends and relatives scoffed in 1990, when I became executive director of a not-for-profit organization that coordinated services for pregnant women and young children whose incomes were low. After all, I'm the person who never wanted kids.

But I saw the lack of prenatal and infant care as women's issues. The job appealed to me as a way to ensure that all pregnant women and children got healthcare, and also gave me the opportunity to be director of a not-for-profit organization.

Maternal-Infant Services Network of Orange, Sullivan, and Ulster Counties (MISN), just north and west of Rockland County, was a new organization. It was funded mostly by the New York State Department of Health to bring together the varied health and human service providers who worked on behalf of pregnant women, new mothers, and their children, and to educate the women about the need for prenatal care and about programs to help them.

We succeeded, to the extent that the New York State systems allowed anyone to succeed.

Many women who were on Medicaid, which is the federal healthcare payor for people whose incomes are below a certain amount, received other government services: food stamps, assistance with heating bills, mental health services, and more. Each service required the woman to frequently meet with a government representative. When I worked at MISN, I met some women who had to meet the requirements of as many as seven different government agencies. Some of those agencies required the women to take different—and sometimes, contradictory—actions. MISN tried to coordinate the way their staffs worked with each woman, which was often impossible—each agency had its own immoveable rules.

We couldn't change that. We did try to get the agency representatives to confer about what each woman needed, which itself was very difficult; the agencies normally didn't talk with one another.

What we could do: mount campaigns to bring women and children into healthcare services. We developed marketing programs, and each year we brought more than eight hundred women and children into funded healthcare and related programs. It's an astounding number, and I was pleased to receive an award for our work from the national Healthy Mothers, Healthy Babies coalition, which had been created to improve the quality and reach of public and professional education related to prenatal and infant care.

We also sponsored conferences and developed educational programs for the many people who worked with pregnant and parenting women. One area we did innovative work in was promoting recognition that women with mental illness and women with developmental disabilities are sexual, and that ignoring their sexuality is unrealistic. Even in the early 2000s, any time a woman in a treatment facility or a group home or even an outpatient program became pregnant, there was an assumption that she had been raped. That sometimes was true, but very often, the sex had been consensual. That raises ethical, and sometimes legal, issues, but they have to be dealt with, not ignored.

The other topic that surprisingly few people talked about then was how the environment was affecting the health of pregnant women and their unborn children. I became concerned about what might be in the air and water they absorbed, and I brought scientists and medical professionals to conferences to talk about it. I was surprised at how few people were researching the issue.

Fighting—and Beating—a Multinational Corporation

That interest led to my participation in the new Rockland Water Coalition (RWC). Initially, I went to its meetings because I wondered what unhealthy substances might be in the county's water, but I learned that the RWC had been created to fight the construction of a desalination plant proposed by the water utility to augment Rockland's limited water supply. I agreed that Rockland could have enough water if it developed a strong water conservation plan, and that the plant was unnecessary. I became active in opposing it.

As almost all of Rockland's water comes from rain that falls within the county, there have been water shortages. In 2006, the private, for-profit water company that then owned the water used by more than seventy-seven percent of the county proposed building a desalination plant in the Hudson River, just off the Rockland shoreline, to augment Rockland's water supply. The New York State Public Service Commission (PSC), which regulates private utilities, gave the project preliminary support.

Desalination plants are used in places like Israel and Saudi Arabia, with deserts and large populations. It's absurd to consider one for a county of a little more than 300,000 residents. Rockland County environmentalists, civic groups, elected officials, and members of the public immediately objected to the proposal. The RWC, which comprised thirty-four local, regional, and national groups, led the community's opposition to the plant, together with many elected officials, including state and county legislators.

Objections to the proposal focused on the extraordinary cost, the impact on critical Hudson River habitat, and placing the plant only 3½ miles (6 km) south of the Indian Point nuclear power plant that was on the opposite shore. Indian Point leaked radioactive water with toxic elements that still leach into the Hudson River.

Masses of people turned out to oppose the plant at public hearings. In 2012, hundreds of Rocklanders attended an overflow public hearing. In 2013, more than 1,600 residents and elected officials, nearly all in opposition, attended a public hearing held by the PSC. Close to 1,800 public comments were filed online, overwhelmingly in opposition. Over 32,000 signatures on petitions opposing the project were submitted to the New York State governor.

We won!

In December 2015, the PSC ordered the water company to abandon the desalination project. The PSC told it to expedite reduction of water losses, to move to a water conservation rate (surcharges for high water use during periods of drought), and to work with a new county-established water task force to develop a water conservation plan (which it didn't do).

Now What?

I've been lucky. I was born in a time and place where I've been able to fight for justice, and when my mother's protests about the plight of being a woman are being addressed. My family didn't encourage me to live my life in the worlds of folk music and social justice, but no one tried to hamper me, and everyone accepted me and my activities. I've been able to support myself by doing interesting, useful work. I've lived with three remarkable men, all of whom recognized my need to be independent.

So, I continue to foster social change, which I think is needed in this time of division and dissention, and to be immersed in the world of music, both of which support my being.

FOLK SINGERS AND RELATED PEOPLE IN NEW YORK CITY, MID-LATE 50s THROUGH MID-LATE 60s

I started to list people I knew in the folk music world in New York, and was surprised at how long the list was; I remembered close to 200 people. Then I added the names of people I didn't know but knew of. And the list grew. At the end, I consulted Dick Weissman, who reminded me of some people I'd missed and some I simply didn't know. Not all of the people listed here were musicians. Some were club owners or managers or photographers or owned a record company or worked for a record company or produced concerts or were poets or owned an instrument store. A few weren't based in New York, but visited often enough to be included. And then there was Izzy Young of the Folklore Center, who brought it all together.

Roger Abrahams
Ellen Adler
Mary Katherine Aldin
Phil Allen
Rick Alman
Joe Alper
David Amram
Eric Andersen
Alan Arkin
Steve Arkin
Moe Asch
Luke Askew
Babe
Ed Badeaux

Jack Baker
Paula Ballan
Bill Barth
Frank Beacham
Eddie Bell
Roy Berkeley
Sid Bernstein
Leon Bibb
Theo Bikel
Alan Block
Lawrence Block
David Blue (Cohen)
Ray Boguslav
Roy Bookbinder

Joe Bossum
Oscar Brand
John Brent
Marshall Brickman
Bob Brill
Harvey Brooks
Dave Bromberg
Ian Buchanan
Sandy Bull
Raun Burnham
Tom Burnside
J.C. Burris
Paul Caldwell
Rolf Cahn
Hamilton Camp
Guy Carawan
Peter Carbone
Bob Carey
Len Chandler
Andy Carroll
Ann Charters
Sam Charters
Robin Christensen
Frank Christian
Liam Clancy
Pat Clancy
Tom Clancy
Paul Clayton
Andrew Cohen
David Bennett Cohen
John Cohen
Mike Cohen
Paul Colby
Judy Collins
Michael Cooney
Clarence Cooper
Elizabeth Cotton
Don Crawford
Marty Cutler

Barbara Dane
Karen Dalton
Erik Darling
Rev. Gary Davis
Augustin DelMello
Art D'Lugoff
Alix Dobkin
Bonnie Dobson
Barry Drake
Monte Dunn
Antonia Duren
Bob Dylan
Jack Elliott
Paul Endicott
Logan English
Billy Faier
Mimi Farina
Richard Farina
Bob Fass
Luke Faust
Pat Foster
Hope Foye
Dave Gahr
Herb Gart
Jimmy Gavin
Lawrence Gellert
Paul Geremia
Fred Gerlach
Tom Ghent
Guido Giampieri, Guido
John Gibbon
Tam Gibbs
Bob Gibson
Ronnie Gilbert
Geula Gill
Allen Ginsberg
Gina Glaser
Tom Glazer
Jean Glover

Folk Singers and Related People in New York City, 50s Through 60s

- Jim Glover
- Tony Glover
- J.R. Goddard
- Sandy Goldfarb
- Pete Goldsmith
- Kenny Goldstein
- Cynthia Gooding
- Elmer Gordon
- Arthur Gorson
- Dick Greenhaus
- Kiki Greenhaus
- David Grisman
- Albert Grossman
- Stefan Grossman
- Woody Guthrie
- Frank Hamilton
- Tim Hardin
- Lee Haring
- Bob Harris
- Emmylou Harris
- Richie Havens
- Lee Hayes
- Fred Hellerman
- Judy Henske
- John Herald
- Carolyn Hester
- Joe Hickerson
- Larry Hoffman
- Lee Hoffman
- Laurie Holland
- Will Holt
- Jac Holzman
- Clarence Hood
- Sam Hood
- John Lee Hooker
- Cisco Houston
- Dakota Dave Hull
- Carol Hunter
- Mississippi John Hurt
- Janice Ian
- Rick Illowite
- Judy Isquith
- Harry Jackson
- Joe Jaffe
- Skip James
- Nancy Jeffries
- Ted Joans
- Larry Johnson
- Danny Kalb
- Lucy Karwowski
- Steve Katz
- Nick Katzman
- Alan Kaufman
- Pat Keating
- Bill Keith
- Lionel Kilberg
- Lisa Kindred
- John Koerner
- Barry Kornfeld
- Kenny Kosek
- Irving Kratka
- Jim Kweskin
- Dave Laibman
- Bruce Langhorne
- Roger Lass
- Dan Lauffer
- Tiny Ledbetter
- Perry Lederman
- Bert Lee
- Bill Lee
- Harold Leventhal
- Howard Levy
- Buzzy Linhart
- A.L. Lloyd
- Sid Locker
- Alan Lomax
- George Lourie
- Alex Lukeman

Ewan MacColl
Rod MacDonald
Doug MacKenzie
Raun MacKinnon
Judy Mahan
Tom Makem
Steve Mandell
Joe at the Jazz Record Center
Jo Mapes
Joe Marra
Jim Marshall
Vince Martin
David Massengill
Margot Mayo
Ed McCurdy
Jimmy McDonald
Brownie McGhee
Neila Miller
Bob Milos
John Mitchell
Artie Mogull
Bill Morrissey
Maria Muldaur
Bruce Murdoch
Fred Neil
Marc Nerenberg
Tom Paley
Phil Ochs
Odetta
Milt Okun
Tom Paley
Felix Pappalardi
Tom Pasle
Pauli
Tom Paxton
Dave Peller
John Pickow
Andy Polon
Mike Porco

Paul Prestopino
Ethel Raim
Walter Raim
Gene Rankin
Gene Raskin
Jerry Rasmussen
David Rea
Jean Redpath
Susan Reed
Aaron Rennert
Michael Resnick
Phil Rhodes
Fritz Richmond
Ben Rifkin
Joshua Rifkin
Ralph Rinzler
Jean Ritchie
Susan Martin Robbins
Robby Robinson
Maggie Roche
Terre Roche
Judy Roderick
Hugh Romney
Jim Rooney
Artie Rose
Art Rosenbaum
Len Rosenfeld
Dick Rosmini
Mark Ross
Manny Roth
Charley Rothschild
Paul Rothschild
Suze Rotolo
Tom Rush
Buffy Sainte-Marie
Ellen Saletan
Irene Saletan
Henry Saposnik
Russ Savakus

Norman Savitt
Stu Scharf
Eric Schoenberg
Paul Schoenwetter
Larry Schrieber
Molly Scott
Dave Sear
John Sebastian
Mike Seeger
Pete Seeger
Brother John Sellers
Alec Seward
Robert Shelton
John Sebastian
Marc Silber
Jerry Silberman
Dick Silvera
Paul Simon
Pat Sky
Harry Smith
Ralph Lee Smith
Jack Solomon
Howard Solomon
Maynard Solomon
Juan Sostre
Mark Spoelstra
Roger Sprung
Peter Stampfel
Andy Statman
Ellen Stekert
Susan Sterngold
Bernard Stollmann
Doris Stone
Noel Stookey
Keith Sykes
Norma Tanega
Sonny Terry
Terri Thal
Tiny Tim
Artie Traum

Happy Traum
Mary Travers
Gil Turner
Ian Tyson
Sylvia Tyson
Matt Umanov
Dino Valenti
Bill Vanaver
Dave Van Ronk
Victor Roland Vargas Mousaa
Ernie Vega
Frank Wakefield
Jerry Jeff Walker
Jackie Washington
Dick Waterman
Hal Waters
Doc Watson
Steve Weber
George Wein
Fred Weintraub
Eric Weissberg
Dick Weissman
Donald Westlake
Josh White
Josh White, Jr.
Dave Wilkes
Dave Wilson
John Winn
Wendy Winsted
Winnie Winston
Noah Wolfe
Al Wood
Hally Wood
Dave Woods
Douglas Yaeger
Peter Yarrow
Bob Yellin
Paul Yellin
Izzy Young
Jesse Colin Young

ACKNOWLEDGMENTS

I told very few people that I was writing this book until toward the end of the process. I did immediately tell my sister and some friends who have written or were in the process of writing books. Everyone was wonderfully supportive and helpful.

First on my *thank you* roster: my sister Joyce Hollman, to whom I babbled all the way through writing this, and who read and approved some chapters. Marjorie Turner Hollman, Richard Kostelanetz, Mark Ross, Laurie Seeman, and Howard Whitehouse, who read the manuscript and made excellent suggestions for revisions. Claudette Green and Peggy Kurtz, who respectively reviewed the copy on working for social justice and fighting the desalination plant in Rockland County. Russell Dale, for checking the sentences on socialism for accuracy. Susan Martin Robbins, for information about the folk music clubs in Greenwich Village that I now regret I didn't go to. Jewell Waldbaum, who consistently assured me that I'd get the book done and that it would be good.

Frank Beacham, Jeannie Myers, Susan Martin Robbins, Kyra Saulnier, and Norman Savitt, who helped me find photos and for the use of their photos. Ann Charters, who took an excellent photo of Dave and me that has been published often. Deborah Robins, who gave me valuable information about intellectual property.

Friends who've written or are writing books, who were generous with suggestions about contracts and the publishing process. Richard Barone's book, *Music + Revolution: Greenwich Village in the 1960s*, is a must-read for anyone who's interested in that time and place. Richard shared information about publishing, and allowed me to announce my future book at his own splendid book launch events. Stevie Trudeau wrote *The Dylan Tapes*, transcriptions of the tapes Anthony Scaduto, her deceased husband, recorded when he wrote the first book about Bob Dylan in 1971. Dick Weissman has written 21 books on roots music and the music industry; his most recent is *Bob Dylan's New York: A Historic Guide*. Others include *Talkin' 'Bout a Revolution: Music and Social Change in America*, and *Which Side Are You On?: An Inside History of the Folk Music Revival in America*, and he gave me the ingenious title for the chapter 'The Revival of the Folk Revival.' He also added to the list of 1950s and 60s folk music people.

People who helped me remember back then: Carolyn Hester, who remembers a lot. Lucy Karwowski, Barry Kornfeld, Tom Paxton, Susan Martin Robbins, Terre Roche, Mark Ross, Peter Stampfel, John Winn. Those who reminded me of what happened in the folk music world in New York City in the 1970s and '80s: Chris Lavin, Rod MacDonald, Terre Roche, who came up with the chapter title, 'There's Life After Folk Music'; Mark Ross, Happy Traum, whom I've known since I was 18 and listening to folk singers in Washington Square, and who has become a wonderful musician.

Special thanks to Jeannie Myers, who organized the annual Washington Square Bluegrass and Folk Music Reunion from 2006 through 2019, when COVID shut it down. It was a wonderful way to visit with people I didn't usually see during the year. Also to Frank Beacham, who posts information on Facebook about many people and events, and who celebrates the birthdays of a lot of folk music people, with interesting information about them.

I'm grateful to my publishers, Caroline Peden Smith, who edited the book and insisted that I delete copy that wasn't relevant to it; and Andy Smith at McNidder & Grace. They asked whether I was writing a book, offered to publish one, were supportive all the way through, and have been a pleasure to work and talk with.

Did I miss someone? If I did, please let me know and I'll add you to the next print run of the book.

BIBLIOGRAPHY

This isn't a scholarly book, and this isn't a scholarly or comprehensive list of books on folk music in the 1960s. These are books I've perused while writing this book either to stimulate my memory or to check a date or just because I've been immersed in that era. Or I took them out of the bookcase or picked them up from a pile and glanced at them. They are listed alphabetically by author.

On Folk Music

Deep Community: Adventures in the Modern Folk Underground by Scott Alarik. Black Wolf Press, 2003.

The Conscience of the Folk Revival: The Writings of Israel "Izzy" Young edited by Scott Barretta, The Scarecrow Press, Inc., 2013.

music + revolution: Greenwich Village in the 60s, by Richard Barone, Backbeat Books, 2002.

The Country Blues by Samuel Charters, New York: Rinehart 1959, Reprinted 1975, Da Capo Press, with a new introduction by the author.

My Red Blood by Alix Dobkin, Alyson Books, 2009.

Bob Dylan in the Big Apple: Troubadour Tales of New York by KG Miles, McNidder & Grace, 2022.

That's the Bag I'm In: The Life, Music and Mystery of Fred Neil by Peter Lee Neff, Blue Ceiling Publishing, 2019.

Making People's Music: Moe Asch and Folkways Records by Peter D. Goldsmith, Smithsonian Institution, 1998.

Folk City: New York and the American Folk Music Revival by Stephen Petrus and Ronald D. Cohen, Oxford University Press, 2015.

Blabbermouth, by Terre Roche, privately published, 2013.

Kin Ya See That Sun by Terre and Maggie Roche, privately published, 2022.

A Freewheelin' Time by Suze Rotolo, Broadway Books, 2008.

Bob Dylan an intimate biography by Anthony Scaduto, Grosset & Dunlap, 1971.

The Dylan Tapes, by Anthony Scaduto edited by Stephanie Trudeau, University of Minnesota Press, 2022.

No Direction Home: The Life and Music of Bob Dylan by Robert Shelton, edited by Elizabeth Thomson and Patrick Humphries, Backbeat Books, 2011.

The Mayor of MacDougal Street, A Memoir by Dave Van Ronk with Elijah Wald, 2005.

Dylan Goes Electric by Elijah Wald, Dey St., 2015.

Which Side Are You On? An Inside History of the Folk Music Revival in America by Dick Weissman, Green Press Initiative, Continuum Publishing, 2005.

Bob Dylan in America by Sean Wilentz, Anchor Books, 2010.

This Singin' Thing by John R. Winn, Copyright John R. Winn, 2015.

Say No to the Devil: The Life and Musical Genius of Rev. Gary Davis by Ian Zack, The University of Chicago Press, 2015.

On Socialism

Gerry Healy and his place in the history of the Fourth International by David North, Labor Publications, 1991.

The ABCs of Socialism edited by Bhaskar Sunkara, Verso, 2016.

The Age of Permanent Revolution: A Trotsky Anthology by Leon Trotsky, Dell Publishing Co., Inc., 1964.

The Permanent Revolution & results and prospects by Leon Trotsky, Red Letter Press, 2010. (First published in St. Petersburg in 1906.)

The Prophet's Children: Travels on the American Left by Tim Wohlforth, Humanities Press, 1994.

Also

Culver, David, (1987), Historical Commentary, Vietnam and Revisionism, *Bridgewater Review* 4(3) 24 – 26, http://vc.bridgew.edu/br_rev/vol4/iss3/11

INDEX

190 Waverly Place 61, 64, 114
219 West 15th Street 53
Abrahams, Roger 50, 189
Adams, Camila
Adams, Derroll 76
Adler, Ellen 25, 289
'Ain't No Grave Can Hold My Body Down' 26
Alda, Alan 91
Almanac Singers 19
American Civil Liberties Union 166
American Communist Party, Communist Party 19, 34, 48, 59, 72, 135, 160–1
American Federation of Musicians, Local 80–2, 94, 99, 141
American Songbag 23
Andersen, Eric 178, 189
Anderson, Maxwell 170
Anderson, Pink 137
Anthology of American Folk Music 23
Anti-Semitism, Anti-Semitic, 10, 11, 91
Appalachia 19, 146
Aran Islands 77
Armstrong, Louis 137, 143
Army-McCarthy hearings 36
Arnold, Jack 62–3, 78, 93, 153
Arnold, Kokomo 137
Asch, Moe 34, 114, 189, 197
'Ashokan Farewell' 105
Auden, W.H. 15, 91
Avalon, Mississippi 97

Babe 108–9, 138, 189
Baez, Joan 101, 104
'The Ballad of Emmett Till' 136
'The Ballad of John Henry Faulk' 136
'Bamboo' 118, 127
Banjo 23, 116, 148, 178, 182
Barone, Richard 141, 195, 197

Basket house, basket houses 69, 88, 94, 105, 133, 138, 139 ,175–6
Beiderbecke, Bix 137
Beller, Dorene 70
Beller, Jack 7–8
'Be My Baby' 122
Berkeley, Roy 50, 59, 189
Best Man at Wedding 68, 92
Bibleland 91
Big Joe, 103, 66, 138, 143–4
Bikel, Theo 22, 61, 189
'Bird Song' 122, 127
Birth of a Nation 19
Bitter End 94, 110, 126, 175
Black 9, 11, 23, 26, 46, 48, 55–6, 62, 91, 96–7, 120, 134, 136, 156
Black Panthers 159
Blind Blake 137
Blake, William 91
Bleecker (Street) 23, 99, 108, 110
Block, Alan 189
Block, Larry 67
Block, Rory 103, 180
Bloomfield, Michael 106
Blue, David
  Also Cohen, Dave 136, 189
blues 23–6, 46, 58–9, 65–6, 78, 82, 94–7, 103–4, 111, 116, 118–21, 134, 137–8, 142–3, 179
The Blues Project 58, 103, 106, 120, 182
Bosses' Songbook 59
Boston 74, 197, 139, 140, 153, 178
'Both Sides Now' 106, 119
Bottom Line 110, 175
Bookbinder, Roy 108, 189
Boudin, Jean 40
Boudin, Kathy 40–1
Boudin, Leonard 38–40

Brand, Oscar 25, 189
Braun, Fred 103
Brecht, Bertolt 116, 135, 152
Brent, John 91, 189
Brill (Bob) 50, 179, 118, 190
Bringing It All Back Home 137
Broadside Magazine 153
Bromberg, Dave 175, 190
Brooklyn Public Library 152
Bruce, Lenny 104
Bukowski, Charles 91

Café Au Go Go 103–4
Café Bizarre 105
Cafe Wha? 105
Café Yana 74, 139
Caffè Lena 74, 141–2
'Cake Walking Babies From Home' 23
Cab Calloway 137
Cambridge, MA 13, 115, 140, 142, 153
Caravan 44
Caricature 23, 44
Carmine Street 168
Carnegie Hall 99, 148
Carr, Leroy 137
Carroll, Hattie 134
Castro, Fidel 152
Catskills 27, 48
Chad Mitchell Trio 106
Chandler, Len 91–2, 94, 98
Chambers Brothers, The 103
Chaplin, Charlie 133
Charters, Ann 65, 116, 190, 195
    Also Danberg, Ann
Charters, Sam
    Also Charters, Samuel 46, 65, 116, 122, 137, 178, 190, 197
Chicago, Chicago blues 51, 91, 103
Child Ballads 45
Chinatown 67, 153
Christian, Charlie 137, 143
Christian, Frank 176, 190
CIA 183
City College 14, 72–3
City University of New York 72
Civil Rights Act 156, 184
Civil War 22
The Civil War 105
Clancy Brothers 76, 99
Clancy, Liam 76, 190

Clayton, Paul 25, 99, 146, 179, 190
'Clouds' 105, 119
Clubs 47, 74, 76–7, 81–3, 92–6, 99, 101–3, 105–9, 113, 117, 140, 142–3, 153, 159, 164, 175, 177, 179–80, 195
'Cocaine Blues' 26
Coen Brothers 85, 87
Coffee houses 44, 57, 74, 85, 91–8, 113, 117, 142, 177, 179
Cohen, Andrew 180, 190
Cohen, David Bennett 182, 190
Cohen, John 49, 182, 190
Cohen, Mike 49, 190
Collins, Judy 99, 101, 119, 190
Columbia Records 142, 144
Columbia University 21, 41
Commons, The 87–9
Communists 12, 22, 36,73
Condit, Tom 63, 78, 121
Coney Island 13
Cooking 3, 48, 67, 68
Corduroy cap, Bob Dylan's 150
CORE, Congress of Racial Equality 37, 114, 156
Cornelia Street Café 178
Corporate Monopoly, Monopoly 67
Cosby, Bill 93
Cotton, James 103
The Country Blues 65, 197
Country Joe and the Fish 65, 182
Crawford, Don 92, 190
Cruddup, Arthur 137
Cuba, Cuban 91, 135 ,152
Cuban Missile Crisis 152
Czechoslovakia, Czech 73

Dalton, Karen 105, 146, 190
Dane, Barbara 104, 190
Darling, Erik 50, 190
Das Kapital 21
Dave Van Ronk and the Hudson Dusters, Hudson Dusters 16, 17, 118, 119, 123
Dave Van Ronk and the Ragtime Jug Stompers, Ragtime Jug Stompers 106, 117–8, 120
Davis, Reverend Gary 87, 92, 97–8, 115, 135, 137
Davis, Miles 104
Delta Blues 103, 143
Democratic Party 31, 73

Index

de Tocqueville, Alexis 47
Deutscher, Isaac 71
Dick, Philip 122
Dickinson, Emily 90
Disneyworld 91
Art D'Lugoff, 104, 107, 190
Dobkin, Alix 63, 96, 102, 104, 107, 156, 190
Dobro 116
Dobson, Bonnie 99, 190
Dodds, Johnny 137
Donovan 76
'Don't Think Twice, It's All Right' 146
'Tom Dooley' 106
Du Bois, W.E.B. 47
Duelling Banjos 181
Duren, Antonia 121, 127, 190
Dylan, Bob 40, 63, 78, 88, 100, 102, 105–6, 119, 133, 139–41, 148, 155, 176–9, 190, 195–8

Eaglin, Snooks 137
East 9th Street 12,54
East Village 158
Easy Rider 122, 127
Einstein, Albert 138–9
Elektra Records 123,125
Eisenhower, Dwight D. 156
Eliot, T.S. 91
Ellington, Duke 104, 137
Elliott, Ramblin' Jack 50, 76, 98–9, 104
Endicott, Paul 111, 190
England 37, 75–6, 159, 160
Engels, Frederich 21
English, Logan 25, 190
Estes, Sleepy John 23
Ethical Culture 166, 167, 183
Even Dozen Jug Band 106, 116

Fanzines 44
Farina, Richard 139, 190
Fast Folk Musical Magazine, The 176
Faust, Luke 25, 48, 50, 190
FBI 35, 36–9, 92, 159, 183
Fein, Naomi 78–9
Feliciano, Jose 92
Figaro 23, 43, 47, 50, 82
Fingerpicking 22, 39
Folk musician 50, 76, 98, 103, 182
Folklore Center 98, 100, 125, 142, 189
Folksingers Guild 24–5, 166, 175

Folkways Records, Folkways 19, 34, 65, 197
Four Winds 105
Franklin, John Hope 21, 47
Frost, Robert 91
Fugs, The 122
Fuller, Blind Boy 137

Gaslight Café
  Also Gaslight 45, 60, 60, 67, 81, 85, 89, 90–1, 99, 105, 108, 119, 125, 138, 139, 140, 152, 158, 165, 175, 177, 179
'Gaslight Rag' 60
Gerdes, George 176
Gerde's Folk City
  Also Gerde's 99, 100, 110, 141, 142–44, 175, 178, 180
Geremia, Paul 63, 83, 119, 161, 190
Giampieri, Guido 108–9, 138, 190
Gibson, Bob 23
Gillespie, Dizzy 104
Glaser, Gina 25, 190
Glazer, Lenny 63, 78, 107, 190
Gleason, Sid and Bob 133
Glynn, Russell 116
goliard poets 134
Gooding, Cynthia 22, 33, 34, 60, 191
Goodman, Benny 137, 143
Goodman, Steve 105
Gordon, Elmer 64,191
Gordon, Max 117
Granirer, Martus 11, 17, 34, 157, 171–4, 180
Grateful Dead 103
Great Depression 19
Green, Claudette 195
Green, Debbie 178
Greenbriar Boys 49, 99, 104, 156, 182
Green Green Rocky Road 91
Greenhill, Manny 113, 139, 140, 192
Greenwich Village 5, 6, 43, 85, 86, 94, 99, 138, 149, 152, 158, 178, 195
Greenwich Village Folk Festival 181
Greenwich Village: Music That Defined a Generation 86
Gregory, Ed 17, 118, 123
Griffith, D.W. 19
Grisman, David 94, 99, 191
Grossman, Albert 63, 112, 116, 138, 144, 148, 191
Grossman, Stefan 116, 191

Guitar 23–4, 58–60, 66, 77, 87, 97–8, 103, 116, 120, 134, 137, 143, 149, 178–80
Guthrie, Woody 19, 20, 133, 140, 142, 169, 179, 181–2, 191

Hamilton, Chico 104
Hammond, John 110, 143–4
Hancock, Herbie 117
Hanks, Larry 180
Hardin, Tim 105, 177, 191
Hardy, Jack 175
Harris, Emmylou 105, 191
Havens, Richie 94, 177, 191
Henderson, Fletcher 137, 143
Henderson, Rick 17, 23
Hendrix, Jimi 105, 123
   Also, Jimmy James 105
'He Was a Friend of Mine' 140
Herald, John 49, 104, 178
Herbert, Frank 122
Hester, Caroline 99, 101, 144
Hickey, Vince 143
Hodges, Johnny 137
Hoffman, Lee 44
Holiday, Billie 104, 137, 143
Hollman, Joyce 2–8, 10, 12, 15, 19, 36, 151
Hollywood 122
'Hootchy Kootchy Man' 103
Hootenanny 89, 104, 125
Hopkins, Lightnin' 23, 59, 65, 94, 137
Holocaust 78
Holy Modal Rounders, 65, 79, 81, 114, 120–8, 160–1, 176, 182
   Also the Rounders
'Hoochie Coochie Man' 120
Hood, Clarence 90, 95–6
Hooker, John Lee 141
House Un-American Committee 22, 39, 104
   Also HUAC
'House of the Rising Sun' 145
Houston, Cisco 19, 34, 99
Howell, Peg Leg 137
Hudson Dusters, The 16–7, 106, 118–9, 123
Hull, Dakota Dave 180
Hurt, Mississippi John 92, 94, 96, 97, 120

I Ching 77
Ian, Janis 105
Independent Socialist League 73
Indian Point 187

Inside Llewyn Davis 86
Intondi, Tom 176
Isquit, Judy 45
Israel, Israeli 11, 91, 177, 187

Jackson, Harry 63
Jackson, Mahalia 157
Jahn's 51
James Webb Space Telescope 7
James, Skip 94, 137
Jazz 23, 26, 58, 66, 78, 92, 103, 103–4, 116–7, 133, 137, 169, 182
Jazz band 22–3, 59, 101, 136
Jazz clubs 169
Jazz musician 23, 97, 118, 120, 143, 149, 177
Jazz Record Center 66
Jefferson, Blind Lemon 59, 137, 143
Jewish 2–4, 9–15, 30, 43, 46–7, 81, 83, 151
Jews 2–3, 9–11, 33, 47, 55
Jim Kweskin Jug Band 106, 116
Joel, Billy 175
John the Conqueror root 119, 120
Jones, LeRoi 91
   Also Amiri Baraka, 91
Johnson, Bunk 59
Johnson, Lonnie 99, 143
Jones, Quincy 117
A Joplin Bouquet 65
Joplin, Scott 65, 137
Hall, Jordan 140
Joseph, Anthea 76, 160

Kalb, Danny 58, 63, 103, 106, 114, 116–8, 120, 153, 156, 178, 182
Kaplansky, Lucy 176
Katz, Steve 58, 103
Kaufman, Bob 91
Keith, Bill 178
Kennedy, John F. 152, 153
   Also President Kennedy 156
Kettle of Fish 85, 90, 93, 96, 108–10, 138, 164–5
Kilberg, Lionel 49
Kindred, Lisa 104
King, Martin Luther 156
   Also Reverend King 157
Kingston Trio, The 106
Kornfeld, Barry 50, 59, 63–4, 78, 97, 116, 153, 182
Kossoy, Ellen 50

Index

Kossoy, Irene 50
Krasilovsky, Bill 129
Khrushchev, Nikita 152
Kunstadt, Len 116, 143
Kurt Weill Foundation 116, 170

Lafayette High School 9, 43
Lake George 74, 75
Lang, Eddie 136
Langhorne, Bruce 136, 143, 157, 178
'The Last Thing On My Mind' 98
Lavin, Christine 176, 179, 182, 196
Lead Belly 19, 23, 59, 137
'Legend of a Dead Soldier' 134
Legman, Gershon 68
Leisure Lodge 4–9, 167, 177
Lenya, Lotte 169, 172
Leonard, Aaron J. 39
Lerman, Eliot 63
Les Cousins 76
Levy, Howard 180
Lewis, Mark 5
   Also my cousin Mark
Lewis, Sandra (Sandy) 5–6
Libertarian League 22
Library of Congress 26, 137
Limbert, Richard 180
Lincoln Memorial 156
Liquor 29, 31, 93–4, 99, 100, 108, 117, 141, 174
Lloyd, A.L. 76, 99
'Lloyd George knew my father' 99
London 73, 75–6, 159–60
Lorrie, George 25
Lovin' Spoonful 105, 176, 182
Lukeman, Alex 63, 114, 120

MacColl, Ewan 76, 179
MacDonald, Rod 176, 196
MacDougal Street 23, 44–5, 50, 52, 87, 98, 107–9, 125, 165, 175
'Mack the Knife' 116
Mahal, Taj 94
Mailer, Norman 44
Malcolm X 91
Manchester, Sue 119
Mandell, Steve 182
March on Washington for Jobs and Freedom 156
Marcuse, Herbert 36

Marijuana
   Also pot, grass, cannabis, hashish 37, 43, 56, 61–2, 64, 74–5, 78, 108, 110, 125, 137, 153
Marra, Joe 106
Marriage 16, 30–1, 66, 69, 70, 79, 81, 130
Marshall, Jim 146
   Also Jim Marshall photographer, cover illustration
Martin, Vince 105
Marx, Karl 21
Marxist 64, 73, 91, 152, 154, 162
Marxist-Leninist 91
Massengill, David 175
'Masters of War' 134
Maternal-Infant Services Network (MISN) 185
Mauldin, Bill 170
The Mayor of MacDougal Street 52, 87, 198
McCarthy, Senator Joseph 36, 65, 73, 159, 183
McCartney, Paul 125
McCurdy, Ed 61, 179
McKenzie, Eve and Mack 133
McGhee, Brownie 94, 111, 137
McSorley's Old Ale House 121
Mercury Records 114, 116
Metsa, Paul 180
Mills, C. Wright 21
Mingus, Charles 104
Mississippi 103, 136, 156
Mississippi Delta 143
Mitchell, Chad 94, 106, 182
Mitchell, John 95
Mitchell, Joni 63, 106, 119
Mohawk, Frazier 123
Monkees 105
The Moray Eels Eat the Holy Modal Rounders 125
Larry 'Mud' Morganfield 104
Morris dancing 98
Morton, Jelly Roll 59, 137
'Mr. Noah,' 99
'Mr. Tambourine Man' 140
Muldaur, Geoff 178
Muldaur, Maria 178, 182
Murray, Bill 91
Music of the Bahamas 65
Museum of Modern Art 34, 172
Myers, Jeannie 180, 181

NAACP 166
NYU 25, 43, 53, 62
Nazis 12
Negro Religious Songs and Services 26
Neil, Fred 104, 177, 197
New Lost City Ramblers 49, 182
New Left 36
1959 Newport Folk Festival 97
Newport Folk Festival 59, 97, 118, 148–9, 181
New York Emergency Civil Liberties Committee (NECLC) 40
NY Post 25
NY Times
   Also New York Times 53, 65, 117, 142 168
NYU 25, 43, 53, 62
Nickel bag 61
Night Owl 105, 107
No Dirty Names 119
North Vietnam 157

Obscure Music 16, 127–8
Ochs, Phil 63, 104, 135, 148, 155, 176, 178
Odetta 94, 157
Oklahoma City 113, 147
Old Left 159
'Old Man, This' 140
Oliver, King 137
Olson, Charles 91
'Onward Christian Soldiers' 99
Operation Sidewinder 123
Oppenheim, Joel 91
Orange Blossom Jug Five, The 116
Orentlich, Paul Solomon 33, 38, 61, 71, 109, 126
Orwell, George 152

Pace University 73
Page, Angela 175–6
Paley, Tom 49, 63
Panties 63, 150
Patton, Charlie 59, 137
Paul Butterfield Blues Band 103, 106
Paxton, Midge 78,110
Paxton, Tom 63–4, 69, 78, 86–7, 92, 98–9, 104, 106, 109, 148, 153, 156, 158, 176
Pearlman, Phil 25
Penderecki, Krzystof 79
Peter, Paul, and Mary 63, 92, 94, 112, 118, 127, 157

Philadelphia Folk festival 181
Piedmont Blūz Acoustic Duo 180
Pied Piper of Hamlin 75
Plyushch, Leonid Ivanovych 167
Porco, Bob 100
Porco, Mike 100, 142
The Power Elite 21
Prestige Records 115, 122
Prestopino, Paul 50, 182
'Pretty Polly' 140
Public Health Service 37
Public Service Commission (PSC) 187
Puerto Ricans, Puerto Rican 9, 11

railroad flat 53
'Ramblin' Boy' 98
Rasmussen, Jerry 59, 63
Redpath, Jean 99
Repertory Theater of Lincoln Center 123
Republic of Vietnam, North Vietnam, Vietnam 1, 71, 122, 157
Richmond Hill 44
Rienzi (coffee house) 46
Rifkin, Ben 25, 50
Rifkin, Joshua 182
Rinzler, Ralph 50
Ritchie, Jean 95, 179
Ritterman, Stuart (Stu) 13, 53
Riverside Church 142–4
Robbins, Susan Martin 105, 177
Robbins, Trina 102
Robertson, Jim 73
Robins, Deborah 195
Roche, Maggie 81, 83, 125, 126, 161, 176
Roche, Terre 81, 83, 125, 126, 161, 176, 180
Rockland Coalition to End the New Jim Crow (RCENJC) 184
Rockland County, Rockland 28, 34, 40, 120, 169, 172
Rockland Water Coalition 187
Romani, Romanis 9, 11
Romney, Hugh (Wavy Gravy) 92–3
Ronettes 122
Rooney, Jim 178
Rose, Artie 116
Rosmini, Dick 50, 63
Ross, Mark 83, 96, 109, 114, 164
Rotante, Cole Quest 182
Rotolo, Carla 78

Rotolo, Suze 78, 102, 134, 147
Royalties
   Also Royalty 16–7, 114, 122–3, 127–9
Rubin, Manny 113, 139
Rustin, Bayard 54

Sainte-Marie, Buffy 99
'Samson and Delilah' 115
Sam Wo 153
Sandburg, Carl 23
Saratoga Springs 74, 141
Savitt, Norman 122, 195
Schwarz, Tracy 49
sci fi fandom 43
Sebastian, John 178, 182
Second City 91
Second Fret 111, 119, 139
Second Red Scare
Second Wave 176
Seeger, Mike 49
Seeger, Pete 19, 20, 34, 104, 149, 169
Sellers, Brother John 99
Sex, sexist, sexual, sexy 6, 7, 13, 16, 27–41, 47, 51–2, 57–9, 64, 67–8, 77–80, 82, 86, 96, 100, 106–7
Shanty Boys 49
Shelton, Robert (Bob) 53, 65, 117
Shepard, Sam 122–3
Silverstein, Shel 91
Simon, Paul 63, 76, 126
Sinclair, Upton 21, 152
singer-songwriters 76, 98, 110, 126–7, 131, 149, 176, 178
Skiffle in Stereo 116
Sky, Patrick (Pat) 63, 78, 99, 106, 177–8
Smith, Bessie 137
Smithsonian Center for Folklife and Cultural Heritage 176
Student Non-Violent Coordinating Committee (SNCC) 37, 113, 155
Socialist Labor League (SLL) 158, 159
Socialist Party 46, 154
Socialist Workers Party (SWP) 154
Soho Weekly News 168
'Solidarity Forever' 20
Solomon, Howard 104
Some Like It Hot 51
South Mountain Road 170, 172
Soviet Union, Soviet, also Russia 2, 3, 6, 11–2, 33–5, 73, 152–3, 161, 167

Spanish Civil War 22
Spartacist League 158
Speakeasy (club) 175, 176
Spencer, Bill 74, 141
Spencer, Lena 74, 141
Spencer, Dr. Robert Douglas 71
'Spike Driver Blues' 97
Spivey, Victoria 137, 138, 143
Spivey Records 143
Springsteen, Bruce 105
190 Spring Street 50
Sprung, Roger 49, 50
Stampfel, Peter 63, 121, 126, 127
Statman, Andy 99
Stone, Doris 118
Stoned 43, 63, 134
Stookey, Noel (Paul) 92, 93, 112, 157
Stravinsky 13
Students for a Democratic Society (SDS) 113
Students for Democratic Action (SDA) 31
Sturdivant, Bozie 26
Swados, Bette 6
Swados, Harvey 6, 21, 68

'Talking Bear Mountain Picnic Massacre Blues' 140
Tatum, Art 137, 143
Taylor, James 131
'Tell Old Bill' 23, 58
Terry, Clark 117
Terry, Sonny 94, 111, 137
Thal, Bernard
   Also my father 2, 4, 5, 9, 15, 75
Thal, Esther
   Also my mother 2–6, 11, 12, 29, 45
Thal, Leon
   Also my brother 2, 37, 62–3
Theatre de Lys 152
This Business of Music 129
Thomas, Dylan 91
The Threepenny Opera 152
'The Times They Are a-Changin'' 134
Tin Can Alley Antiques 168
Tompkins Square Park, Tompkins Square 47, 158
Tork, Peter 105
Traum, Happy 50, 99, 104, 178, 180
Travers, Mary 112, 157, 178

Trotsky, Leon
  Also Trotskyist, Trotsky's, Trotskyism 35, 37, 46, 62, 63, 71, 73, 78, 102, 134, 153–61
Troubadour 76, 160
Trumbauer, Frankie 137
Turner, Gil 50
Turning Point 180
Tyson, Sylvia 182

Ubaldini, Michael 180
Ulster County 167, 169
Umanov, Matt 98, 182
Ungar, Jay 105

Valli, Frankie 122
Van Ronk Sings (recording) 103
Van Ronk, Dave 1, 5, 10, 15, 16, 19–26, 33, 34, 37–9, 43–90, 92–101, 103, 106–109, 111–21, 125–31, 133–50, 152–61, 165, 170–2, 179
Van Ronk, Terri 115
Vega, Susanne 176
Velvet Underground 105
Verve/Forecast, Verve Folkways 119
Village Gate 104
Village, Greenwich 5, 6, 43, 85, 86, 94, 99, 138, 149, 152, 158, 178, 195
Village Vanguard, Vanguard 117
Village Voice 25, 86
Villager 25
Vivian Beaumont Theater 123
Vietnam, North Vietnam 1, 71, 122, 157
Voice of America 73
Von Schmidt, Eric 103, 150

Wald, Elijah 52, 179
Walrus 150
Washington Square 23, 47, 49–50, 178, 181, 195
Washington Square Bluegrass and Folk Music Reunion 181, 196
Waters, Muddy 103–4, 120
Watson, Doc 94, 95, 103, 175

Waverly Place 61, 64–5, 78, 114, 150
Waverly Theatre 50
WCBS-TV 184
Weather Underground 40
Weavers, The 20, 34
WBAI 25, 125
Webb, Chick 137
Weber, Steve 121
Wedding 13, 69, 81
Weill, Kurt 116, 170
Weissberg, Eric 49, 178, 182
Weissman, Dick 89, 118, 127, 189
Westlake, Donald (Don) 67
West Side Story 67
West Village 146
'When Johnny Comes Marching Home' 135
White, Bukka 137
'Who's Gonna Buy Your Ribbons (When I'm Gone)' 146
Why Not 105
Wilkins, Robert 95
Williams, Big Joe 103, 138, 143–4
Williams, Robert Pete 137
Wilson, David 153
Winn, John 1, 63, 92, 99
Wohlforth, Tim 155, 158, 161
Woods, Dave 17, 63, 118
Woodstock, Woodstock Folk Festival 92, 96, 149, 178
Woolworth 45, 156
Workers League 37, 154–62

Yarrow, Peter 157
Yellin, Bob 49
Young, Izzy (Israel) 98, 100, 125, 142, 178, 189
Young, Lester 137
Young People's Socialist League (YPSL) 46, 51–2
Young Socialist League (YSL) 20, 35–6, 73
Youth March for Integrated Schools 156

Zeisel, Eva 170